PRAISE F

DEATH ON THE ISLAND

"I loved this book. Eliza Reid is so assured in her plot, her characters that it's hard to believe this is her first novel. *Death on the Island* is compulsive and propulsive reading. Not only wonderfully evocative of a little known area of Iceland, it is also surprising, with twists even a seasoned crime reader won't see coming. A brilliant debut that promises more to come."

—Louise Penny, #1 *New York Times* bestselling author

"An intriguing mystery, an exotic setting, and a Christie vibe—what's not to love?"

—Shari Lapena, international bestselling
author of *What Have You Done?*

"Now, here's something new: *The Good Wife* meets Agatha Christie beneath the Northern Lights of Iceland. In *Death on the Island*, Eliza Reid—who served as that country's First Lady for eight historic years—evokes its extraordinary atmosphere, its cultural rituals, even the quirks of its language; better still, her protagonist—the intrepid yet vulnerable wife of a diplomat—is tactful but fierce, a heroine to thrill fans of *Scandal* and *Madam Secretary*. And the mystery, cunningly structured as a series of tick-tock countdowns, pays homage to locked-room classics while blazing a path that's defiantly modern. This is a fresh, transporting, emotionally involving suspense debut, that rare crime novel you'll want to discuss with friends. Maybe even beneath the Northern Lights."

—A. J. Finn, #1 *New York Times* bestselling author of *The Woman in the Window* and *End of Story*

"*Death on the Island* is a wonderful and compelling debut, welcoming a new and unique voice to the Icelandic crime fiction genre."

—Yrsa Sigurðardóttir, international bestselling author

"With its twisty Golden Age plot and a fascinating Nordic noir setting, this novel is perfect for lovers of each."

—Ann Cleeves, *New York Times* bestselling author

"An addictive and edgy murder mystery with wonderfully quirky characters and razor-sharp dialogue. You'll turn the pages faster than you ever thought possible."

—Jann Arden, bestselling author of *The Bittlemores*

"Eliza Reid's take on a locked-room mystery is an island off the coast of Iceland during a perfect storm—for the perfect murder. Among the suspects are an ambitious chef, an award-winning writer, an ambassador, and a captain of industry. Skullduggery in high places! A most enthralling, entertaining, and intriguing mystery."

—Liz Nugent, bestselling author

"So this is what Eliza Reid was thinking about during all those diplomatic dinners."

—Anthony Horowitz, *New York Times* bestselling author

SECRETS OF THE SPRAKKAR: ICELAND'S EXTRAORDINARY WOMEN AND HOW THEY ARE CHANGING THE WORLD

"Riveting."

—*New York Times*

"*Secrets of the Sprakkar* is a fascinating window into what a more gender-equal world could look like and why it's worth striving for. Iceland is doing a lot to level the playing field: paid parental leave, affordable childcare, and broad support for gender equality as a core value. Reid takes us on an exploration not only around this fascinating island but also through the triumphs and stumbles of a country as it journeys toward gender equality."

—Hillary Rodham Clinton

"With warmth, wit, and insight, First Lady Eliza Reid explores the reasons why Iceland is one of the best places on earth for women, as well as the challenges still ahead in achieving full gender equity. *Secrets of the Sprakkar* is an illuminating, inspiring, and absorbing book about how a more equitable society could elevate us all."

—Cheryl Strayed, #1 *New York Times* bestselling author of *Wild*

"What a world of possibilities Eliza Reid unveils in this warm and wonderful book! It made me want to pack my bags and move to Iceland."

—Ruth Reichl, *New York Times* bestselling
author of *Save Me the Plums*

"The fact that the Icelandic language includes the word 'sprakkar'—an ancient term that translates to mean 'extraordinary women'—in its lexicon tells you a great deal about the country of Iceland. And in her marvelous memoir, Eliza Reid tells us a great deal more: not only about her life in Iceland but also about gender equality in action and the sense of purpose that all of us seek. This is a charming and necessary book."

—Meg Wolitzer, *New York Times* bestselling author

"A warm and intimate exploration of what one small country can teach the world about gender equality. Eliza Reid charts her personal journey from a Canadian farm to Iceland's presidential residence and along the way proves to be the best possible guide to the historical, geographical, and cultural factors that helped women thrive and build a vibrant modern society."

—Geraldine Brooks, Pulitzer Prize–winning author

"Everyone who visits Iceland quickly learns that the little country contains some of the world's most extraordinary women, their lives rooted in a social and political culture that nurtures equality between men and women without ignoring the pleasures and complexities of family life. It's a pleasure to see that culture marked out for us through the sometimes wry but always beautifully personal and perceptive lens of the remarkable Eliza Reid."

—Adam Gopnik, *New Yorker* staff writer

"A breath of fresh Icelandic air! Eliza Reid crafts a highly original, warm, and honest journey into the heart of the small Nordic island nation and its rich culture and history, creating an empowering read on how striving for equality can improve everyone's lives."

—Katja Pantzar, author of *The Finnish Way*

"Charting her own love of the nation and her journey to becoming its First Lady, alongside histories of other formidable women, Eliza Reid's *Secrets of the Sprakkar* sheds light on Iceland's unique approach to gender equity—an emblematic look at what's possible in the fight for women's rights worldwide. A fascinating, hopeful, and inspiring read."

—Esi Edugyan, bestselling author of *Washington Black*

"Reading *Secrets of the Sprakkar* is like sitting down with your favorite, smartest, warmest girlfriend and hearing all about the extraordinary women, history, and culture of her tiny adopted country. Reid celebrates Iceland and its attitudes toward women while also discussing where it has some room for improvement. By the time I finished this book, I felt I had traveled to Iceland and gotten to know its beauty and quirks and, most importantly, its *sprakkar*."

—Ann Hood, bestselling author

"Laced with frank discussions of domestic abuse, intersectionality, and other complex issues, this is a winning portrait of a country at the forefront of the fight for gender equality."

—*Publishers Weekly*

"Reid…is uniquely placed to observe the country which leads the world in gender equality, providing generous parenting leave, abundant childcare, and free prenatal services… The tiny country of Iceland should serve as an inspiration to the rest of the world."

—*Booklist*

"Reid's style is amusing, her thoughts are honest, and the issues she discusses are becoming more important by the day."

—*Washington Post*

"Reid artfully weaves incisive, relatable observations into her impressive new book on gender equality… An accessible, highly personal read."

—*Star Tribune*

"Eliza Reid has compiled here a daring, insightful, often humorous, and often fascinating look at women in Iceland… A real page turner and one that everyone should read, regardless of gender."

—*Reykjavik Grapevine*

"The sometimes funny, always insightful episodes really put you in touch with Icelandic culture and its attitude toward women—an uplifting and inspiring memoir that reads like a novel."

—*Condé Nast Traveler*

"Insightful and encouraging."

—Maria Shriver's *Sunday Paper*

"Her debut is a wonderful read. "

—*Lögberg-Heimskringla*

"The book is peppered with lively personal anecdotes about Reid's life as First Lady, interviews with notable local women, and observations about daily life in the beautiful country… It's interesting to hear so directly and unguardedly from an active First Lady."

—*The Kit*

"[A] delightful love letter to [Reid's] adopted nation, in which she employs an engaging blend of reportage and memoir."

—*Quill & Quire*

ALSO BY ELIZA REID

*Secrets of the Sprakkar: Iceland's Extraordinary
Women and How They Are Changing the World*

DEATH
ON THE
ISLAND

DEATH
ON THE
ISLAND

A NOVEL

ELIZA REID

Poisoned Pen
PRESS

Published by Poisoned Pen Press, an imprint of Sourcebooks
P.O. Box 4410, Naperville, Illinois 60567-4410
(630) 961-3900
sourcebooks.com

Library of Congress Cataloging-in-Publication Data

Names: Reid, Eliza, author.
Title: Death on the island : a novel / Eliza Reid.
Description: Naperville, Illinois : Poisoned Pen Press, 2025.
Identifiers: LCCN 2024046714 (print) | LCCN 2024046715
 (ebook) | (trade paperback) | (epub)
Subjects: LCGFT: Detective and mystery fiction. | Novels.
Classification: LCC PR9143.9.R45 D43 2025 (print) | LCC PR9143.9.R45
 (ebook) | DDC 813/.6--dc23/eng/20241031
LC record available at https://lccn.loc.gov/2024046714
LC ebook record available at https://lccn.loc.gov/2024046715

Printed and bound in the United States of America.
VP 10 9 8 7 6 5 4 3 2

NOTES ON ICELANDIC

People in Iceland generally refer to each other by first name, even in formal circumstances, so in this story characters such as the mayor, the ambassador, and the police officer are usually referred to in this way, and not using a surname.

The Westman Islands, where this story takes place, are located just off the south coast of Iceland. They are known as Vestmannaeyjar in Icelandic (literally "Westman Islands"), and this word is used in the book except when two English speakers, who would use the foreign term, are talking together. The main island of the archipelago, and the only inhabited one, is called "Heimaey" ("Home Island") and the island's community is called "Vestmannaeyjabær" ("Westman Islands Town"), although, to add to a visitor's confusion, the community is usually referred to simply as "Eyjar" or "the islands." I have attempted to keep these references as close as possible to how they would really be used, unless to do so would cause undue confusion for the reader.

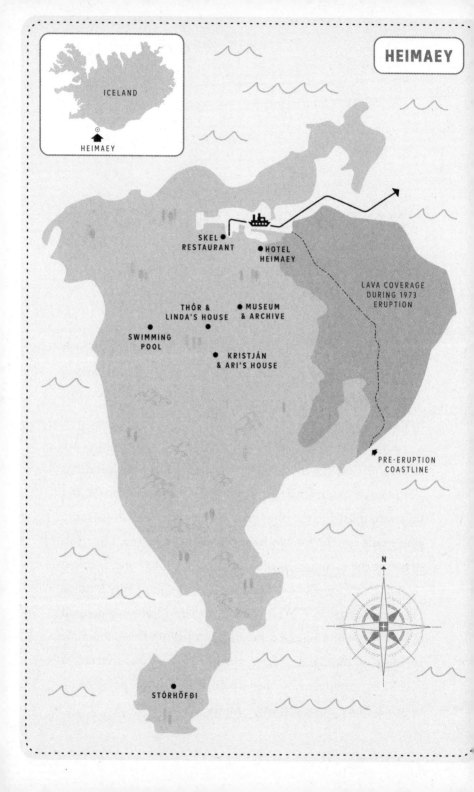

PROLOGUE

Kristján's world went dark on a sunny Wednesday.

But before that, there was light. Common snipes were calling cheerfully to each other, their long beaks popping in and out of damp grasses in search of a fat worm. Children squealed in delight as they chased each other around a playground. Tourists in hiking boots ambled along the community's sidewalks, gazing into store windows. At the entrance to the folklore museum and town archive, the summer breeze swirled ocher leaves on the ground. Kristján crunched his way through them.

Once inside, he hurried down the building's main hall, past the sepia photos of early twentieth-century fishermen, faces worn and serious, aprons stained with fish entrails and blood.

He came across it at the end of the hall. The body was on the hard stone floor, arms splayed to the side. The dead man was wearing expensive fitted jeans, brown leather oxfords, a tailored pale-pink shirt, now partially untucked, a white undershirt peeking out near the undone top button. The dead man's cell phone was a few feet away from him, its screen cracked. The head of hair was still as impressive as it had been in life—plentiful, wavy, salt-and-pepper—except for a patch above the right ear, matted with congealing blood.

The still face was remarkably smooth for someone of middle age. That single, perfect cleft on the chin, the light stubble. But now, his eyes were glassy, his blue lips parted, as if his soul had left his body via the softest exhale. Still, whatever had immediately preceded death had not come painlessly.

Kristján looked down at the corpse on the floor. He dropped to his knees. He laid his head on the familiar torso, picked up the cool and stiffening hand and held it in his, stroking the palm with his thumb. Was he allowed to do this? Touch a body? Caress it? He didn't care. He would stay this way until someone told him he couldn't.

A chasm opened in his heart, like the volcanic rifts that had devastated this tiny community half a century ago, spouting ash and fire from the earth's belly. And like that real fissure, the one within him would cause untold damage. There was no coming back now, no words of sorrow or regret or forgiveness or love that could change anything. There was only shock, and that brief, final text sent only half an hour ago.

Komdu. Come.

PART ONE

PART ONE

ONE

Jane Shearer took a large swig of white wine, hoping it would mask the strong anise flavor of the angelica in the appetizer. Skel restaurant was known for creating dishes that showcased plants native to Vestmannaeyjar, and in her single day here she had already seen plenty of angelica growing on the nearby hillsides. Its local allure did nothing to increase her interest in the dish, though. Nothing could taste appealing after the day she'd had.

This two-day trip to the photogenic Vestmannaeyjar, the archipelago that lay just a few nautical miles south of the "mainland" of Iceland, was officially to open an art exhibition with a Canadian connection. But Jane knew the real reason her husband, Graeme, was here: to carefully influence the largest employer on the islands to open its next facility in Canada's Maritime Provinces.

It was always like this with diplomacy. Graeme's missions appeared to be about one thing on the surface but were often about something else. As she grew older and more cynical, this two-facedness galled Jane more than ever.

It's not that she had been dreading this trip. Vestmannaeyjar had been on her wish list ever since she, Graeme, and their teenage twins had moved to Iceland just over fourteen months ago, when Graeme began his post as Canada's ambassador to the small island nation.

Jane had read about the beauty of the grass-topped mountain islands that encircled Heimaey, the only populated one, like a verdant shield. She had learned about the name, Vestmannaeyjar, or Westman Islands, so given because the main seventeen-square-kilometer isle was where enslaved Celts—known as "Westmen"—had fled from attacks in Iceland during the area's settlement in the late ninth century. And she knew about the devastating volcanic eruption fifty years ago that had destroyed much of the town.

Despite the increasingly treacherous autumnal weather, the beauty and history of the islands had exceeded her expectations. Still, Jane could not enjoy it. Until a few hours ago, she could think only of how this might be her last trip with Graeme, their conversation on the ferry over replaying in her head like one of those Instagram videos her children were forever watching. Then there had been the argument just before this dinner—Graeme and his deputy screaming at each other like a married couple in full view of the hotel bar—and the threats that followed. Now it wasn't just Jane's marriage that seemed balanced on a knife edge. The tension in the dining room was stretched so taut it felt like it might snap at any moment.

Two seats away from her at the large table in Skel's private dining room (why was it protocol to separate couples at working dinners?), Graeme was locked in conversation with the community's mayor, Kristján Gunnarsson. Graeme's balding head nodded in agreement with whatever the dapper mayor was saying. The mayor seemed cheerful enough, but Jane suspected this was a front. It was common knowledge that Kristján's husband had died suddenly only eight weeks ago. Kristján gave little away with his demeanor, but Jane had to wonder whether running a town was a noble distraction or one stress too many.

"What is this, some kind of trout?"

Jane glanced at the man to her right, who was prodding tentatively at the delicate cut of fish in front of him, and grinned. Given everything that had happened this afternoon, she was particularly grateful that she'd had the good sense to invite her friend Ben Rafdal along.

His dinner small talk left something to be desired, but he added some cultural glamour to their delegation. It wasn't every day that an internationally famous author, especially one with a strand of Icelandic ancestry, visited a tiny town on a remote island.

"It's arctic char," Jane replied.

"Why does it taste like celery?"

"I think that's the angelica."

Ben gave a shrug and put a forkful into his mouth. Jane returned her attention to the assembly gathered about the table.

Across from Jane, Graeme's deputy at the Canadian embassy, Kavita Banerjee, was staring intently at her boss and draining her

wineglass fast. *Sip, stare, sip, stare.* Jane knew Kavita harbored griev-
ances against Graeme, but she feared that after today's events, the
feeling was mutual. And though Jane couldn't blame the deputy
ambassador for her antagonism toward Graeme (after this morning Jane's own emotional pendulum had swung violently away from
affection for her husband), she also didn't trust Kavita.

Kavita, her long, dark hair fixed in a tight bun, was accompanied by her husband, Rahul, along for his first overnight diplomatic visit. Naturally, he wasn't seated next to his wife but two
places to her right. Jane had noticed that Kavita often treated
her other half as no more than a well-dressed accessory and Jane
respected his ability to refrain from escalating tensions. But something was up between them now; throughout the day he had been
casting troubled glances in his wife's direction. Not, Jane thought,
that she was in any position to be casting aspersions on other
people's marriages.

Rahul was in conversation with Linda Jónsdóttir, the wife of
the CEO of Bláhafið Seafood Products, Thór Magnússon. She
was an attractive, middle-aged woman in a figure-hugging black
dress, shades of gray in artistic patterns adding lift and texture to
its darkness. Her shoulder-length blond hair, perfectly tinted with
three complementary highlights, was full and thick. Jane couldn't
make out what they were saying, but Rahul's face showed an ear-
nestness that Jane hadn't seen before. Rahul was clearly trying to
get an important message across, but Jane had no idea what that
could possibly be. After all, Rahul had only just met the woman.

Meanwhile, Linda's husband was the person Graeme most

needed to impress on this visit. Thór was smiling at the Canadian envoy to his left, his six-and-a-half-foot frame radiating confidence.

And the person who this dinner was supposed to be about, the one who *should* have been attracting the most attention because her exhibition was opening in the morning, was the artist seated to Jane's left, Hanna Kovacic. Jane was struggling to mask her dislike of the woman.

"That angelica is quite an assertive flavor," Jane commented to Hanna as she nudged the food on her plate with her fork to make it appear as if she had eaten more than she really had.

"That's what this is for," Hanna said, lifting her wineglass with a smile. Jane pasted an identical grin on her face and lifted hers too.

Rain began to pound against the windows, hitting the glass diagonally as the wind blew it in great whooshes.

"Fall in Iceland," Hanna commented. "When I lived in this town, it once poured nonstop for forty-eight hours."

"How bad is this storm going to get?" Jane asked.

Hanna shrugged. "That's out of our control."

Graeme delicately tapped his water glass and cleared his throat. Conversation stopped as the ambassador stood.

"Good evening, everyone. I wanted to give a few words of thanks to our host for this evening, Mayor Kristján Gunnarsson." He launched into generic lines about the beautiful Vestmannaeyjar, the value of art, and the importance of the strong bilateral relationship between Iceland and his home country, Canada. Jane was relieved that official visits such as this one usually followed the same cookie-cutter format: a mix of cultural tour, visit to local business, and dinner with speech to cement friendship. Graeme could mostly perform his duties on autopilot despite the shock Jane had delivered to him earlier.

Jane caught Kavita rolling her eyes as her boss spoke. The diplomat's impatient nature had gotten the better of her at various points during the day. Jane used to have more sympathy for her than many. How many times had Jane herself stifled an identical gesture during her husband's boilerplate discourse? Now it was difficult to feel any sympathy for Kavita.

"Mayor Kristján"—Ambassador Graeme nodded in the man's direction—"it is a joy to visit this special town and to get to know its special people. To my new good friend, Thór Magnússon, I was immeasurably impressed by Bláhafid's cutting-edge technologies and your approach to sustainability. You are a true visionary in your field. I am told that the word *bláhafid i*s Icelandic for 'the blue sea,' and I know that protecting our oceans and their resources is a guiding principle of your organization."

Thór nodded in the practiced manner of someone used to such tributes. On the other side of Graeme, Mayor Kristján looked down at his plate. Did Jane imagine it, or did a muscle in his jaw twitch as Graeme praised the fishing company?

"So let us raise our glasses and toast to Hanna Kovacic and her art, to the people of the Westman Islands, and to friendship." Graeme lifted his glass, prompting the group to take sips, some more enthusiastically than others. He sat down, and conversation picked up once again.

Ben leaned across Jane to Hanna. "Nervous about the exhibition opening tomorrow?" he asked and arched an eyebrow.

Jane groaned inwardly. Ben began all conversations with women flirtatiously, and his cavalier charm sometimes rankled her, maybe because, even now in her early forties, she could never speak to strangers or even acquaintances with the same confidence.

Hanna did not appear in the mood for coy games, though.

"I'm not nervous about my work," she answered Ben calmly. "I'm looking forward to tomorrow. And I'm grateful for the embassy's support, for Graeme's—Ambassador Shearer's—hard work."

"I bet," said Ben. "I can't imagine what it was like to live here like you did. Since we came over on the ferry today, I've already met several people who know others I know. It must be impossible to keep secrets."

"Not if you know how to do it," Hanna replied.

Was it the candles flickering, or did Jane notice Hanna wink at Ben as she said that?

Ten minutes later, as staff brought around the meal's next course, Skel's owner and head chef, Piotr Tómasson, stumbled slightly as he rounded the corner, and some sour cream from a side dish dribbled onto Hanna's thigh. She gave him a sharp look and began dabbing at the stain with her napkin.

"Sorry," he blurted. "The sous-chef made the emulsion too runny."

Hanna waved him off. "It'll be fine."

The chef moved on to the other side of the table and Ben turned to Jane. "That was no accident. Some men can't handle a breakup."

Jane raised her eyebrows. "I saw them together earlier today," Ben explained. "I've attuned myself to human chemistry and nonverbal signals with all my research." If he was attempting to look modest, he was failing. "It's totally obvious with them, believe me." He took a sip of his drink. "No question they've seen each other naked."

Jane's jaw clenched. How could Ben possibly know that? She recalled what she'd seen on the boat that morning and tried to keep her revulsion at bay. The less time she spent thinking about Hanna's private life, the better.

She looked across to her husband, but Graeme and Thór were still talking, lost in some nitty-gritty details about fisheries, dual taxation agreements, and terms of trade.

"Yes, yes, exactly!" exclaimed Thór. "Then, after you conclude the second agreement, there's even more scope for long-term investment and expansion."

The two men looked up, surprised to see that others in the group were paying attention to their dialogue. Kavita set down her utensils with an audible clunk. Spots of color blossomed on her cheeks.

The rain continued to pound against the windows. The candles flickered on the table, and the electric light remained dim. Was that hail hitting the building like bullets? Wineglasses were refilled. No one declined.

Kavita finished her drink and turned to Kristján. Her eyes were glassy as she spoke at a volume that made the rest of the diners fall silent. "So, Kristján, how has this evening been for you? I heard this used to be your husband's favorite restaurant. Losing him must be hard."

Jane cringed at the diplomatic misstep. Those gulps of wine the deputy had been taking had added up.

Kristján looked at the deputy ambassador in shock. People had been tiptoeing around the subject of the mayor's husband's sudden demise. All Jane and the other visitors knew was that Kristján's husband had been found dead by the mayor himself at the very museum they had visited earlier in the day. The official report concluded he'd died from cardiac arrest, a result of the cardiomyopathy he'd been living with for years.

The mayor stammered. "I–I…" He took a deep breath. The others watched him.

"It's as if all the warmth, all the light, all the laughter that I kept with me has been taken away. I don't know how it will ever return." Kristján's eyes filled with tears. He dabbed them with his napkin.

Jane's eyes welled in sympathy. It was refreshing to see how close the mayor's emotions were to the surface. No matter how many self-help articles advised men to speak openly of their feelings, to share their emotions, tears, and fears, the real world adhered to different norms. Even in Iceland.

Ben leaned close to Jane and whispered, "God, this is the worst, isn't it?"

It was. In fact, Jane couldn't remember the last time she'd been at a diplomatic dinner this fraught.

Meanwhile, across the table, Graeme made a vague grunt of commiseration, but Jane knew that tone and all it implied. Kristján had crossed a line of masculinity, and her husband did not approve.

"A tragedy," muttered Thór gruffly, in a tone that suggested he was keen to move the conversation on as quickly as possible.

A glint of something Jane couldn't put her finger on appeared in Mayor Kristján's eyes.

"A tragedy," he sniffed. "Yes, so everyone keeps saying."

"Kristján." Was Jane imagining it, or was there a strange tone of warning in Thór's voice? "Now is not the time or the place."

An uncomfortable silence descended upon the table. Linda, Thór's demure wife, stared down at her plate and looked as though she wished she were anywhere else.

Hanna was the first to break the tension. "Ari was a lovely man, and we all miss him," she said.

Chef Piotr walked in then and whispered something in the mayor's ear. The mayor straightened, his eyes suddenly clear and focused again, as though none of the previous exchange had happened. He cleared his throat, and when he spoke his voice was even and composed.

"Dear guests," he said. "I'm afraid to say that our weather forecast is not improving. All flights and ferries to and from our island have been canceled. We're staying here until further notice."

TWO

"We can't return late!" cried Kavita. "Isn't there a way to take a helicopter tomorrow after the exhibition opens? I *have* to get back to Reykjavík."

There were murmurs of agreement, though none as strident as the deputy ambassador's.

Chef Piotr shrugged his shoulders. "We cannot control the weather. But—" He paused dramatically. "We can control how we wait it out. Dear guests, our other patrons have now left. May I invite you into the main dining area for our special after-dinner cocktail?"

He glanced at Kristján, whose eyes brightened.

The main room of Skel was decorated in similar fashion to the private dining area, with unfinished plaster walls and a few paintings hanging from them, so eclectic that Jane could only presume they were family heirlooms. The tables were minimally adorned, and small pots of wildflowers and local herbs stood in the windowsills. At the far end from where they entered, a large table was arranged with bottles of rum, brandy, and an Icelandic schnapps. A large punch bowl of ice stood to the side along with several empty whiskey tumblers. One completed cocktail, full of crushed ice and elegantly garnished with a large sprig of angelica, sat near the front, ready to be captured for a viral Instagram story. Jane's heart sank a little at the sight of the herb.

"You're in for quite a show," Linda confided to Jane as they walked toward where the generously tattooed chef had relocated to get a few final details ready behind the bar. "The chef and the mayor have this routine down to an art. It's the same every time but somehow never gets boring. Piotr loves to mix this cocktail in front of guests. And Kristján loves to drink it."

She reached for a teacup. "I think I'm at my limit, though."

Jane gazed into the pitch-darkness out the window. "This isn't getting any better, is it?"

"No, but I've seen worse. Just Westman Islands weather. It's been like this my whole life, all half century of it."

Jane looked up as Ben strode into the room toward the group. He appeared flushed. It seemed everyone had been enjoying the alcohol this evening.

Standing next to the long table, Kristján picked up the completed cocktail, lifting it to his lips and twitching his nose. "That garnish always tickles." He laughed and took a sip. "Aah," he sighed to no one in particular. "Just as potent as ever."

Piotr smiled. "Do you think the others dare to try this?"

"Many people don't have the stomach," Kristján replied. "But I think you'll find this group amenable."

"We certainly are!" exclaimed Graeme in a burst of enthusiasm. "Can you make one for each of us? We're all brave. Aren't we?" He looked from Jane to Ben.

"I thought you'd never ask," exclaimed Piotr in a tone that implied he had been waiting for this exact request. "Come closer, everyone, please. Kristján, can you help me with this?"

The mayor put down his glass, ready to assist, and the group clustered tightly around them.

"You won't find it on our menu. This drink is only for our most exclusive guests. And it's Mayor Kristján's favorite! Excellencies, ladies and gentlemen, I present to you Skel's signature drink, the Flaming Viking!"

"Why is it called the Flaming Viking?" asked Graeme. "Does it burn one's insides?" He laughed at his own joke.

"Just watch and see," replied Piotr. "This drink is a secret combination of my own house-spiced rum, birch-bark liqueur, and traditional Icelandic *brennevín,* or 'burning wine.' You need to be strong as a Viking to enjoy it!"

He laughed heartily as he stirred and shook various components. On occasion he wordlessly held his open palm out, like a surgeon in the operating theater, and the mayor handed the chef whatever bottle or spice was next needed. It was indeed a finely choreographed performance, and after a minute, Piotr poured the concoction into a row of waiting glasses. Several members of the group had their phones out, snapping photos and taking videos.

"And now, the pièce de résistance," the bald chef announced with a flourish. "Lights, please!" Kristján dashed to the opposite

wall of the room to turn off the lights, and the room was engulfed
in darkness. Small tea lights flickered in one corner. The shift in
illumination caused the group to go quiet, the wind howling outside. Jane had to squint to watch the chef at work.

Suddenly, a loud clatter shattered the silence.

"What was that?" someone shouted. Jane looked around. Her
eyes had not yet adjusted to the darkness and she couldn't see who
had spoken, or even where the sound had come from. Instinctively,
she reached her hand out to grab the arm of the person nearest her.
Was that Ben? He didn't seem so nearby anymore. Jane felt the soft
fabric of a blouse and jerked her arm away.

"Don't worry, only me," Hanna said to her. "I'm just trying to
get a good angle for this. Hard to get the right shot in this light."

"Sorry, everyone. I dropped my phone!" called Linda. "Didn't
mean to startle you. Keep going, please, Piotr."

Piotr threw some more herbs into a metal jug, pouring liquid
from a bottle over it. Something smelled spicy. Was that aroma
cinnamon? Orange peel? Jane couldn't see all the drink's components. Piotr struck a match to set the alcohol on fire and poured
it over the drinks one by one. A bright-blue flame lit a path from
glass to glass.

"He's like a teenager showing off a new car," Hanna muttered
to Jane, who forced herself to laugh out loud. Jane lifted her phone
and took a picture, the flash exploding light into the room.

There were oohs and aahs, more camera flashes. Jane felt
woozy, just as she had on the ferry ride to get here. But this time
she knew the cause was the wine, not the sea. In a few moments,

the flame subsided, and the lights went back on. The chef sprinkled some chopped chervil over each glass.

"*Gerið þið svo vel*," Piotr said triumphantly, gesturing grandly to the row of cocktails. "Be my guest."

Hands quickly reached out to the table with the row of Flaming Vikings. Hanna grabbed the glass in front of her and turned to Jane. "I think we need to capture this moment. Linda, can you take a photo of us?" Hanna handed her phone to Linda, who looked put out, but accepted the device.

Jane picked up a glass and stood rigidly as she felt the artist's arm draped sloppily around her shoulders. Hanna was the last person Jane wanted to appear online next to.

"I think this deserves a toast," announced Graeme.

"I agree," said Thór. He picked up a drink in front of him while Graeme handed the remaining glasses around to the group. Kavita and Ben both took large swigs of theirs.

"To art, to friendship, to Canadian-Icelandic relations!" proclaimed Graeme.

The ambassador raised his glass and took a sip. He blinked, and then coughed as he swallowed. "Wow, that burns on the way down!"

The others all sampled their Flaming Vikings. Kristján pursed his lips through the pungency, while Ben gave the mayor a look of surprised admiration.

"Reminds me of my undergrad days," remarked Jane as she slowly worked her way through the cocktail. She could taste the wintry spices and the rum, warm and gentle, but before she knew it, the subtleties were obliterated with a sinus-clearing blast of strong alcohol. That must be the Icelandic schnapps. Tiny fronds of the chopped chervil lingered on her tongue. Next to Jane, Hanna downed hers in two efficient gulps.

"Excuse me a moment," Linda turned away from Hanna and Jane and spoke to her husband, lowering her voice a notch and looking pointedly at his already empty glass. "I thought you weren't drinking tonight?" Jane didn't catch his reply but saw him glare at Linda.

"Cheers," Rahul said as he lifted his glass and looked into his wife's eyes. "Kavita, darling. Well done today." Something was off about his tone. It had no warmth.

"Cheers!" Kavita replied, lifting her near-empty glass to her lips. Jane saw her mouthing what looked like "I'm sorry."

Kavita tossed back the dregs of her Flaming Viking and began to cough. Jane wasn't surprised; she couldn't imagine the earnest deputy ambassador was used to this kind of concoction. Tears appeared in Kavita's eyes. She blinked them away and, with an air of determination, swallowed the last drops of liquid in her glass. She coughed again, more violently this time, her mouth gaping. Jane was reminded of the fish they had seen earlier in the day at Bláhafid. Something was wrong. The deputy ambassador's eyes were bulging, as though invisible hands were pressing at her neck. Then she dropped her glass, which shattered on the floor.

That caught everyone's attention.

"Kavita?" Rahul said. He put a hand on her back.

"Kavita, are you all right?" Graeme stood next to her, looking concerned.

Kavita collapsed, seizing and foaming at the mouth.

"Somebody do something!" Rahul cried.

"Call an ambulance!" Jane shouted. She looked around her to see who could help. Linda picked up her phone.

Ben knelt to Kavita, two fingers pressed against her convulsing neck. "There's a pulse. It's rapid and faint, but it's there!" he cried.

"The ambulance is on its way," said Linda. "Three minutes out."

But within two minutes the diplomat had no pulse. The small group helplessly watched as Kavita lay still, her lips blue and eyes glassy.

THREE

Mayor Kristján Gunnarsson stood in front of the art deco mirror in his front hall, lifted his chin, and straightened his tie. It wasn't every day that a man wore a tie in Vestmannaeyjar. Come to think of it, the last time was probably forty-seven days ago, that tempestuous Tuesday when the clouds draped themselves low over the hills, and the chill of the sea permeated deep into his bones. The day when he and most of the community bid a formal farewell to the love of his life.

Today's was a different tie, though. Softer, less expensive, equally professional yet simpler, brighter. A tie for a happier occasion. And indeed this was—or at least, it should be.

Kristján had been looking forward to meeting Ambassador Graeme Shearer again, this time on home turf. It wasn't all that uncommon for ambassadors resident in Reykjavík to pay one visit, or more, to the islands during their tenure. Usual postings were four years, and the trip involved only a ninety-minute car ride and the forty-five-minute ferry or, in a pinch, a twenty-minute flight. The prospect of inclement weather dissuaded some of the less hardy. No one wanted to be stranded on Vestmannaeyjar or forced to endure a three-hour ferry ride in rough seas if the regular route was considered too dangerous.

But now it was autumn. Winter's unreliability had not yet arrived, the days not yet depressingly short. As the seasonal darkness and the unpredictable weather encroached, this was the perfect time to invite the ambassador to the islands. And what better occasion than to officially open his compatriot Hanna Kovacic's new exhibition of images inspired by Icelandic nature. During the winter, people would begin to look inward, to stay inside and away from the elements, and they grew more culturally alert, seeking theater, readings, song.

Vestmannaeyjar had a rich cultural life for its size, but with only a few thousand inhabitants it was inevitably limited. With shorter days, people would be thirsty for art. And Hanna's images showcased the birth of an island, the infinite power of life to find a toehold everywhere. The way her light was beginning to shine in the art world, it would not be long before this town would be far too provincial for her talents, though Kristján doubted Hanna would ever treat these townspeople with such conceit. After all, she had spent years living on Vestmannaeyjar as a scientist. Even though she had moved away rather abruptly three years ago, its landscape and its people were surely now part of her soul. He thought she must be excited about her much anticipated return.

Tie in its proper place, Kristján sat down on the smooth

wooden bench next to the mirror and turned his attention to his shoes. For the second time in forty-seven days, he took out the black polish and began to burnish them to a shine. He was still shaken after what happened at the budget meeting the previous morning. When his assistant had swept all the papers into a brief-case, without even tidying them first, Kristján felt as if he had been slapped. That carefree, disorganized motion. It was as if Ari had been chairing the meeting himself. For a moment, he could see his dead husband's face, crooked smile, dimpled chin. As if Ari were about to gently chastise him for fretting over a minor detail.

All the books on grief cautioned about this. Grief had no end point. It was like floating on the sea for eternity. Sometimes, it came in waves and knocked you off course. The only way to deal with it was to accept it, to try and remember that those waves would gradually reduce in both severity and frequency, though never entirely disappear. Thank God for that. He couldn't face the thought that life without Ari could ever be normal.

While his grief never came at a convenient moment, Kristján knew he couldn't postpone the Canadian ambassador's tour. Kristján couldn't say, "Excuse me, Your Excellency, can we take the folklore museum off the schedule? I fear I'll have a panic attack if I walk into that building where eight weeks ago I discovered my husband's dead body."

For the millionth time, Kristján allowed his mind to wander to the period immediately following Ari's demise. The local doctor told him it was a "sudden cardiac event." Nothing anyone could do. She was very sorry, she said with shoulders almost shrugging. Ari had been on the right meds for cardiomyopathy, but sudden death was still a risk. Ari may have felt acutely unwell in the moments leading up to the event. The doctor suggested this might be why Ari had summoned him with a one-word text. But Kristján wasn't sure. The doctor didn't know about Ari's work and the enemies he may have made from it. They didn't know how many secrets Ari had uncovered about this community's inhabitants. And while Kristján was unaware of precisely what Ari had been working on before his untimely demise, he was sure of one thing: his husband's death could not have been from natural causes. His death had been a murder.

The mayor heard something being pushed through the letter box of the front door, disrupting his train of thought. He snatched the thin envelope from the floor. Who even received real mail anymore? Tearing it open, he read in haste and exhaled a sigh of relief. The letter finally confirmed some of his suspicions. He was on the right track. A little more detective work, some digging through the mountains of documents Ari had left behind, and he could blow the lid off corruption in his community. The next two days would not really be about art and diplomacy. They would be about finishing what Ari had set out to prove.

Kristján already knew that he would have to stomach a few encounters with one of his least favorite people in the country. But this letter confirmed his suspicions that he would also need to have words with Canada's deputy ambassador to Iceland. She had a lot to answer for.

FOUR

Jane felt seasick. She hoped the nausea would not last long into their two-day visit to Vestmannaeyjar.

She was sitting upright, her low-heeled leather boots crossed at the ankles, gently twisting the ferry's rotating chair from side to side to distract herself from the unpleasant sensation of the ferry riding the waves. When she focused out the triple-glazed window to the horizon, the *Herjólfur*'s rhythmic lurches through the churning North Atlantic were more bearable. Jane wore a tailored but unremarkable gray suit, a pastel-shaded patterned silk blouse, and small hoop earrings. A single strand of pearls encircled her slim neck, while simple diamond engagement and wedding rings completed her jewelry. She looked her part, with no extra fuss. Her companions—Graeme, Kavita, Rahul, Ben, and Hanna—sat in identical chairs near her.

Outside, it was cloudy and winds were increasing. It had been an unusually sunny summer, and the autumn weather, some felt,

was nature's way of evening the scales. Iceland's national mete-
orological station had issued nearly daily weather warnings for
some part of the country or another. Daylight each day shrank by
many minutes, a visual noose tightening around their chances to
experience the outdoors.

Jane silently chided herself for allowing self-pity to creep into
her thoughts; only a landlubber like her would feel overcome by
what was surely no more than a sea breeze. The locals around her
were oblivious. They played on their phones, chatted with each
other, or queued to order fries or even a pint of lager, despite the
morning hour. Jane unzipped her purse and popped a mint into her
mouth to help the nausea pass.

She shifted her glance away from the sea to Graeme. As usual,
he was impervious to discomfort. He had ridden ten agonizing
kilometers on the back of a camel in Mongolia, landed in rain-
storms with airlines that no longer had accreditation to fly into
Europe, even put the finishing touches on a visiting deputy minister's policy statement in a 4x4 bumping next to a field strewn
with land mines. She knew that Graeme would never complain
about a few waves. He was intently studying the speech he would
be delivering at the exhibition opening the next day, his blue eyes
sharply focused. On occasion he paused, scribbling a note or two in
the margins with a blue-ink fountain pen that Jane thought both
impractical and ostentatious.

The briefing documents the Canadian team had received were
vital to an understanding of, as the Global Affairs parlance had it,
the *key stakeholders* for the visit. As usual, Jane had committed the

memo to memory. She knew all about Hanna, from her ground-breaking research to her art to the unofficial rumors that she'd temporarily shacked up with a married local. Now that Hanna was sitting directly across from her and next to the ambassador, Jane took a moment to size up the woman to whom her husband had been referring as "remarkably talented" for several weeks now. She appeared to be in her midthirties—and that would fit, given that those same briefing notes mentioned a child she was raising on her own. Like Jane's, her hair was short, but while Jane's was a straight silver gray, Hanna sported lush curls in a deep auburn. Each ear was pierced three times. She wore Doc Martens with a fashionable black top and pants, both of which made her cherry-red raincoat pop.

Graeme shifted in his seat, his knee brushing Hanna's. The artist looked up from her phone, smiled at the ambassador, and languidly crossed her legs. Graeme glanced up at his wife and shifted his reading glasses so he could see her.

"Is the sea getting to you?" he inquired.

"I'll be fine." Jane forced a tight smile. "You should focus on those remarks. Hopefully this weather will calm down soon."

But the *Herjólfur* continued to lurch, while heavy clouds limited the view and only the sea, topped with frothy waves, was a deeper gray than the sky.

As Graeme focused on his notes, on Jane's other side Kavita also appeared unaffected by the *Herjólfur*'s movement. The embassy deputy was talking loudly into her phone, seemingly without a care as to whether she might distract her boss. Rahul sat placidly next to her.

"Of course," she barked into the handset. "We discussed this earlier." She glanced at Jane and rolled her eyes as if to say, *Is there no one competent who lives on that island?*

Graeme looked up from his notes. "Do you think you could take that elsewhere?"

Kavita merely turned her back to him and continued speaking. "No, the ambassador is *very aware* of the situation. He has given me full authority to insist that—" Kavita stared at her phone in disbelief as if the person had hung up. "Great," she muttered. "What a way to start the day."

"Kavita, we've discussed this," Graeme said. "I know how important your side project is, and I support that, but this trip is about other things. Let's try to calm down, shall we?"

"I'm getting a coffee. Thirsty?" Rahul asked his wife. He then turned to Jane with a look that said *I need a break from the tension here.*

"Get me a sparkling water, thanks. That one with lemon," Kavita replied.

"Black coffee, one sugar. Thanks, mate," called Ben. Rahul rounded the corner to the small bar on the other side of the cabin.

"At least he's being useful," Kavita said to Jane. "I don't really know why he wanted to tag along here, of all places. Computer programmers aren't known for their love of the great outdoors and posting images of puffins on Instagram. He has no real role to play, but he was so insistent on coming, I didn't want to say no."

"Icelanders love the optics of a man trailing his wife, don't worry," replied Hanna. Jane thought that despite the stereotypes of Rahul's profession, he had scrubbed up quite suitably. Classically tall, dark, and handsome, he resembled more a brooding film star than a vitamin D–deprived computer nerd. Especially when he wore a perfectly tailored suit, as he did now.

A few minutes later, Rahul dutifully handed his wife an opened can of lemon-flavored sparkling water and returned to his seat with a small sigh.

"Do you feel the waves too?" Jane asked him.

Rahul shook his head. "No, I spent a lot of time on the water when I was younger. But I confess this day is starting out a little differently than I had expected." He looked pointedly at his wife, who ignored the gesture and busied herself on her phone.

"How so?" Jane asked.

"I've never joined Kavita on one of these official tours. I mean, I've been to some cocktail receptions with her, but usually she does her thing and I do mine." He looked around him. "It's a bit more mundane than I expected."

"You ain't seen nothing yet!" Jane said teasingly. "Glamorous it is not. But, from one spouse to another, I'm sure you'll find something interesting about today and tomorrow. What appealed to you about this trip?"

Rahul paused for a moment, as if debating whether he knew Jane well enough to give her more than a boilerplate answer. "I've never been inside a fish factory before, yet they are ubiquitous in this country. Plus, it's an opportunity to get to meet the legendary Thór Magnússon."

Kavita looked up from her phone and raised her eyebrows. Clearly, she was not expecting this response from her handsome husband.

"Also your new exhibition, Hanna, obviously. And I'm looking forward to eating at Skel. I've heard excellent things," Rahul added as an afterthought.

Curious, thought Jane. Was Rahul going to say more about Iceland's leading "fish baron," and was Kavita's raised eyebrow her attempt to stop him? Was the beauty of these islands really enough to entice a very busy computer engineer from his own job, or was there another reason Rahul wanted to make this trip with his wife?

"You don't have anything to drink," Graeme commented to Hanna as the others sipped their beverages. "Let me get you something. Tea, perhaps?"

"That's very kind of you, but you're busy with your speech," Hanna replied. Jane bristled as she saw how Hanna, who had hardly spoken with any of them on the drive to the ferry or since they had begun sailing, was now smiling and engaged.

"It's no trouble. I need to stand up anyway." The ambassador rose, his arm lightly brushing Hanna's as he maneuvered his way out of the seat and around the corner.

Jane tightened her grip on the seat's armrest. Surely it couldn't be happening, not again, not after last time. Graeme had promised. But she'd just heard the tenderness in his voice and saw the "accidental" physical contact with the attractive artist.

"Thanks again for asking me to tag along." Ben's voice was in Jane's ear. "This is the only area of the country I have yet to visit; it'll be great to get somewhere new. My publisher would have me chained to my desk if they could."

With an effort, Jane forced her attention away from Graeme

and Hanna and on to Ben. He was sitting to her right, sipping his coffee. He had perfected the rumpled but charming writer look. Soft beige loafers and comfortable pants that could be dressed up or down, overpriced thin wool V-neck over a Thomas Pink shirt, the thickness of which mostly managed to conceal the slight paunch that was developing around his middle. He wore a durable TAG Heuer watch with a well-worn leather strap. Ben's dark wavy hair carried a light dusting of distinguished gray, and his blue eyes, while not exactly piercing, were deep and warm. He was enjoying his success, not taking it for granted yet utterly unsurprised at its arrival.

"How is book two coming along?"

Ben gave her a withering look. "You know better than to ask that."

Jane smiled. She may not have read the Canadian author's Booker Prize–winning debut, *Every Good Man*, but she had followed the culture section enough to know that it had ended in a way that teed up a sequel and that Ben's many publishers around the world had been crying for it with increasing vehemence ever since. Ben had even moved to Reykjavík a few months earlier to research the follow-up in the country where it was set.

"Tell the truth about why you're here. You want the cachet of traveling with an ambassador and escorted by the mayor." Jane's tone was friendly. She recalled that they had first met at an embassy function, where he'd been the only one to talk to her about anything besides Graeme, and she'd refused to fawn over his literary achievements. A fast and candid friendship had quickly formed between them.

Ben grinned. "Exactly. And I bet it will be an adventure!"

What an optimist, Jane thought. She twisted uncomfortably and again fixed her eyes on the shifting horizon.

"Not far now," Ben said to her. "You'll feel better as soon as we arrive."

Would she, though? At that moment Graeme returned with a mug of tea, which he handed to Hanna. She smiled up at him, and Jane's stomach churned in a way that had nothing to do with the sea.

"Could I have a word?" she said softly to her husband.

"Right now? I'm trying to get these notes finished."

But you've just stepped away from them to get Hanna a drink, she thought. "Yes, now."

They both stood and navigated their way past a group of schoolchildren to the back of the boat. Jane pulled Graeme inside an empty room lined with bunk beds and closed the door. Once inside, alone with her husband, she wasn't sure she could say what she wanted to.

"You were mouthing the words of your speech as you reviewed it," she opened, and immediately chided herself for her lack of courage.

"Again?" Graeme sounded surprised. "A juvenile habit. It doesn't look good. You should have told me earlier."

"I'm telling you now." Jane took a breath just as the boat lurched. "I don't know how much longer I can do this, Graeme."

"We're not far—"

"Not the ferry, Graeme. Our marriage." There. She'd said it.

Graeme stared at her as if she'd just slapped him, and Jane felt her temper rise. How could he not expect this, when he was just fawning over Hanna?

"The foundations are crumbling. You mouth the words of your speeches when you're practicing them. You ask me how I take my coffee every time you pour me a cup. Your idiosyncrasies are no longer adorable; I find them irritating. And that's a sign of some deeper unease."

"Hang on a moment. You're saying the foundations of our marriage are crumbling because I can't remember what you take in your coffee? What's wrong with you?" Consternation creased her husband's brow.

"It's not that. It's not the coffee. It's not your speeches. Maybe it's not even you making doe eyes at a certain woman on this trip. It's just—everything."

"Who are you—"

"I can't keep going on like this. Acting as if your selfishness, your obsession with your career doesn't matter to me, as if it doesn't affect the whole family. I cannot keep acting as if you haven't committed some serious mistakes. As if you aren't about to commit some more."

"Me? As I recall, I'm not the one who nearly destroyed—"

"Stop," she hissed. "Just stop. *This* is what I cannot stand. This condescension. It was you who had the affair, as I recall. The most clichéd cliché. The middle-aged man who couldn't keep it in his pants the moment an attractive woman turned up at work."

"I don't know how many times I can apologize for the same mistake. It was four years ago. I have never strayed since and never will."

Jane inhaled sharply. Was he telling the truth? Could that chemistry between him and Hanna be all in her mind? Before she had time to ask him, he continued: "I was referring to what happened *after* you found out. You cannot say you forgive me and then hold my sins over my head again. I don't do that to you."

Jane felt the words cut into her. Graeme knew exactly where her will was weakest: her need to believe that their marital crisis was solely her husband's making.

"I'm not trying to destroy this visit for you. God knows you need a professional win, and convincing Iceland's biggest seafood exporter to set up shop back home would be perfect. You could finally get an ambassadorship that 'would mean something,' as you put it. But what does it mean to me? I can't keep playing the role of supportive spouse just to soothe your ego. If you can't show me that your marriage is more important than your career, then I cannot stay in it."

Graeme stared at her as though she were a stranger rather than his wife of over twenty years. Beads of sweat glistened on his forehead, genuine worry finally showing itself on his face.

"Jane, please. Please don't threaten me with this. Not now."

"There is no good time for this. But I have reached my limit."

She thought of Hanna and how attentive Graeme was to her. Jane felt her nausea increasing, her convictions far weaker now than a moment ago. It was too late. She had put her cards on the table. Unlike the world of diplomacy, so steeped in nuance and doublespeak, she needed to be clear and direct.

Now, it was up to him.

FIVE

"*Kurwa!*"

Kristján held the phone away from his ear as Piotr Tómasson cursed loudly in Polish. The chef couldn't speak his mother's language well, but Kristján had borne witness to a range of Slavic profanities that Piotr used on his friends and foes alike with regularity. With only nine hours before a major VIP dinner, Chef Piotr had brought out the linguistic guns.

In any case, the artistic whims of Skel's head chef were the perfect distraction from Kristján's own spiraling thoughts. As he clutched that morning's letter in his hand, he heard Piotr slam something at the restaurant.

"Last night at closing there was still plenty of angelica," fumed Piotr. "Now, it's mere hours before we are serving a four-course dinner for nine, including an ambassador, and all I can find are a few flaccid stalks in Tupperware. No dried root at all!"

"Oh dear." Kristján was impassive. It was always best to allow these creative types to blow off steam before trying to soothe their egos.

Skel had been Ari's favorite restaurant. He had loved the conceit of Skel, its menu that seemed to magically elevate the culinary value of kelp to something TikTok foodies were willing to fly across an ocean for. Since Ari's death, Piotr had stayed in closer contact with the mayor than Kristján had necessarily wanted, calling him at strange hours of the day and sharing details of his own job stresses and personal woes. Kristján was too kindhearted to put a stop to it. Besides, he felt he owed Piotr, who had, after all, once shared useful information about the town's biggest employer.

"So what do you want me to do, Kristján? Should I remove the arctic char as the second course tonight, or hike over to the mountainside to forage any wild angelica still growing at this time of year? And can I dry the roots in time? *Niech to szlag trafi!* There are plenty of other details for tonight I need to complete. I don't need this hassle now."

"Piotr, as usual, I have every confidence that this menu will offer the best of what Vestmannaeyjar has to offer from both sea and land, and at a world-class standard no less. After all, who's the only Icelander spotlighted in the most recent Nordic Guides 'Chef to Watch' series?"

Kristján could picture it now. The article praising Skel's "eclectic combination of ancient wisdom and contemporary presentation" was framed and hanging on Skel's wall, in the direct eyeline of customers who never blinked about paying $30 for an Across the Street (glorified gin and tonic) or $50 for a starter of grilled carrots garnished with seasonal herbs. Piotr stood cross-armed in the accompanying photo, his bald head and pose reminiscent of an epicurean, heavily tattooed Mr. Clean.

The mayor could sense that Piotr's anger had begun to plateau.

"You're right. That was an honor. 'At Skel, Chef Tómasson has melded centuries-old flavors with modern twists and international influences.'" Piotr paused. "I memorized it."

"Well, those twists and influences will be on full display this evening, I'm sure. What are we having?"

"We will begin with sea sandwort with roasted kelp vinaigrette, bites of sea urchin, dried dulse with a sour cream dip, then dung-smoked arctic char on angelica-flavored flatbreads. The main is reindeer fillet with beetroot, and for dessert, a bilberry and arctic thyme sorbet with yarrow. Of course, we'll wrap it up with my famous Flaming Viking at the end!"

"That will be unforgettable for our visitors," Kristján said, with an emollient tone. "It already sounds like a triumph."

"It will be," agreed Piotr. "The arctic char is Hanna's favorite. But I must tell you, I should be charging you extra for accommo-dating all the dietary requirements of this group. I know sometimes it is necessary to create something vegan"—Piotr said the word as if he had tasted something rotten—"and I realize that some people get anaphylactic reactions to some foods. But a claim that stir-fried mushrooms would cause gastric upset, when raw mushrooms would not? That Canadian embassy deputy is driving me nuts. She says she has a shellfish allergy and that the ambassador won't eat real butter, but that dairy is all right. That he has an intolerance for nuts but not an actual allergy. What does that even mean? Do you think she realizes how irritating she is? No one wants to go out of their way for someone so rude. Ari never spoke to me like that, you know, even though I had to tweak many dishes to suit his diet." Piotr paused for a moment. "Kristján, I didn't mean to mention Ari so abruptly."

"I know," Kristján answered gruffly. "Speaking of the dinner, can you make sure I sit near your picky Canadian? I need to talk to her."

"We got a seating plan from the embassy a few weeks ago," Piotr answered. "So I don't have control over that. But if you don't catch her at dinner, talk to her when I do my Flaming Viking performance. It's the perfect moment for some excitement."

SIX

TEN HOURS BEFORE SHE DIED

The wind was relentless as the Canadian delegation pulled up to a dull, off-white, two-story structure whose practical architect wisely had endurance rather than aesthetics in mind during its creation. An equally plain sign in Icelandic and English above the entrance announced: "Vestmannaeyjar Folklore Museum and Municipal Archive."

"I thought the museum was up on the mountain over there," Ben said to Jane as they dashed from the vehicle inside. He pointed to a dark, modernist structure high up on the hill overlooking the town, barely visible through the fog. Jane was not surprised he had not read their briefing documents. Ben was a fly-by-the-seat-of-his-pants guy at the best of times. He could charm his hosts, but he wouldn't put himself out for them.

"You're thinking of the newer museum that commemorates the 1973 eruption," Jane told him. She lowered her voice. "That museum is apparently much swankier than this one; it was built by some glamorous architects from the continent. All part of the plan to position the Westman Islands as the 'Pompeii of the North,' even though there was only one casualty."

"It was still devastating though," Rahul chimed in as they stomped their feet and began removing coats. "It's an unbelievable story, really. In the middle of a dark winter's night, a huge chasm just opened up in the earth somewhere right over there"—he pointed toward the grassless summit outside the window—"and began spouting lava high into the sky. Within a few hours, the whole town was evacuated to the mainland. But what locals thought would last a few hours, or perhaps a few days, turned into five months living as refugees. When they returned, a third of their town was buried under lava and another third had been destroyed by the ash that had rained down. I can't begin to imagine the impact that had on the locals."

"You really did your homework." Jane was impressed.

"This folklore museum is some sort of anemic older sibling to the newer volcano center," commented Kavita. Jane hoped the mayor, standing nearby, couldn't hear them. "It has far fewer visitors, but the ambassador wanted us to stop here."

Jane gave her a questioning glance.

"Hanna's exhibition will be held here," Kavita explained.

"Where is Hanna?" Ben asked. "She was on the ferry, but I haven't seen her since."

"She mentioned having to prepare something before the big opening," Graeme replied hastily.

Just as he spoke, a tall, blond woman with puffy, styled hair and dark, thinly plucked eyebrows greeted the group with a warm smile and introduced herself as Stella Finnsdóttir, director of the museum. Stella looked like a Hollywood stereotype of a Nordic beauty. Jane could practically feel the waves of attraction emanating from every heterosexual man in the group.

"I'd like to begin with a brief introduction to Vestmannaeyjar, or as you may know them, the Westman Islands," Stella began in warm tones. "The Westman Islands are one of the most well-known areas of Iceland, and even though our population is still only 4,500 souls, we like to think we have an outsized impact on Iceland. Most of us can trace our ancestry back centuries on this teardrop-shaped island. Our forefathers and -mothers were sheep farmers and fishers who eked out a living from the short grazing season and frigid ocean. Follow me and I'll show you some of the exhibitions we are most proud of."

Stella led them toward the first permanent exhibition of the small museum. As the crowd clustered together, she directed them toward a series of large, illustrated tableaux, a sort of wall-sized comic strip.

"In the seventeenth century, the Westman Islands' population was about five hundred, and people generally worked in agriculture. During what is colloquially known as the 'Turkish Raid,' Algerian pirates attacked the island in July 1627. Over three agonizing days, they tore children from mothers, raped women, and murdered priests, either killing or kidnapping almost half of the population.

"Incredibly, the Westman Islanders who remained raised enough money via the king of Denmark to pay a handsome ransom for their countrymen. Eventually, about fifty people were freed although they did not all return to Iceland.

"These illustrations tell the story of the raid," concluded Stella. "We chose to portray it this way so that young people would be interested in learning about this tragic part of our history."

Jane peered more closely at the rudimentary paintings. The first panels depicted people going about their daily business—hanging up washing, milking a cow, drying fish in the sun. But later, when the marauders arrived, the panels changed. The oil colors were just as bright, the illustrations as simplistic as before, but now, instead of a PG recounting of Middle Ages Iceland, each panel showed the unvarnished violence of the attack: a man raping a woman in the grass, blood spurting from the neck of an elderly farmer who had been stabbed, children wailing as they were torn from their mothers' arms. How easily their tranquility had been shattered without warning, transforming all their lives forever.

This was Icelandic storytelling, Jane recalled—the unvarnished truth. There was no attempt to sugarcoat the brutality of history.

Jane leaned closer, focusing on the weather-beaten faces of the islanders in the images. Dragged from everything they had ever known, how could they possibly begin a new life in a new world? What compelled some of them to stay in Algeria when they had a chance to return to Iceland? Did they feel guilt for their decisions? Were they seen as heroes or cast away as traitors?

The others in Jane's group didn't seem to be as affected by the story and its depiction. Ben had listened in a practiced but unemotional way. He held a battered notebook in his hand and was looking elsewhere, scribbling a few notes. These were just as likely to be character sketches of people among this modern-day group as facts about a seventeenth-century attack on the island.

Kavita and Rahul stood together, she with a serious face, listening politely but also looking like she had more important places to be. Jane knew Kavita to be prompt and sometimes overly fixated on rigid schedules, but she was always a consummate professional. Yet on this trip, she seemed more jittery than usual. Jane caught her looking at her watch and checking her phone often. It was as if she had left the limited patience she possessed back on the mainland to collect after their visit to Vestmannaeyjar.

Graeme too seemed fixated on the images in front of him, and Jane couldn't figure out whether he was paying attention to the story or merely lost in his own worries. There was something almost endearing about the frown etching his brow, and she felt a sudden rush of regret for what she might be giving up. Graeme noticed the expression and touched his wife's wrist, whispering softly in her ear. "Why are you doing this now, Jane?"

"Please, you know exactly why."

Yet Jane let his hand remain softly against her arm.

"I'd like to show you our other permanent exhibit," said Stella, shattering the moment of chemistry. "We'll move from the Middle Ages up to the twentieth century."

As they walked through a dimly lit hall and past old pictures of dirty fishermen, Jane saw the mayor approach Ben and tap him on the shoulder.

"I just want to say that we're thrilled to have you with us,"

Kristján said effusively. "You're quite the celebrity in these parts, you know. And if there's one thing Icelanders love more than a visiting celebrity, it's a visiting celebrity with Icelandic ancestry!"

Ben responded with a friendly grin. No doubt he had heard this before. "Yes, my grandfather moved to Gimli in Canada from Borgarfjördur eystri when he was just a boy." He lifted his wrist. "Actually, this old watch was his. Costs a fortune to keep it working, but it keeps me close to my roots, I guess."

"Oh, we know all about the Eastfjords connection!" exclaimed Kristján. "When you moved to Iceland to write, there was a feature article on you in *Mannlíf* magazine. Photos from the farm where your grandfather was born and everything. But there is a Westman Islands connection too. Did you know that?"

"No, actually, I didn't." Ben sounded genuinely surprised. "My great-grandfather left from a valley in the northeast of Iceland. With due respect, I thought Westman Islanders here on the other side of the country were known for keeping to themselves."

"My husband, Ari, was not from around here. After you got famous, Ari used to boast that you had the same great-grandfather, the guy who ditched the old country and set up anew in Gimli, Manitoba. His oldest son was Ari's grandfather, who stayed behind after his father emigrated." Kristján blinked something from his eyes. "I used to tease Ari about how often he brought this up. I mean, every Icelander is related to someone famous."

"So I've discovered."

"And you both got the writing gene," Kristján continued. "Your great-grandfather had the nickname Jón the Learned. Legend has it that on dark winter nights in those damp turf huts, he could keep people spellbound for hours with the most engaging stories. My Ari could captivate a room too." Kristján gazed at some point far in the distance and then appeared to return to the present. "I mean, it's nothing so impressive as a Booker Prize." He shrugged his shoulders. "But it's a source of pride all the same. We're counting the days until *Every Good Man*'s sequel comes out."

They were interrupted by a delicate cough from Stella. Her tour was continuing. "As many of you may know, Iceland was officially neutral during the Second World War. But the country was occupied, first by the British and then the Americans. They claimed it was for our own protection, so the Nazis wouldn't arrive to claim a foothold in the North Atlantic.

"This exhibit showcases life for the Westman Islanders during the war years." She gestured to a series of more traditional museum displays. Long, framed posters of wartime propaganda hung along one wall. Small captions next to them provided context in Icelandic.

There was also a lower, glass-covered case with memorabilia from the time: a record player, a typewriter, old bottles of after-shave, tin coffee mugs, and silk scarves. Above this hung maps from the era, of Vestmannaeyjar, of maritime currents.

"This is one of our showcase pieces," said Stella proudly as she gestured to a mannequin clothed in a British soldier's khaki uniform. "One of our residents found it among the possessions of her late grandmother. The older woman never revealed where she acquired it, or from whom. Within the family there is lore of a romance gone awry." Stella grinned.

"What's particularly interesting about this uniform is its condition. There are no moth holes, no wear and tear." Stella pointed to a satchel hanging over the right shoulder of the mannequin. "This bag is full of items soldiers here may have had: a ration card, a small photo of a loved one back home, even some rock-hard chewing gum. Then up here," Stella's hand pointed higher on the mannequin, "you can see the chain, missing its dog tags but with a small cyanide capsule encased in thin metal."

She paused to make sure she had the room's full attention. "And here's the ongoing mystery. A soldier who wore cyanide around his neck must have been tasked with such secret information that he would have been instructed to pop it in his mouth if he were captured and threatened with torture. He would protect his secrets with his life; chewing the capsule would cause near-instant, but agonizing, death."

Jane caught the skeptical glance that Rahul threw to Kavita. She looked to Graeme, who shifted his feet uncomfortably.

"We've never discovered who owned this uniform, this satchel, and this chain," Stella said. "And as you see, the dog tags that would have listed the soldier's name, rank, and serial number have been removed. I suppose that's all right, though," she said. "We Westman Islanders like our little mysteries."

Jane turned away to look at the next exhibition but stopped in her tracks when, instead of the next display case, she saw Graeme and Kavita locked in private conversation.

"I think the mayor might know," Graeme was saying to her urgently. "That would ruin everything. I know you're impatient, but we have to wait. We only have one shot at this. You have to find out what information he has."

Kavita's lips were a tight line. "I'll let you know if he says anything to me."

Jane wasn't sure what they were discussing, but she wished Graeme would not take out his impatience on the deputy ambassador. Kavita lacked emotional intelligence, but she was devoted and smart. And why was Graeme keeping a secret from a small-town mayor? And using Kavita to help him?

SEVEN

NINE HOURS BEFORE SHE DIED

Half an hour after the visiting delegation left the warmth of the folklore museum and archive for their next destination, Hanna Kovacic marched into the area's foyer. She stomped her Doc Martens on a welcome mat, removed her cherry-red rain jacket and shook as much of the water off it as she could, strode behind the unmanned ticket booth, and hung the jacket up on a worn hook.

"Stella!" she called into the empty space. "I'm here. Is everyone gone?"

The museum's curator appeared in the room a moment later, running up to give her friend a hug.

"Gone and happy," she said. "I told them all the good stories we locals know: the Turkish Raid, the mysterious World War Two spy." She paused. "Looks like it's coming down out there."

"The weather's atrocious!" complained the artist. "No wonder you have dozens of words for wind in Icelandic. What's this outside? *Manndrápsveður?*"

Stella chuckled. "'Man-killing weather'? Not quite. You've become weak since you left Iceland. This is nothing special. But I do know something that'll help make you feel better. Hang on." She rushed out of the room and returned a moment later with a bottle of room-temperature sparkling wine and two plastic champagne flutes.

"Cheers! Here's to the rebirth of the liquid lunch."

Hanna returned the gaze, taking a generous sip of bubbly. "I'll say," she replied. "Been looking forward to this all week. So, this is the space, eh? It looks great." Hanna smiled as she studied the final setup. "Thanks again for hosting the show here. I know moss paintings by a Canadian aren't exactly within the educational remit of this place."

"Well, I like to help out a friend," replied Stella. "This is art, and just the name Hanna Kovacic is going to have both the great and the good—and the gossip-eager locals—rushing to see what the fuss is about. It's wonderful publicity for us."

Hanna knew it was going to be perfect. The room was sparse, clean, and bright, an ideal venue for the international debut of the hotly anticipated Kovacic exhibition *Focus*, which was an homage to the nearby island of Surtsey, a rocky teardrop that had sprung unannounced out of the Atlantic in 1963, formed from an undersea eruption. Hanna was one of the lucky few scientists who had been allowed to visit the blossoming ecosystem—and only then under strict conditions. Her art was inspired by what she discovered— scenes that at first glance appeared to be simplistic, yet only after setting preconceptions aside could their true value be gleaned.

They were also a way for her to deal with the sudden manner in which she had left her position—left science altogether, in fact.

"We got the brochures this morning too." Stella showed Hanna a trifolded pamphlet in Icelandic and English with a few prints of the paintings and photos and bios of both Hanna and Stella as museum curator.

"Check out this description of you: 'Dr. Hanna Kovacic has a doctorate degree in microbiology and has been published widely in the fields of taxonomy and ecophysiology. She spent two years in Vestmannaeyjar researching the developing species of lichen on nearby Surtsey Island.'" Stella looked up from the folded paper in her hand and smiled. "It should *really* say something like: 'Dr. Kovacic is spontaneous and fun and knows better than anyone the importance of wearing bright colors…' People would really relate to that more, don't you think?"

Hanna chortled and snatched the program from Stella's hands.

"Well, what about your bio? It's all about your record-setting grant from the Ministry of Culture. Oh, and it brags about your glowing profile in *Museum Monthly*." She looked up for a moment with an ironic twinkle in her eye. "*Museum Monthly?* I can't believe you never told me. These blurbs always forget what makes people people. Here's how yours should go."

Hanna took a sip of her drink and cleared her throat: "Following almost a decade in university and work in the capital, Stella returned to the village of her birth, enticed by the prospect of managing her own museum. After ending a four-year relationship with a fellow historian back in Reykjavík, Stella surprised many by packing up and buying—not even renting!—a small, one-bedroom apartment near the elementary school on Vestmannaeyjar. Her heart healed quicker than she expected. Now, Stella has found her niche."

Stella lightly applauded to her friend's praise.

Hanna relished her friend's humor, her lighthearted ways. She was surprised at what good friends they had become ever since that chance encounter at the local swimming pool a few years ago, given that Stella was at the older end of Gen Z, tall, and gifted with thick, golden locks, while Hanna was petite, auburn-haired, and a single parent of a preteen boy who spent more time with his father than with her. Yet beneath their physical differences, their camaraderie was entirely logical. They were both comfortably free spirits but tight-lipped and loyal. Hanna knew that Stella would store any secrets she shared with the same care she used to protect the museum's most valuable artifacts. Of course, there were also some secrets Hanna would not ever divulge.

The rain pounded against the windows as they contemplated the artwork around them.

Stella leaned toward her friend. "You emailed last week that one of these pieces was a reference to one of your local hookups. Which one?"

Hanna pointed to a one-meter-by-one-meter canvas on the wall opposite the window. It featured a green gently undulating mossy field, the sky above Surtsey a gentle blue.

"It's called *Come Hither*," she told her friend. "You know, like to my boudoir." They cackled in delight.

"Speaking of which, the dinner tonight with all the diplomats... That's at Skel, isn't it?" Stella asked Hanna.

"Hmm, I think so."

"Is it going to be awkward for you, seeing Chef Piotr again?"

Hanna shrugged. "Not for me. For him maybe. But I can't miss dinner because the restaurant owner was once hoping for more than a one-night stand."

She looked back down at the exhibition brochure. Small text at the bottom proclaimed: "This exhibition has been made possible through the generous support of Bláhafid Seafood Products."

"Stella, what's this?" The artist held the paper up and pointed to the text.

Stella shrugged. "Bláhafid. They're the main sponsor. Didn't you know that? They're covering the costs of advertising this event, even paying a teenager to do an extra evening shift or two. Why? Is there a problem with that?"

"Thór? Why didn't I know about it before? You know what I think of that company. I don't want to have anything to do with them."

Stella shrugged again and held up her hands. "Hey, I'm just the venue. Talk to the Canadian embassy. They're the ones coordinating it."

Hanna felt a pang of hurt. "The embassy?" she asked. "Graeme never mentioned this cooperation. I didn't think he'd—"

"What?" Stella asked. "Was the ambassador involved in this? Wouldn't his deputy look after that sort of thing?"

Hanna didn't respond. The situation was too complicated, too raw, to explain. She sighed and took another sip of her sparkling wine. It didn't taste so refreshing anymore. This unpleasant development changed things, possibly even put the whole exhibition in jeopardy. She couldn't let that happen after all the sacrifices she had made.

"Earth to Hanna?" Stella was nudging her with her foot. "Is this really the end of the world? This is just a bit of money to help you get on your feet."

Hanna took a deep breath. Stella was right. It was just money. Wasn't it? She looked at her friend, who saw opportunities and not threats, who trusted in people's potential, instead of bemoaning the unfairness of blighted dreams.

Hanna finished off her drink. "You're right," she said, standing up to collect her coat. "Thanks. I'll figure out a way to put Thór in his place tonight."

"Do you mean *a way* like when you were almost charged with arson after that accountant messed up your taxes?"

"Nah. My dealings with law enforcement are behind me. What I have in mind is perfectly legal. Well, *probably* legal."

"Don't do anything dangerous, Hanna." Stella looked around her. "You're on the cusp of greatness. What would be worth risking that?"

Hanna shrugged. "I just want tonight's dinner to be memorable."

What she didn't say was that tonight's dinner was now intricately entwined with the success she so desperately craved. In fact, without it, everything she had worked so hard for might evaporate.

EIGHT

EIGHT HOURS BEFORE SHE DIED

A dapper assistant hit Play on the corporate introduction to Bláhafid Seafood Products, and Jane swiveled her leather boardroom chair to face a new OLED screen. Over sweeping orchestral music, a voice-over central casting would have dubbed "rugged male" began recounting the plucky story of two brothers with a rickety trawler and a dream to make their fortunes.

Expensive drone shots zoomed over the handsomest, trimmest, and most muscular members of Bláhafid's fishing crews hauling tubs of glistening fish from the shimmering seas under cloudless skies. The narration explained that the company had grown from owning a few vessels to a three-hundred-person processing facility, with additional staff elsewhere. The company was named one of Iceland's top employers five years running, and Bláhafid's current CEO and majority owner, Thór Magnússon, had been named Entrepreneur of the Year by the national business magazine twice in the last decade.

The message conveyed by the video was one of confidence, safety, sustainability, and pride in Iceland's fishing heritage, combined with the latest in technical know-how and modernization.

It was impressive how inspirational—even aspirational—a generous budget and a creative marketing team could make a fish factory seem. They were extolling the virtues of a place where blood literally spilled on the floor. Jane leaned back in the soft chair. She imagined those Viking seafarers smelled like fish guts, weathered as they had been by the North Atlantic's brutal winter storms. Then she wondered whether, despite all the advances in radar locators, inflatable lifeboats, and fluorescent personal flotation suits, they still got scared during a Category 3 storm and how many of them had lost someone to the sea's unforgiving clutches.

She shuddered. Seafaring life was not as glamorous as this video made it out to be, and Thór Magnússon could not be as glamorous as he seemed either. Still, he was one of the country's legendary quota barons, a man whose family had ended up on the right side of the ledger book a few decades before, when the government decided to impose restrictions on one of the nation's most valuable resource, its fisheries.

"Does anyone have any questions before I give you a little tour?" Thór asked the visiting delegation. Approaching two meters in height, he commanded a room not so much because of his size, but because of his voice—a deep, buttery baritone. He knew how to captivate and how to endear even the most cynical visitor to Bláhafid Seafood Products HQ.

Kavita immediately began asking detailed questions of the

CEO; Jane tuned out when she heard "annual tonnages" and "ISO certifications" and looked around. Mayor Kristján was typing something on his phone. Next to him was an empty seat that had been reserved for Ben, until he announced as they left the folklore museum that he was skipping the factory tour to go and sign copies of his novel at the local bookstore. In the center seat, the one unofficially designated for the most senior guest, Graeme had been taking notes, reading glasses bobbing up and down as he alternated between examining bullet points on the video and his own handwritten scribbles in front of him. He had always been an extensive note-taker, telling Jane that the simple act of writing down a new fact helped one to retain it. "Little tip," he'd say, tapping her on the shoulder or nodding his head gently. But Jane knew the truth. He wrote things down to avoid making errors, to protect himself and his team.

Of course, Graeme had no idea how patronizing his various "little tips" came across. (What a relief when the term *mansplaining* entered the lexicon.)

Jane's mind drifted to their conversation aboard the *Herjólfur*. Would she discover proof of what she suspected to be true about her husband and Hanna? And even if, somehow, he managed to produce a plausible explanation for the obvious intimacy between them, would he understand that their own problems were about more than that? Would he be prepared to change, and was she prepared to stick with their marriage if he was?

Jane had no idea what was said during the rest of the speeches, but ten minutes later, when they were completed, the group donned the unflattering but compulsory garb of any food industry facility and were guided to the action on Bláhafid's factory floor.

"I had no idea it was so large-scale," Rahul said in awe as they walked gingerly between row upon row of women gutting and trimming what seemed to be cod shuttling along a conveyor belt at alarming speed. The visitors' company-issued rubber boots squeaked on the cement floors, wet with spray from the water that constantly kept surfaces clean and bacteria-free.

"All this noise, these conveyors, and these fish smells… It's a cacophony for the senses," Rahul said to Jane.

Thór, who was leading the group, occasionally picked up a slick, beheaded fish from a conveyor belt to highlight something to do with size, or quality, or safety. Thanks to the noise, only Graeme, and perhaps Kavita, could hear him.

Kristján looked as if he had stopped listening to Thór's lecture, presumably because he knew the inside of Bláhafid's facility almost as well as its employees, having escorted VIP visitors on an almost monthly basis since taking over as mayor. He instead made attempts at small talk with Rahul and Jane.

"Have you seen a facility such as this before?"

"It reminds me of a plant we saw in Ólafsvík," recalled Jane. Only a few weeks after their arrival in Iceland, she and Graeme had made their first trip to a fish-processing facility, meeting and talking with people whose livelihoods depended on the riches of the sea. These factories were not only the lifeblood of small, maritime communities, she told her husband later, but also the backbone and muscle. But that power, granted through economics rather than democracy, often gave the factories a disproportionate influence over a village, as if Amazon or Meta had based their global HQ in a remote northern harbor town.

They moved past the conveyor belts, where women worked wearing sound-reducing headphones to minimize distraction. Graeme stopped and smiled at everyone with whom he succeeded in making eye contact. Kavita, meanwhile, kept her eyes on her watch as each brief interaction, however well intentioned, added to the odds that her well-structured schedule would go off the rails.

As they moved from the main processing hall over to a quieter but equally busy packing and distribution area, Graeme turned to Thór.

"By the way, thank you for your support of Hanna's exhibition," he offered. "I doubt the event would be happening if it weren't for Bláhafid, and it's so important to Hanna—to Canadian artistic promotion—that it get off to a good start."

Thór smiled, familiar with the diplomatic dance of appreciated offers and favors obtained.

"My pleasure. We value a dynamic arts scene here on the Westman Islands."

Only Jane noticed Kristján roll his eyes.

"You really are the lifeblood of this town," Graeme said to Thór. "Its skeleton and muscle."

"Brilliant metaphor. You've hit the nail on the head," Thór said.

Jane knew Graeme would not acknowledge that it was, in fact, *her* metaphor, but still she felt a surge of irritation when he didn't. He and Thór stood together, two tall men turning toward each other, blocking out the rest of the group as they moved from opening gambit to professional tête-à-tête, eyes and ears only for each other.

The remaining guests waited awkwardly for the dialogue to conclude.

"Do you think we'll have an opportunity to talk privately later today?" Kavita asked the mayor.

Kristján's eyes lit up. "Yes, definitely. At dinner? There is something I'd like to review with you."

Jane thought she saw a flicker of puzzlement pass across Kavita's face, but a moment later the deputy ambassador's phone buzzed, and her attention snapped to her screen.

The CEO's and ambassador's hearty chuckling drifted over to the hangers-on. This was a good sign. Jane gritted her teeth and resigned herself to another few minutes of boredom. Establishing a relationship of respect and trust between Graeme and Thór was one of the key objectives of this trip. If Graeme could finesse an expansion of Bláhafid's operations into Canada, he'd be praised by the higher-ups for his promotion of Canadian trade interests.

Finished on her phone, Kavita turned to Jane with a worried look on her face. "This storm is worse than predicted, and the weather office has issued an orange warning, effective immediately. I've never heard of that happening so quickly before. If it delays transport beyond our scheduled ferry after the morning's opening, I won't be able get my latest group of refugees to Canada. I'm supposed to sign and seal all their documents at the embassy tomorrow, and if I can't, we lose our place in the queue."

Jane recalled some discussion of refugees in Iceland awaiting approval to reside in Canada. Thanks to some clever work by the embassy, they were granted permission to stay and work in Iceland while the paperwork cleared. This must be what Kavita was referring to.

"Would that be the end of the world?" Jane asked. "They're in Iceland now. Safest country in the world."

"You have no idea just how bad it would be," Kavita responded grimly. "Your husband knows something about it. He's been greasing the wheels back in Ottawa. That's a good thing," she said, then glanced in the direction of Graeme and Thór. "When I was setting up this Bláhafid visit I never realized that…"

She hesitated, so Jane coaxed her. "What didn't you realize?"

"That everything comes at a price," Kavita told Jane. "Though by now I should have clued in to that."

"What do you mean?"

But Kavita merely shrugged, and Jane saw from the thin, determined line of her lips that it was pointless to press her.

"I've only ever known you to do the right thing," Jane said. "Keep your game face on, your eyes on the prize."

"What, are you a boxing coach now?" Kavita asked, allowing herself a small smile.

"We have all had to make sacrifices and hope that the payoff is worth it." Jane replied. "But let me tell you, it can be fucking frustrating sometimes."

Kavita raised her eyebrows.

"Yes, diplomatic wives swear too," Jane said. "It's healthy on occasion. Look, I'm happy to hear Graeme has been helping with your refugee initiative; I know that's not usually something Global Affairs would handle. I'm just a bit jealous, I guess. You still have time to change the world. My idealism is long extinguished, I'm afraid."

"Sometimes I wish mine would take a back seat," Kavita replied. "Everything seems to have suddenly become so complicated. I thought if I just did the right thing for the right people, it wouldn't really matter how I got there." She shot Jane a rather desperate glance. "But now even Rahul is disappointed in me."

At the mention of marital discord, Jane subconsciously touched the pearls around her neck.

Kavita frowned. "You don't strike me as a pearl-wearing woman."

"They were a gift from Graeme the week after the twins' births," Jane answered. "At the time, I couldn't stand for more than fifteen minutes at once, and post-labor pains made me double over. I was young and fragile, and he made me feel stable then."

"And not now?" Kavita prodded.

Jane hesitated. Professionalism and loyalty to Graeme cut her short of laying bare her marital problems to his deputy, but neither could she bring herself to lie. The truth felt lodged in her throat: that these pearls now felt like an albatross around her neck, yet she couldn't bring herself to take them off, to acknowledge what that would mean.

Kavita looked at the floor and was silent for a moment, then seemed to come to a decision.

"Jane, can I ask you something personal?"

Jane didn't want Kavita prying into her private life, but something about the deputy ambassador's tone gave her the impression that Kavita was seeking advice rather than nosing into Jane's business.

Jane glanced at her husband, who was still deep in dialogue with his new best friend. The mayor was sending a message on his cell phone, and Rahul was sitting quietly in the corner, apparently waiting for this stop on the tour to be finished. Jane nodded to Kavita.

"It's about Rahul. And me. I'm not sure why I'm telling you this, but time is running out."

"What is it?"

"I may have gone too far with this refugee initiative. The ambassador doesn't know the compromises I've had to make to move things forward, but I have told Rahul. He's usually the most easygoing guy in the world, but he was furious. He asked me what happened to my sense of right and wrong, if I remembered why I chose a career in diplomacy in the first place." Her tone was one of bemusement rather than hurt.

Jane stared at her. What could Kavita possibly have done to make Rahul, who seemed prepared to put up with being treated like a spare part most of the time, so enraged. Should Graeme know about whatever Kavita had done? She glanced again at her husband, then back at Kavita. The deputy's eyes were wide, frightened, vulnerable.

"I may not have battled my way up the diplomatic ladder, but I do have some life experience," said Jane quietly. "If you think you're right, you need to talk it over with Rahul and make sure he understands your point of view."

"But what if he doesn't? What did Graeme say to you when he messed up? What made you forgive him?"

Jane looked at Kavita sharply.

Kavita froze. "Jane, I…"

"I forgave him for what?" Jane asked coldly.

"I… That was just an expression. Hasn't everyone done something stupid in their relationships?"

Jane felt her anger rising. "That was no slip of the tongue. You were referring to something specific. Tell me what it is."

Kavita cast a glance to the others in the room, as if wishing the other discourses were winding up and she could race out the door. But Thór and Graeme were still in conversation and the others busy on their phones.

"Jane, look, I'm sorry. I thought it was something everyone knew about."

Jane knew exactly what Kavita was referring to. But the deputy needed to learn not to be so careless with her words, and she wasn't going to let her off the hook this easily. "Kavita, I'm losing patience. Tell me what you know."

Slowly, Kavita took out her phone and found a screenshot of an email dated a year earlier. Wordlessly, she handed the device to Jane, who read the email's contents:

Global Affairs sure isn't a pure meritocracy. You're posted to Reykjavík now, right? Isn't Graeme Shearer the ambassador

there? He's the guy I told you about last year, the one who
was reprimanded for sleeping with his boss. The boss hasn't
been promoted since, but Graeme seems to be going strong.
Of course. Thought you'd want to know. He shouldn't be able
to get away with shit like that.

Jane felt as though icy fingers were dancing along her spine.
She looked for the name of the sender, but the screenshot hadn't
captured it. She stared at those awful words a while longer, then
looked up from the phone, fighting to keep a neutral expression on
her face. "Who sent this to you?"

"It doesn't matter. A colleague back in Ottawa. It's another
example of the double standard." Kavita paused for a moment.
"Wait. Didn't you know about this? Somehow I thought you must
have, if it reached me."

Jane knew all about Graeme's infidelity, that poison that had
seeped into their marriage four years ago and whose effect had
never quite been excised. She did not know that it had been water-
cooler gossip. In fact, Graeme had promised her that only he and
the person involved knew about it. Yet here was the evidence to the
contrary, her humiliation passed along the diplomatic grapevine
like juicy fruit to be devoured. In this too, she had been deceived.
Jane felt the old writhing of shame in her belly.

She couldn't succumb to this now, not here. She forced her
attention back to Kavita.

"Did you cheat on Rahul and now regret it? Is that what you're
getting at?"

"No, no," Kavita answered hastily as she shoved her phone back in her purse. "It was more about the idea of forgiveness. If you could do something your partner didn't like and be forgiven for it."

Jane snorted and patted the diplomat condescendingly on the shoulder. "Kavita, you can't ever turn back the clock. You can only put one foot in front of the other and hope that your mistakes haven't fucked things up for too many people." She put her coffee on the table and pasted a smile on her face. "Well, gentlemen, isn't it time we got a move on?" she asked the group pointedly.

Inwardly, her heart pounding, she felt the firewalls she had built around her life start to crack. Graeme had made it sound to her like nobody knew about his affair, but clearly it was common knowledge. If he was lying to her about that, what else was he lying about?

NINE

SEVEN HOURS BEFORE SHE DIED

Hanna sank her shoulders into the warm water and pressed a button unleashing a surge of bubbles. She inhaled the pristine air. She was sheltered here from the violent wind; high plexiglass sides surrounded the hot tub.

Vestmannaeyjabær's public swimming pool was Hanna's favorite in all of Iceland and a source of pride for the community; swimming pools were some of the nation's most popular gathering places. Open from early morning and often until late in the evening, hundreds of pools around the country hosted a revealing cross section of Icelandic society. Senior citizens talked politics before or after 7:00 a.m. laps. Exhausted parents stopped by with their toddlers for a couple of hours of healthy, energetic play. Hungover teenagers compared stories from the night before during dreary weekend noon hours. The swimming pools were the great equalizer, one of the only locations in the nation where one would be just as likely to exchange small talk with a TV celebrity as with a recently arrived refugee.

Despite the weather, this pool was the perfect place to relax after her lunchtime drink with Stella. Hanna didn't usually succumb to nerves, but something about this exhibition was different. There had been a lot of buzz surrounding Hanna's transition to the artistic world, a lot of chatter about whether a lauded researcher could actually make the shift to creator, or rather *why* she would choose to do so. She'd heard all the gossip: Was it an attempt to earn extra money for her son? To run away from something in Canada? To prove something to someone?

While she could turn a blind eye to idle chat, and she knew that her art was innovation and would really say something important, Hanna couldn't help but worry that her acquaintances and friends from these parts might be her harshest critics. After all, many of them knew, or at least suspected, why she had abandoned her career as a scientist and her position researching Surtsey. Not all of them agreed with her tactics.

And then there was the issue of the sponsorship. Hanna had been turning it over in her mind since Stella's revelation. That she should be indebted to the likes of Thór Magnússon made her sick to her stomach. But what could she do? It would be disastrous to pull the exhibition now; everyone would be furious. She would be asked to justify her decision, but she had no substantive evidence for what she knew to be true. Which was how she had arrived at her plan for dinner this evening. One that just might pay dividends in the long run, risky as it was.

After ten minutes of solitude, a new male body clad in a blue Speedo entered Hanna's vicinity. She nodded a greeting.

"Nice bathing suit."

"I rented it at the check-in," the man replied.

"I know," Hanna answered. "The rental ones are all the same and certainly not a style anyone would actually spend money on. I wouldn't have said anything except we already got to know each other a bit on the ferry."

"Indeed we did." Ben smiled. "Though we weren't so scantily clad then as we are now."

Okay, two can play this game, Hanna thought. Step one, flatter. "So I hear you won a Booker Prize and then produced the Emmy-winning series based on it?"

"It was only nominated for an Emmy actually, though the book has been published in thirty languages." Ben looked quizzically at Hanna. "You're also Canadian. Are you a Vestur Íslendingur too?"

"A 'Western Icelander'?" Hanna corrected. "No, afraid not. Though I know I'd have earned more cred from the locals if I were of Icelandic descent. I used to live here, though. Spent a couple of years on this island until I changed jobs and returned to Canada." Hanna paused. "Aren't you supposed to be touring Bláhafid now? I bowed out of the program to get ready for the exhibition." She paused and splashed some water on her shoulders. "As you can see, I'm doing just that."

"I was supposed to be," acknowledged Ben. "But I went in to sign copies of my book and someone at the store told me there was a trampoline in this pool and that sounded a bit more exciting. Plus, I like to visit a community's swimming pool whenever possible. It's great fodder for my writing—a soup of humanity."

"The weather isn't bothering you?" Hanna asked.

"This is nothing compared to Gimli's minus 40°C windchill winters. Even dashing from the house to the car is an exercise in endurance against the elements there. Actually, it reminds me a bit of the climax of my book."

Hanna looked at him blankly.

"When the hero escapes the glacial flooding right before a volcanic eruption?"

"I haven't read it, actually."

"Of course, I haven't seen much of the island yet," Ben conceded as if she hadn't spoken. "But traveling with the ambassador does give me a special perspective on the place. I haven't necessarily taken advantage of all opportunities, though. I skipped the tour of that fish factory."

"Believe me, you didn't miss anything there." Hanna lowered her voice. "The owner of the facility, Thór, is what the locals call a *monthani*, an 'arrogant rooster.' He wears the right clothes, he knows lots of fancy words. But he's not particularly trustworthy."

"Good word, *monthani*," said Ben. "And isn't Thór's company the main sponsor of your exhibition tomorrow?"

Wow, I'm really the last to know, thought Hanna, though she wasn't about to admit that to her poolmate. "Doesn't mean I have to like him, though," she continued. "In my old age, I have learned that life is all about compromises. I'm sure Kristján would have made a huge fuss about Bláhafid sponsoring my exhibition if he hadn't been drowning in grief and unable to focus on anything. The mayor positively seethes with resentment when he sees Thór."

"I only chatted with him briefly, but the mayor seemed perfectly fine to me," countered Ben.

"He's used to pretending," said Hanna with a sigh. "Ari's death was such a shock for him, such a shock for the whole town. They were such a great couple, so close, and then to have to identify his own husband's body in that state…" Her voice trailed off.

"What state?"

Hanna looked quizzically at her bathing companion. Could it be that Ben didn't know? It had been all over the news. Then again, foreigners usually didn't pay much attention to local goings-on. She only knew because Stella had been keeping her updated on everything in the islands since she left. And though she would never have called herself a gossip, she knew that guys like Ben liked to take credit for insider knowledge others had passed on. For now, it was entertaining to see how easy it would be to use that to her advantage.

"He had some sort of heart attack, or so they think. Apparently had cardiomyopathy, but no one knew it was that severe. Banged his head on a sharp marble corner of an exhibit on the way down," explained Hanna. "He must have felt unwell. He texted Kristján right before, but by the time the mayor arrived at the folklore museum there were blood and brains all over the floor, and Ari was dead."

"Wow. I had no idea. What a bizarre way to go."

"Poor Kristján is convinced Ari was murdered. He's the only one, though."

"Murdered? Here in the Westman Islands? Sounds like a story I would write."

Hanna laughed. "I'm sure you are more original than that. Ari was an investigative journalist. Or at least as close as people get to them here in Iceland. He worked on small stuff, local interest pieces. But Kristján said in the weeks before he died he was focusing on something big."

"Wow, really. Did he say what?"

Hanna shrugged. "The mayor said Ari hadn't even told him what it was—and as it turned out, he took that secret with him to the grave. I think Kristján wants to prove that Ari was murdered and that Thór had something to do with it."

"Thór?"

"Kristján's never really said why, but there was no love lost between that couple and Thór."

"What a lot of secrets this town has," marveled Ben.

You have no idea, thought Hanna. But instead she said: "I can't stay long in the pool in this weather. If you're finished with your swim, I can go back into town with you."

Ben nodded, and half an hour later they were trudging along Strandvegur Street, sleet pummeling their faces. In the distance, now shrouded by fog, was the steep hill formed from the eruption a half century earlier: a wide swath of hardened lava, now with pockets of weeds and wildflowers peeking through the jagged rock, forging a trail all the way to the sea. The waves were roiling. Down in the harbor below, small privately owned vessels bobbed and turned like corks.

"This is unusually harsh," Hanna yelled against the screaming wind. "There definitely won't be any ferry service until the storm quietens down. Even the three-hour journey to the bigger harbor closer to Reykjavík will be canceled under these conditions. Flights too. We'll be cut off from the rest of the world for at least a day or so until the low-pressure system passes through."

"Remind me why we're out and about then?" Ben asked, the wind nearly gobbling his words.

"We're visiting! No car!" she yelled in reply, miming the gesture of driving in case Ben couldn't hear her. In truth, Hanna wasn't really sure what had enticed her to invite Ben to walk back downtown with her. Was he a distraction from her concerns about the exhibition? An opportunity to show off her local nous with a high-profile visitor? Having now studied Ben's near-naked body in the hot tub, Hanna could attest that Ben likely never accomplished more than a handful of push-ups each morning, yet that signaled its own keep-it-real appeal. Her little game of flirtation had served as a stronger aphrodisiac than she had intended, and she disliked how charmed she was by him.

Head down to shield her face from the worst of the sleet, Hanna's thoughts meandered to what kind of kisser Ben might be, until she slammed into the pedestrian walking toward her.

"*Fokk!*" exclaimed the man. "*Hvað í helvíti…*" He stopped himself as he saw Hanna's face above her cherry-red jacket. He stammered for a moment.

"Hanna! Is it you?" He squinted through the sleet.

"Piotr, you're drenched!" she exclaimed. Rain had dripped from his windproof pants and leaked into his so-called waterproof hiking boots. His woolen *lopapeysa* sweater should in theory have kept him warm from the damp, but the bright-blue windbreaker on top was too flimsy for this storm. Same for the matching toque he wore on his bald head.

Despite the dreadful weather, despite his less-than-ideal outerwear, Piotr broke out in a broad smile. "I wondered if I might see you on this visit."

Before she could reply, Piotr noticed that his satchel had fallen to the ground. With an exclamation he dove to his knees. "My angelica!"

Ben leaned down to help him gather up what had fallen. Hanna stayed where she was. "What is all this?" He peered at the green plant in his hands.

"It's angelica root," said Piotr, his voice calmer now. "Cooking for the ambassador of Canada tonight," he added with a touch of pride in his voice.

"I'll be at that dinner!" exclaimed Ben. "Who are you?" He looked more closely at Piotr. "Wait, are you the celebrity chef who does all the foraging?"

"Yes, exactly. Piotr." The chef put out his grubby hand. Ben accepted it and shook it firmly.

"Ben Rafdal."

"Ah, the famous Canadian writer of Icelandic descent. We know all about you too." Piotr looked from one sopping person to the other and his eyes narrowed. "Why are you out walking with Hanna?"

Ben glanced awkwardly at her. At least he had the decency to be embarrassed by the fact that the conversation was happening as though she were invisible. "We met at the swimming pool and didn't have a ride back into town."

"Well, my restaurant is just around the corner. Come in to warm up for a moment," offered Piotr. "Hanna knows it very well," he added pointedly. Hanna ignored the barb.

"That'd be lovely, thanks," Ben agreed. Ten minutes later, he and Hanna were comfortably ensconced, sipping strong black coffee and taking bites of a sweet, jam-filled square Piotr had placed in front of each of them.

"This sofa is just like the one back at my *amma*'s in Gimli," Ben commented with satisfaction. He and Hanna watched as the chef continued his dinner preparations.

"I'm a fan of your work, by the way," Piotr said, eyes trained on the carrot he was peeling into delicate curls. "Daníel is such an impressive hero. When is the next one out?"

Hanna grimaced inwardly. In all the time she had known Piotr, he had never once more than leafed through a battered copy of Anthony Bourdain's memoir.

"That's kind of you. I hear we're in for quite a treat tonight," Ben said as Piotr tenderly unpacked the now-soggy and muddy angelica root from his satchel and laid each piece out on two sheets of paper towel. Ben's avoidance of the question of his sequel was skillful, Hanna thought. It must be both tiring and stressful to be weighed down by expectation of the next project the moment you completed the first one.

"Absolutely! This angelica is the finishing touch, and I finally managed to find some." Piotr launched into loving detail about the menu he had created specifically to showcase Vestmannaeyjar's fish catches and inspire what he dubbed "Canadian resourcefulness." He used terms such as *umami* and *emulsion* on the assumption that a prolific author would have an encyclopedic vocabulary, while his guests sipped their coffee and took bites of the squares.

"The ambassador will enjoy all this, I'm sure," said Ben. "His wife will too. She's a real foodie. Told me all the best places to eat in Reykjavík and has only been there a few months longer than I have!"

"Then there is dessert..." Piotr was not only fully immersed in his recitation; he was also managing to organize the ingredients needed for the evening as he spoke. The chef was using different-sized sharp knives to prune and thinly slice various vegetables, placing the shavings in a small container and then expertly rinsing several bunches of fresh herbs.

"With just a light dusting of powdered egg yolk!" Piotr finished this chapter with a flourish. "Finally, we get to one of my favorite parts, and it's a surprise actually."

Piotr placed another slice of *hjónabandssæla* on Ben's empty plate. Hanna had barely touched hers.

"Go ahead, Piotr," Hanna said with a sigh. "You can tell him about the show."

"It's called a Flaming Viking. It's a postdinner cocktail. I make it when we have important foreign visitors. It's Mayor Kristján's favorite too."

"Sounds strong," commented Ben.

"Yes," Piotr shrugged. "But not like you would think. It's a whole performance. You will see tonight."

Hanna knew all about the Flaming Viking and tried to suppress her memories involving that very drink, some fur-lined handcuffs, and her first glimpses of Piotr's most intimate tattoos.

"Will you do the same show as usual?" she asked him.

Piotr nodded, looking straight at her. "Exactly as you remember it, but even better. This will be a night no one will forget."

"But that root? Angelica, was it?" Ben asked Piotr. "I thought that was toxic. Can you use it in the supper?"

Piotr looked quizzically at Ben as if wondering from where he might have gleaned this knowledge. "Nah, that's just murder mystery stuff," he said casually. "The root would only cause death if you ate huge quantities and didn't prepare it properly by roasting or drying it thoroughly." He smiled. "Don't worry, I'm here to impress you, not to kill you!"

TEN

Jane arrived at the town's only wine bar for a refreshment with Ben a couple of hours before the big dinner at Skel. She knew it wasn't a good idea to drink when she was under stress, but today had gone from bad to worse, and she needed an emotional crutch. Doubts and fears blew around her head like embers wafting in the breeze, threatening to set everything aflame the moment they settled.

What was behind Hanna's obvious comfort with her husband this morning on the ferry? Why was he so attentive to her needs? They clearly knew each other better than mere acquaintances would. But was it enough to justify threatening to leave her husband, risking everything she had been building her adult life for? When she began thinking of her marriage, her twins, now on the awkward cusp of adulthood and independence, she wasn't sure if she was being selfish with her threats to Graeme. Perhaps she needed to be more patient with him, more understanding of the sacrifices he made as he traveled the world to kindle relationships, only to leave their nurturing to a replacement every few years.

But then she thought of the email Kavita showed her at Bláhafid. That nightmare was meant to be behind her, and now the deputy ambassador had casually flung it in her face, implying that Graeme's affair was common knowledge. She wanted that chapter of her life shut and locked with a desperation she hadn't fully acknowledged until this afternoon.

So a drink was most certainly in order now. And some distraction with her writer friend.

As soon as they ordered—dry white wine for her, scotch on the rocks for him—Jane told Ben about the trip to Bláhafid.

"And of course it's the largest employer on the island," she concluded. "So the livelihoods of a significant number of local families are intertwined with its successes or failures. These employees have spouses working other jobs in the community and children in the local school, so they essentially live at the whim of the company's owner. If Thór ever felt the need to pack up and start afresh elsewhere, the effect on the town would be devastating."

"The very survival of an ancient community often depends on the caprices of a single owner or small family," Ben said.

"It's a shame, don't you think?"

"Not necessarily. It's simple economics. Private companies are generally a good thing. They're keeping everything running."

Jane grudgingly agreed. If these enterprises weren't there, some of the towns would have been abandoned long ago. She took a sip of her drink. "How was your time playing hooky?"

"Fun, thanks. You know, I used to think everyone in Reykjavík knew each other. But the capital has nothing on the Westman Islands. *Everyone* here is either related or old friends. The mayor told me his dead husband was some sort of cousin of mine. I ran into Hanna in the hot tub. Then I met the chef from Skel just walking on the street. I went to the local bookstore too, signed a few copies of my book, had some great *plokkfiskur* stew for lunch."

"Who was the most interesting?"

Ben recounted his meeting with Piotr and they laughed when Ben described what would go into the Flaming Viking drink that evening.

"Sounds lethal!" Jane joked. "What did you think about the others?"

Ben shrugged. "I like Hanna. She's dynamic and fun. I found out she doesn't like Thór, even though he's the main sponsor of her exhibition."

"Interesting. Kavita doesn't think highly of Thór either. She also seems desperate to talk to the mayor about something."

"Listen to us, gossiping like two old women!" exclaimed Ben. "In all seriousness though, I liked Hanna a lot. She seems very comfortable with herself—"

"Oh, I'm sure," Jane said sarcastically. "Honestly, Ben, do you have to appraise every woman you ever meet? Especially her."

She glanced out of the window and sighed. She watched the rain spatter against the pane, flinching when a car drove by the road at speed and splashed a torrent of water toward her.

"Is something wrong?" Ben asked gently. He sipped his

whiskey. "You don't seem yourself. You're my favorite, you know. Of all the women." He flashed her a silly grin.

Jane responded with an uneven smile. Ben didn't know the half of it. She was still trying to process the bombshell that Kavita and half the foreign service knew about Graeme's affair and didn't want to talk about that yet. But she could use some emotional support as she struggled to come to a decision. "I sort of jumped off the proverbial cliff this morning." She started to tell Ben about her conversation with Graeme on the boat.

"I'm an introvert, and I never used to mind the anonymity of being Graeme's shadow. I was content to be a human-sized shape on a bus, or a tour, or a museum who rarely reached the consciousness of those whose attention was always on my husband. But something about living in Iceland has made it all feel so constrictive."

"How so?"

Jane tapped her fingers on the table as she thought. It was hard to articulate. "I think Iceland is small enough that it has made me feel I could make more of a difference here," she said. "That probably makes no sense to you. I mean that I never wanted to change the world. I like the status quo. But in this country, I feel like people are more tolerant of my flaws and more willing to let me try new things, even if I don't always have the confidence to think I can succeed."

"Try new things?" asked Ben. "Like picking up knitting?"

"No," Jane smiled. Before Graeme's posting she hadn't realized that knitting was practically a national sport in Iceland. "I don't know, maybe it's as the twins get older and more independent too. But I feel like I can do something—whatever *something* is—beyond the mold of diplomat's spouse. I want more. I think that's what feels constrictive. I've only really noticed it in the past few months. Also, it feels like Graeme never learns. Well, maybe *we* never learn. And then with everything on the boat this morning."

"The boat?" asked Ben.

"You know," said Jane. "The 'accidental' arm brush. The rush to get Hanna anything she needs."

"Jane, at the risk of patronizing you, aren't you maybe overreacting a bit? Seeing things that aren't there? Hanna isn't the type to go for an older man like Graeme anyway, no offense."

Jane frowned. Maybe Ben was right. Was she seeing things that weren't really there? She had no idea anymore. "I'm just running out of patience, I guess." She finished the remainder of her drink, feeling Ben's eyes scrutinizing her.

"Anything else troubling you?" he asked.

Jane's thoughts returned to the earlier conversation with Kavita. Ben probably didn't know about the affair—although after today she felt as if the whole world was aware—and she should exercise caution, but at the same time the urge to speak to someone about it all was overwhelming.

"I just found out Graeme hasn't been entirely honest with me—again. About something that happened a few years ago. It's embarrassing. He told me nobody at work knew about it, but Kavita knows."

"Ah. She is his deputy, though."

"She wasn't at the time. Plus it turns out it was doing the rounds of the gossip mill throughout Global Affairs."

"You know these rumor mills. They change quickly."

"I guess. Possibly. But it can't become *public* knowledge. Graeme's colleagues are one thing, but to think of all the people we know back in Reykjavík. Our friends. I couldn't bear it."

"Do you want to tell me what it was?" Ben asked.

Jane shook her head. "I can't, but it's clichéd enough that I'm sure you can guess."

A stomach-churning thought occurred to Jane, and she froze. If Graeme's affair was known among his colleagues, did that mean what happened afterward was too? She suddenly felt as nauseous as she had earlier on the rough Icelandic sea.

"It's not really that important, though." The lie slipped out easily. "Your comment just made me think about everything from today."

"I'm sure Kavita will be discreet," Ben said uncertainly, and from his tone Jane wondered if he too was thinking about the deputy ambassador's loud and confrontational phone call on the boat.

"But how can I be sure of that?"

If Ben had any response to this, he didn't offer it, and Jane thought she probably wouldn't have been able to hear it over the howling of the wind.

The storm was imminent.

ELEVEN

FOUR HOURS BEFORE SHE DIED

Hanna dashed along the street toward Hotel Heimaey, her red raincoat a bright flash in the dimming light. The afternoon hadn't turned out quite as she expected. There hadn't been time to finish planning what she wanted to achieve before the exhibition opened tomorrow, but on the other hand, the distraction was not unwelcome.

Hotel Heimaey was the island's only establishment with en suite baths, and therefore the only place where the VIP guests were accommodated. Hanna was grateful an acquaintance who worked at the hotel bar had called her when the ambassador had appeared about twenty minutes earlier. It was good to have allies throughout this town. She didn't want to cause a scene with Graeme, but perhaps she would find a moment now to speak to him. She needed to try, at least, before it was too late.

Hanna entered the small foyer and headed to the hotel bar, spotting Graeme sitting in a dimly lit corner across from Kavita, two half-filled pints of beer and a pile of papers scattered on the table in front of them. Both appeared to be already dressed for dinner, though the ambassador looked somewhat rumpled.

Graeme was scribbling some notes with an old-fashioned fountain pen, while the deputy ambassador looked at him with disdain. Hanna hadn't met Kavita in person before today, but she had dealt with her on the phone, and she knew how prickly she could be about enforcing the rules. If Kavita was busy with the ambassador now, it might make it more difficult to catch Graeme alone. Hanna ordered a gin and tonic from the bar and took it to a nearby table. She was close enough to hear their conversation, but they hadn't noticed her come in and were so engrossed, they paid her no attention.

"Remind me again," Graeme was saying. "How many jobs would Bláhafid create if they open a facility in Halifax?"

"We should be talking contingencies, not economics," Kavita replied in a tone that implied she had done this a million times before. "The flights have already been canceled in this weather. It's likely the ferry will too, and if this low front lingers, we'll be stuck here for another day. You know what that means."

Graeme looked blank. "Kavita, I'm not sure I do."

"It means my refugee project will have to be rescheduled! The government deadline is expiring, and they won't give extensions for any reason. I can't bear to see more victims, Graeme. And I know you can't either. You've been so supportive of my work, contributing so much of your own time, your own money. To be honest, I'm not sure why you insisted on this visit here on these specific days. It's as if this relationship with Bláhafid is more important than the refugees."

"No ferry at all tomorrow?" Graeme asked his colleague, as if he hadn't been listening.

"No, that's what I've been saying."

"Oh. I see," he answered, nonplussed. "Well, let's not make too big a deal of a theoretical possibility."

Hanna was unimpressed. She'd heard plenty of praise about Canada's ambassador, and she bore strong affection for him herself, but he was not showcasing his most competent side now. Despite her animosity toward the deputy ambassador, if she were Kavita, she would be seething. *Come on,* she silently willed Kavita, *tell him where to go. You're young and clearly ambitious, and you shouldn't have to put up with this.*

Graeme took another sip of his beer.

"Tell me again who will be at this dinner tonight."

"All of us in the delegation, of course. Unless Ben goes AWOL again," Kavita said. "From their side it's the mayor, Thór from Bláhafid, and his wife, Linda. And Hanna; I guess she's both a local and a visitor. She can be quite pushy sometimes." She paused. "But you already know that."

The ambassador said nothing. *Good,* thought Hanna, best to stay quiet. She didn't care what Kavita thought of her.

"It's not a huge group, and I don't think it will run too late," continued Kavita. "Except the chef at Skel said there is some surprise at the end of the meal."

"Fine, good."

A server walked by with a small dish of mixed pitted olives and put it down at the table. Kavita speared one with a toothpick and popped it in her mouth.

"By the way, please don't jump in so much when I'm talking to Thór tonight," Graeme said.

Kavita stopped midchew and glared at her boss.

"Bláhafid, earlier today," he continued. "You kept asking all those questions, like you also did on the phone this morning. It sounds a little confrontational. It'll reflect badly on us, and ultimately the relationship." Graeme speared his own olive. "Little tip." He gave her a small smile that seemed to say, *Don't worry, I'm only here to save you from yourself.*

Kavita put down her toothpick. She waited two beats, then spoke calmly, but with rage quivering in her voice. "A little tip?" she began. "I give my four-year-old niece little tips. I gave some server I'll never see again a little tip."

From her table a few meters away, Hanna felt the air freeze.

"I am not a four-year-old," Kavita continued. "I'm not service staff. I'm your *colleague*, Graeme. I've got a master's degree in international development; I've received a distinguished service award for God's sake. I am not someone who welcomes little tips." She spat the words out. Graeme's face began to redden, but he remained silent.

"I know you're the ambassador, and I'm the deputy. I know you have been working in foreign service far longer than I have. I know I am not perfect. But none of that, *none of that*, justifies the patronizing, condescending, sexist way in which you speak to me. I have spent all day giving you the same details, over and over, reminding you not to ask Kristján how 'his wife' is, not to forget Hanna's exhibition is about an island near here. I have asked questions so you don't look like a fool when you need that information later on. I have taken the blame for *your* incompetence when you have forgotten, been confused, or lost your temper. And I have done so competently and efficiently."

"Watch yourself, Kavita. This is utterly unprofessional." Graeme spoke with a firm tone and at a volume raised to match Kavita's. Hanna recognized it as one many men reserved for people with whom they had no further patience.

Kavita leaned closer to the ambassador, speaking in so low a voice that Hanna had to strain to hear.

"I know *all about you*," she hissed. "I know who has propped up your success and why. How can your wife possibly stand being married to you?" She leaned even closer and said something Hanna couldn't catch.

"I would advise against that," Graeme replied with a coldness that sent a shiver down Hanna's spine. "Such a move would mean the end of you."

Though there were only a handful of other patrons in the restaurant, most were now following the drama at the small table in the corner. If someone recognized these two people as representatives of the government of Canada, it could unleash a media firestorm. And if Kavita had some secret information that could threaten Graeme's reputation, that was only bad news for Hanna. He had been integral in getting everything off the ground, and her name was now firmly tied to his.

Kavita stood up and stormed out of the bar, leaving Hanna alone with a terrible fear building inside her that the deputy ambassador might just have ruined everything.

TWELVE

THREE HOURS BEFORE SHE DIED

"Is that what you're wearing tonight?"

Thór Magnússon gave his wife, Linda, a stern look. He stood in their en suite bathroom in his underwear and undershirt, shaving in preparation for the dinner that was to begin in less than an hour.

Linda looked up from affixing a pair of dangling beaded earrings.

"You don't think I look okay? You liked this the last time I wore it, at that sporting gala."

She stood up and smoothed the fabric over her legs and her abdomen, taut from a rigorous regimen of strict eating, jogging, and daily yoga.

"It was fine for a party with drunken athletes, but this is serious. You know how much is riding on our possible expansion into Canada. We were lucky when Ari died. He isn't a thorn in our side anymore, and I know exactly how to tackle Kristján. I've been in contact with the embassy deputy for months, and she's on our side. We can make this business deal happen. So I don't want the ambassador thinking my wife can't dress the part."

Linda sat back down on the bed, deflated. Every time she felt she had a handle on Thór's caprices, he shifted once again. This was a nice dress. She felt—no, she knew—that she looked good.

A three-decade marriage to Thór had made Linda a good listener. It had also given her the ability to turn a blind eye when required and to stand her ground when she felt it would be to her benefit. These skills helped make her one of the most respected counselors in her job at the child protection center. In tiny Vestmannaeyjabær, where everyone knew each other's history and had a personal connection, the ability to keep secrets was both rare and highly prized. Linda could have blackmailed half the town for some transgression or another. But blackmail was such a bourgeois habit.

"*Elskan*, this dress will be fine. Ambassador Shearer will be interested in what you have to say about investment in Canada, not in what I'm wearing."

Thór grunted. "Do me a favor, though. Talk to the ambassador's assistant. Find out exactly what kinds of tax concessions the government can offer us to open up a branch in Halifax. Remind her how much help I've been to her off-the-record project; she'll know what I mean. Tell her that can end at any moment. Maybe it'll stop her from acting so arrogantly."

Linda didn't respond. She knew women whose drive and ambition were derided as arrogance and ruthlessness. If Thór thought Kavita was pompous, Linda suspected she'd find her decisive and full of personality. But keeping her husband happy was important to her. Linda played a long game and that sometimes meant biting her tongue.

"Of course, *elskan*," she said, smiling disingenuously. "And remember, don't try the cocktail tonight. You know how you get when you've been drinking hard liquor. Also, try to keep it civil with Kristján," she reminded him. "Everyone feels sorry for him right now. In a popularity contest, you can't compete with a widower."

Thór grunted again. "Why would I? You only need to have a five-minute conversation with the mayor to realize he has become utterly ineffectual in the role since Ari died. He has no talent of his own to fall back on."

Linda didn't bother to reply. Thór wasn't really interested in what she had to say, only that she didn't harm his future plans. Nevertheless, she was looking forward to this dinner. Opportunity to meet an ambassador? A famous writer? Even the "assistant" sounded like she had some gumption. This evening might just be one to remember in this sleepy town.

THIRTEEN

THREE HOURS BEFORE SHE DIED

Drinks finished and Ben departed, Jane was standing to put her coat on when her phone rang.

"Jane, something's happened." Kavita's voice was breathless.

"Tell me," Jane replied.

"It's about Graeme. I'm sorry it's you that I'm calling, but after our conversation this afternoon I thought you'd understand. We were supposed to meet at the hotel bar to go over everything. I was there for an hour before him, drafting a summary of our Bláhafid meeting, preparing a thank-you letter for Stella at the folklore museum, extending our stay at the hotel in case we're stuck here longer, fine-tuning the ambassador's remarks for tonight. He showed up late, with all the signs I have seen so many times before: rumpled trousers, messy hair, dry rasp in the throat. Jane, he had been napping. While I'd been doing all this work."

"Napping?"

"I know it's not a big deal. It's just one more in a long line of micro-irritations, but I'm sick of it. How can men like him rise to the top of Canada's bureaucracy, while highly educated, dynamic women have to fight to climb up even one rung on the ladder and earn reputations as bitchy, overaggressive attention seekers?"

Jane was silent. She couldn't really disagree, and Kavita clearly needed to vent some anger, though Jane did wonder whether it wasn't time for Kavita to find her own network of close friends.

"Jane, I lost my temper. I yelled at him, in front of everyone in the bar. The floodgates just burst. I've managed to elevate the dispute by several degrees."

Jane could picture the scene. What would people think of this public outburst involving *diplomats*? Had anyone taken photos to share the scoop on social media? No, they weren't so recognizable. It looked like what it was: a work meeting argument gone too far. But why was Graeme so insensitive? And how could Kavita lose her cool so dramatically?

"I know Graeme has his imperfections, but you work with him; you also know how he can be. I'm not asking you to accommodate him, but you must manage your feelings. Once things calm down, I'm sure he'll be able to forgive you for this. And hope that no one in the bar recognized you."

"There's more," Kavita answered with concern.

"More? More than you losing your temper with your boss?"

"I told him about the email I showed you. And then I threatened to send it to the media. I couldn't stop myself."

Jane closed her eyes.

"It made him really angry," Kavita continued. Jane understood;

she wanted to scream at Kavita too. How could she do such a thing? Newspapers loved a juicy public-service sex scandal, even an old one. The deputy was meddling where she had no business, without understanding the full consequences. Yes, Graeme had strayed, but hadn't she done worse after she found out? Kavita didn't realize the delicate equations involved, all of Jane's planning to avoid a public altercation just like this one.

Kavita had opened a Pandora's box of emotions. How could Jane possibly stop everything from escaping now? How could Kavita risk ruining things so spectacularly?

Jane forced herself to bite her tongue; she knew it would not help to yell. She would have to find a moment after dinner to warn Kavita about her careless temper and dangerous threats. Meanwhile, Jane could hear Kavita trying to catch her breath on the phone.

"He told me if I went public, such a move would be the end of me. Jane, I'm worried what Graeme might do next."

FOURTEEN

FIFTEEN MINUTES BEFORE SHE DIED

If there was anytime for the lighthearted spectacle of the Flaming Viking show, this was it, Kristján thought. The day had gone as well as could be expected and the dinner was delicious, but the mayor knew his guests were not happy about the weather. Kavita seemed downright panicked. And now, as Piotr was organizing the cocktail ingredients, she was looking pale too.

Kristján saw Kavita grimace and put a hand to her stomach.

"Are you all right?" Kristján asked the deputy ambassador.

"Something in the meal didn't agree with me," Kavita replied. "I'm sure I told the chef about everything I can't eat."

Kristján had to suppress a smile as he remembered Chef Piotr's earlier diatribe.

"Maybe it's the wine?" he suggested.

Kavita merely shrugged and turned to Linda, speaking loudly enough for the mayor to follow along.

"Tell me the truth: is this Bláhafíd expansion into Canada going to go ahead?"

Kristján was taken aback by the confrontation in Kavita's tone. What was she doing? Nobody had seemed keener on the Canadian embassy's connection with the fishing company than her. In fact, that was just what he was desperate to talk to her about. So why this sudden aggression?

"How should I know that?" asked Linda.

"You're married. And Bláhafíd is a family business. I know it's not protocol to have these things decided quickly, but today has not been a good day for protocol. I need to know what to expect."

"I'm sorry," Linda said. "We just don't talk about work that much. I'm sure Thór and the ambassador have much to discuss, though."

Again, Kristján was perplexed. Thór and Linda had been married for decades. The mayor knew that Linda was Thór's confidant. Linda would likely be the first person to know once Thór had made a decision about expansion. In fact, it was unlikely to be made in the first place without her approval. So why lie to Kavita? And why indeed was it all so important, almost personal, to the diplomat in the first place?

Kristján had only taken the smallest sip of the cocktail Piotr had prepared for him, but as he set it down on the table, he could feel the burn of it in his belly. It really was lethal. This was a routine of theirs. Kristján was always given the first drink, accompanied by warnings of its potency, designed to pique the curiosity of the guests.

Their introduction to the cocktail concluded, Piotr was now industriously assembling the remaining drinks, and the guests clustered around him.

"Lights, please!" Piotr called and Kristján knew that was his cue. He moved to the corner of the room, flicked the switch.

It was darker than he expected it to be. Not pitch-black, but the small candles shimmering in one corner provided only a meager light, and the room was suddenly all shadows. It was oddly disorienting, and from the direction of the table he could hear gasps of surprise and alarm. Something clattered onto the floor.

"What was that?" a man yelled.

"Sorry, everyone. I dropped my phone," came a woman's voice in reply. Linda's?

A bright-blue flame appeared as Piotr lit the first cocktail, then another and another. This time the gasps from the table were of delight, and even though he'd seen this performance many times before, Kristján marveled at the spectacle of it. He waited until the flames had burned out, then switched the lights back on.

He found when he arrived back by the bar that the circle had closed, and it took some effort to squeeze himself back into the ring. People were reaching in to take glasses from the table; Kristján searched for his.

"Mayor?" He turned to see the writer, Ben Rafdal, holding out a glass to him and accepted it gratefully.

"I think this deserves a toast!" Graeme handed a glass to his wife, another to Kavita, then picked up one for himself and lifted it into the air.

Kristján took one more sip of his drink and grimaced. Perhaps it was all the wine, but he didn't feel he could stomach it tonight. Instead, he watched as people began sampling the Flaming Viking. Their reactions were nothing new to him. Until Kavita began to choke. Then everything became a blur.

As he saw Kavita sprawled on the floor, Kristján's mind shot back to that summer day eight weeks ago when he had discovered the love of his life on the floor of the museum. Kristján felt his own throat begin to close, felt his heart rate quicken, struggled to control his own breath. There was shouting around him, someone yelling into a phone for an ambulance. Someone else was leaning over the deputy ambassador, feeling for a pulse, loosening the collar of her blouse.

Shards of shattered glass surrounded her on the floor.

But as each agonizing second passed, it became increasingly clear that whatever had befallen Kavita was fatal. He would not need to confront her about the contents of that morning's letter.

"Has she…has she choked on something?" Thór asked helplessly. He looked at Piotr, who flushed a deep shade of purple.

Next to a prone Kavita, Rahul stood, his face a picture of fear and anger. He turned, ever so slowly, as he faced Canada's ambassador to Iceland.

"That was not choking," he said, his voice quaking with emotion. "You, Ambassador, you gave her the drink. What did you put in it?"

PART TWO

THE NEXT DAY

FIFTEEN

THIRTY-SEVEN HOURS BEFORE HE DIES

Jane sat stone-faced at breakfast at 7:30 a.m., her hair dull and unwashed, her pearl choker resting over a wrinkled blouse. She hadn't bothered with makeup, and her eyes felt puffy from tears. It had been impossible to get any sleep. From the second Kavita fell, Jane had replayed the moments before her death as an endless loop in her mind. The collapse, the feeling of futility as she and the others watched the deputy ambassador writhe in agony, the late arrival of the medics. Jane couldn't help but wonder whether more immediate, effective assistance could have made a difference. And though she knew it was irrational, that of course the accusation was groundless, she couldn't get the image of Rahul from her mind, teeth bared, trembling finger pointing at her aghast husband.

Shortly after Kavita's fall, Jane saw Kristján in the corner, his face in his hands. Perhaps he was remembering his own partner's death. Meanwhile, Rahul had knelt on the floor next to his wife after his outburst, talking gently to her, stroking her hand, with tears streaming down his face. When the paramedics arrived, Jane got up to fetch some water for Kristján and Rahul, but the officials stopped her.

"Don't do anything right now," one of them said firmly. "You mustn't touch anything." And so Jane clustered with most of the others a few steps back from Kavita's lifeless body.

A few minutes later, the police arrived. Well, a single police officer arrived. Jane would never have identified him as an officer of the law had he not been wearing his black uniform with the yellow lettering on it. He held a walkie-talkie, and a whistle hung from his belt holster. From the almost baby face to the bright, eager eyes, Jane could feel his inexperience—and his enthusiasm to prove his mettle.

"Is *he* the police officer?" Jane heard Thór whisper to his wife. "It's Jónas from up the road. I thought he was still finishing secondary school!"

"He's probably the only person on duty tonight," Linda replied. "I read that most officers are at some conference in Reykjavík. They aren't due back until tomorrow." She shivered and looked outside. "Or whenever this island opens up again."

The first thing the officer did upon his arrival was to get a glass of water for Rahul, who had become mute after his outburst at the ambassador. The officer sat quietly with Rahul for several minutes in the corner, murmuring something Jane could not hear, while the others stood around awkwardly, as if waiting to be told what they should do.

"What's he doing?" Thór asked with impatience. "Is he going to take charge or not?"

"He's trying to calm Rahul down," Hanna said. "I wish the rest of us could too." Her face was pale.

After speaking with Rahul, the officer asked for everyone to go back to the room where dinner had been served. Piotr stood in the corner, his eyes darting from one person to another, then to the door. He looked desperate to leave.

"Obviously, we don't yet know what happened here tonight," the young man said, looking directly at Graeme. "But in a sudden death such as this, it is protocol to involve the police. My name is Jónas Jónasson. I am the senior officer on duty tonight."

"I bet he's the *only* officer on duty tonight," Hanna whispered to Jane.

"I would like to hear exactly what took place this evening after supper ended," Jónas continued. Rahul stood slowly as if to say something, but Jónas silenced him with a raised hand. "But given the late hour and all the alcohol that has been consumed, I'll allow you all to return to your hotel rooms or homes and I will be in touch early tomorrow morning." Jónas shuffled his feet. "I am very sorry for your loss."

Now, several hours later, as she recalled the night before, Jane wondered again why Jónas had let them leave the premises. Surely there was no curfew for collecting testimonies with such a sudden death?

"We shouldn't be eating breakfast," muttered Graeme, in the seat opposite Jane, as he broke his wife's train of thought. "We should be doing something, helping in some way." He dropped his fork on his plate, pushing the dish of nearly untouched scrambled eggs away from himself.

"You're right. I can't eat anyway." Jane sipped some tepid coffee. "But it's natural; we're all in shock." She could barely sit. Her instinct was to find an outlet for her frustrated energy, for the surprising anguish she felt.

She and Graeme were sitting with Ben. Rahul was nowhere to be seen, and Jane thought perhaps they should soon check on him.

"Kavita had a shellfish allergy, didn't she?" Ben asked no one in particular. It was the third time one of them had brought it up.

Jane nodded. "And she never wore a medical bracelet," she added. "She once said she thought it would indicate some sort of weakness."

"Don't be ridiculous; that must be irrelevant," snapped Graeme. "Do you think there was shellfish in a *cocktail*?"

"Of course not." Jane bristled. "Perhaps she choked."

"Choked on a *drink*?"

"I wonder what will happen to Hanna's exhibition," mused Ben.

"It'll be canceled. Obviously," Graeme replied. His face was pallid, its lines etched deeper overnight. He was wearing the other dress shirt he had brought for the trip, tie intact, even though there would be no formal events today. He looked away briefly as he reached into a pocket and dabbed at his eyes with a tissue. Jane felt some sympathy for Graeme begin to trickle back. He said a lot was riding on this trip, and she had piled on more. His colleague had just died in front of him, and her widower had laid the blame straight at Graeme's feet. Everything was in shambles. She put a hand on her husband's forearm.

"Has Rahul notified Kavita's family members? You'll have to speak to them too."

"It doesn't sound like he wants me near anything," Graeme replied brusquely. Yet they began to talk through some of the inevitable practicalities that surrounded sudden death in what was essentially a foreign country—who to contact, when and where they might get access to repatriate the body.

Graeme spoke about these details with frustration because there was nothing he could do to fix the situation. A member of his team had died on his watch. Jane could almost see the wheels grinding in his mind: What would his superiors say? Naturally, he would be thinking of how Kavita's death affected him. So that's what the deeper lines on his face were about. Not genuine distress for his colleague's death, but concern about his own position. Her mind returned to Rahul's accusation. It was beginning to fester in the recesses of her mind where Graeme's betrayal lay.

"And we're stuck in this fucking town for at least another day!" Graeme concluded roughly, looking out at the still-stormy weather.

He was losing his cool. Graeme never swore.

As they sat mutely, Officer Jónas Jónasson entered the restaurant and made his way over to their table, his thick red hair disheveled and his cheeks ruddy from brisk walking. Had he been out all night in the storm?

"Good morning. I'm going to have to talk to all of you. I heard some tentative news overnight about the possible cause of death. We can't get anything confirmed because we can't take any samples to the lab on the mainland yet, but I sent over photographs. In the meantime, we want to gather some standard information."

"Photographs? Of what?" asked Ben.

"I can't elaborate, but I have reason to believe there is something suspicious, something criminal, about Kavita Banerjee's death last night. It is not natural to expire so rapidly unless someone ingested a poisonous substance. We are therefore operating under the assumption that Kavita's death may have been the result of foul play."

"Just like Rahul implied last night," Ben said to himself. Jane looked at him sharply.

"What's that about Rahul?" Jónas asked.

Ben cleared his throat. "Nothing. Just, Rahul was angry."

Jónas continued to stare at the writer and tapped something into his phone. But he continued: "Can I begin by speaking with you, Ambassador? You worked closely with the deceased, but I understand you had quite a heated argument with her in this very location yesterday afternoon?"

Graeme was stony-faced. "Yes, of course I can speak with you, though I don't know what our disagreement has to do with anything. Why? Did Rahul tell you something else?"

Ben turned to Jane and whispered quietly, "'Expire so rapidly'? Does the child cop think he's Sherlock Holmes?"

Jane ignored him. This was not the time for glib remarks. But she did wonder how the officer knew about the argument. Who told him?

Jónas took out an iPad—the new generation's notebook and pen, Jane assumed—and began to tap away on it.

"You might prefer to take notes with a pen and paper. It will help keep things clearer," Graeme commented. "Good little tip for you."

Jónas ignored the suggestion. "This isn't a formal interrogation, of course. But I'd like to begin by asking you some questions, Ambassador."

"I think that's our cue to go," said Ben, rising to his feet. Jane got up with him, but Graeme turned to her, and Jane saw something in his eyes she hadn't seen in years. Vulnerability. And, did she imagine it, fear?

Graeme looked at Jane. "Stay. Please."

She nodded.

"I'll give you my statement later," Ben said, then smiled at the duo and left.

Jónas waited until the door was closed before continuing. "I have been asked to get as much information as possible from all the witnesses as we put together our report." He paused and glanced down at the iPad as if looking for some sort of investigation flow chart. "I mean, I think you are allowed a lawyer if you want, but…?"

"That would delay things somewhat, given the weather, correct?" finished Graeme. "That's fine. I am deeply regretful about what happened last night. I doubt I have much to add, but I hope that whatever I say might be of help."

Jane watched silently as her husband spoke. She knew that when Graeme didn't have the bandwidth to focus, to remember details, he felt trapped and confused. It would make him speak too bluntly, could make him appear suspicious.

"Can I just begin with how you knew Kavita, what you thought of her?" ventured Jónas.

"Well, she was my deputy, of course. We worked together every day here in Iceland. She was very hardworking, smart, focused. I have had many colleagues over the years, and Kavita was certainly above average. Yes, overall, very capable."

"She was excellent," Jane interjected. She turned to Jónas. "Graeme is speaking cautiously. But from what he has told me before, Kavita had wonderful potential." There was no need to share what Kavita had threatened to expose about her husband. No one else need know now.

"What were her main qualities, would you say?"

Graeme cleared his throat. "At work, you mean? She was driven and focused. When she wanted something, she worked hard to get it. Ambitious. Though maybe a bit impatient to get to where she wanted to be. It takes a while to earn a promotion in the foreign service. She and I were working closely on a scheme to bring over refugees from Yemen and Afghanistan—that is, to help those who are on their way to Canada travel via Iceland and wait here, even find a job, while their final paperwork is processed. Kavita was very passionate about all these projects to help the less fortunate. She worked in East Timor before she joined Global Affairs Canada, and that I think is what encouraged her to go into public service."

Graeme's voice sounded hoarse to Jane, and now she noticed his mildly bloodshot eyes. Had he been more emotional about the death in private?

"How did this immigration scheme work, exactly?"

"You can also ask Thór that. Bláhafid was involved too. They hired many of the refugees on a temporary basis. And it's why Kavita was so desperate not to be stranded here when the weather worsened. It would ruin all her plans. The deadline for filing the final paperwork is—was—today, and she needed to do that in person at the embassy, so we had to leave immediately after the exhibition opened. Because this was Kavita's side project, no one else was working on it other than a bit of extra help from me, and there was no one else to cover. But I suppose the schedule change shouldn't have been a huge surprise. The weather is often bad here."

"What will happen to that work deadline now? Weather or not, there is no deputy to complete the paperwork."

"I'll speak to the people in Global Affairs," Graeme answered. "These are extenuating circumstances."

Jónas nodded, seemingly satisfied with that response. "And outside of work?" The officer looked to Jane again.

"I didn't know her well, but I would argue the project Graeme just mentioned demonstrates her compassionate side," answered Jane.

"What about her weaker qualities?"

Graeme hesitated. "I don't want to speak ill of the dead."

"It's important," Jónas insisted.

Graeme answered slowly. "She was quick to judge. If she thought you weren't doing something well, then she told you in no uncertain terms. Me included."

"What about her husband? Were they happily married?"

"As far as I know," Graeme said. "I didn't speak often to Rahul, but he struck me as smart. Patient with his wife too."

Jónas was busily tapping away as Graeme spoke. He took his time, didn't prod him for more when Graeme paused to consider his wording or recall details. He let Graeme steer the pace of the conversation, or at least made it appear that way. Jane wondered if he was perhaps more perceptive than everyone seemed to give him credit for.

"And why were you visiting in the first place?"

Graeme outlined the art exhibition and visits to the museum and Bláhafid.

"All right, let's move on to last night specifically. Can you walk me through the evening?"

"Of course." Graeme described the dinner. He then told Jónas about the prospect of cooperation with Bláhafid and Thór Magnússon.

"Thór's assertive, ambitious, and his company will do well in the Maritimes."

"Are there any downsides to the potential partnership?"

"Well, we have yet to finish the due diligence," admitted Graeme. "I got the impression that Mayor Kristján is not a supporter. Kavita seemed rather hesitant at first too, but more recently she had been one of the biggest proponents of this potential deal."

Jónas made a note on his iPad. "And after dinner you went into the other room for the cocktails?" he prompted.

"Yes, that's right. I can't remember what time that was. But we were all in good spirits, though Kavita was quite tense about the fact that we were not going to get back to the mainland tomorrow—I mean today, now, as planned."

"Can you recall what happened when she died? Or immediately before?"

"I was standing near Kavita. The mayor was on her other side. We were all tasting that horrible drink. I don't know why they make it. But we toasted, and drank, and then she seemed to choke or something." He paused and stared at his coffee cup. "It all happened so quickly."

"Do you remember where everyone else was at that moment?"

Graeme considered. "Jane was next to me and the mayor was near Kavita. He tried the drink before the rest of us. He and the chef seemed to have some well-practiced routine to introduce this cocktail. After Kristján had the first sip, the lights went out while the chef lit the rest of them on fire. Rahul was near his wife. I don't know about the others. Who else was there?"

"Ben. And Hanna, Thór, and Linda," Jane reminded her husband.

"Right, yes. I'm sorry, I'm not sure where they were. I was busy talking with the mayor about tomorrow's plan—today's plan now, I suppose. But we were all close to each other. It was a bit disorderly."

Jónas typed for a moment or two. "There's just one more thing. Can you tell me about the argument you had with Kavita yesterday?"

Graeme's brows furrowed. "Well, 'argument' is rather a strong word for it. Yes, we had a disagreement. Kavita was upset that the schedule was delayed and that we would be missing the journey back this morning. She took it out on me. But we talked at dinner, and there were no hard feelings."

No hard feelings? Jane couldn't believe her ears. She could recall Kavita's desperate phone call to her from the previous evening almost word for word, the visceral fear in her voice.

"There are a few things to understand about Kavita," Jane

said to Jónas. "At thirty-six, she was the youngest-ever deputy at the embassy here. When Graeme was away, Kavita took his place. She even represented Canada at the gathering of NATO countries hosted by Iceland's prime minister when Graeme was rushed to hospital with appendicitis. She was finally hitting her stride and getting some attention for many years of thankless effort. It's understandable that she would not want anything to go awry at this stage. I'm sure that's all this slight disagreement was."

Graeme shot his wife a grateful look and turned back to Jónas. "Anything else?"

"Yes, actually," he answered. "Other witnesses last night told me that Rahul claimed you were responsible for Kavita's death. Do you care to explain why he might have said that?"

In any other circumstances, Jane would have been impressed. This officer smiled innocently for all, and then, like a wild animal pouncing on its prey, he attacked. No one could have seen it coming.

"Well, I handed Kavita the cocktail," Graeme admitted gruffly. "But it goes without saying that I didn't tamper with it, or whatever Rahul is implying. Yes, as I've said, we had a minor disagreement, but it was about something from the past, nothing that concerns anyone anymore." He shot a glance at his wife.

Jónas said nothing and tapped away. As Jane and her husband sat rigidly, waiting for the next assault, Jónas looked back up.

"Well, that's about it for now," he said. "Thanks for taking the time." Then, turning off his tablet and scooping his coat into his arms, he strode out of the hotel restaurant, leaving the couple alone.

"What just happened?" Jane said to Graeme the second Jónas

was out of earshot. "At first, the kid looked like he'd been up half the night reviewing police training manuals on protocols and interrogations. Then out of nowhere he goes in for the kill?"

"He's the officer in charge," Graeme replied. "Even though he's wet behind the ears. Let's just hope he doesn't jump to the wrong conclusions. It might have helped if you had defended me a bit more."

"You're chastising me? How could you just downplay the argument you had with Kavita yesterday? That cop will obviously discover the truth. Kavita called me after that fight and she sounded terrified. And she showed me an email earlier in the day. She knew about what happened at work back in Ottawa with you and that woman, and she told me she'd threatened to go public."

Jane looked her husband in the eye and before she could stop herself, she blurted, "Graeme, *did* you have something to do with Kavita's death?"

"Of course not!" Graeme exclaimed. An older couple sitting nearby glanced over at them. Graeme lowered his voice, but he could barely contain his rage. "How can you say such a thing? I need your support now, not this."

He stood up and marched out, leaving Jane alone at her table. She stared at her coffee and tried to calm her breathing. She had just said it out loud—she'd just accused her husband of murder.

"Fight? What fight? What was Jónas talking about?" A voice broke through her mental fog. Ben was standing next to her table. He must have been lurking nearby for a while to have overhear Jónas's remarks.

"I wanted to check on you," Ben said by way of explanation of his return. "But I didn't want to interrupt a conjugal discussion. What fight was Jónas talking about and how did he find out?"

Jane had been wondering the same thing. She supposed it would have been easy in this small place. But was that enough for the police to give credence to Rahul's accusation? Or did they know something else about her husband that she didn't?

She briefly explained the previous afternoon's conflict and Kavita's desperate-sounding phone call to her. Ben put a friendly hand on Jane's shoulder.

"This is just procedure, remember. Graeme is the most senior person here; they have to speak with him first. I know everyone was talking about that argument last night, and I know that's unlike Graeme."

"An argument, yes. But Graeme hasn't been himself for a few months now. I know you think it's just an art opening and some factory tour, but this trip is really important to him. Getting more investment in Canada is a crucial part of his legacy. At his age, if he isn't successful as ambassador to this small nation, he'll never get a bigger posting. And he seems extremely interested in Hanna's work. I can't figure it out. She seems to know him very well. Then, of course, I sideswiped him yesterday with that ultimatum about our marriage."

Jane picked at her food. Ben was letting the silence hang. After a long moment, Jane made up her mind. Her friend deserved the full picture—or at least some of it. She looked Ben straight in the eye.

"Remember that 'incident' I told you about at our drink? With Graeme?"

Ben nodded. "You didn't really tell me. But I can guess. An affair? Forgiveness? That kind of stuff happens all the time, Jane."

Jane cringed. Ben didn't need to be quite so offhand about it.

"It may happen all the time, but it had never happened to me." Jane paused. "Kavita knew about the affair too. And Graeme knew that she knew."

"That was a long time ago, though. How could it possibly have affected Kavita?"

Jane gave a cynical laugh. "Not like it did Graeme and me anyway. But she had this moral compass and a standard to which she held everyone. I don't want to think she was naturally the resentful type. But perhaps after years of being underestimated…"

Her voice caught and tears filled her eyes. She wiped her nose with a napkin. "What if? What if he thought his career would be under threat if Kavita filed some sort of formal complaint or went public on social media about it? If this is a serial problem, he'll be fired. It's overwhelming to think about."

"We'll figure this out, Jane. I'm sure you are imagining the worst-case scenario. I mean, an old affair that doesn't even directly affect Kavita can't possibly be a motive for murder. First, tell your kids what happened. They already know you're stuck here for a while, and they'll be fine on their own a while longer. Come on. You're the toughest woman I know. You'll be fine, no matter the situation with Graeme."

Jane forced herself to smile. Ben was probably right. But Ben didn't know that something else had been eating away at Jane's trust of her husband. That affair was more complicated than he knew, and he did not realize just how nervous she was about Graeme's and Hanna's connection. Was history repeating itself with Graeme? Had Kavita found out about it?

"We will need to check up on Rahul," she said, twisting the corner of a sugar packet from the small dish on the table. "Help him with whatever he needs." Really, she thought Rahul could maybe tell her why he had made this accusation against her husband. Surely Graeme handing Kavita the glass wasn't his only reasoning?

"There are probably some counselors or something with him now," replied Ben. "And Mayor Kristján seemed to be in shock last night too. It must have brought back the experience of his husband's death, a déjà vu."

"I'm sure it did. I just can't imagine," replied Jane with a shudder. "Being so close to two sudden deaths on a little island in a country known for its peacefulness. The man must be traumatized."

She paused for a moment. Jane knew she worked best under pressure and hated waiting for other people to fix problems, usually incompetently. There must be something she could do. If Graeme was suspected of committing a criminal offense, he would be the last person who could adequately defend himself. Jane was used to being the proverbial shoulder to cry on. And, she thought, the best way to divert any suspicion from Graeme was to uncover any other secrets this community was hiding. She turned to Ben.

"You know, maybe we should pay Kristján a visit. Wherever he lives, he's all alone. I know we just met him, but I bet he could use some company, and he might be able to tell us more about connections on this island. I suspect they are somehow important. What do you think?"

Ben looked out the window. The wind had begun to abate, but the rain continued and the sky was slate gray.

"I'm not so keen on venturing outside, but you're probably right," he said. "At the very least, maybe Kristján can tell us more about the secrets of the Flaming Viking."

Jane rolled her eyes at him.

SIXTEEN

THIRTY-FIVE HOURS BEFORE HE DIES

At the entrance to Skel, Hanna stomped her boots and shook off drops of rain from her jacket. Under her red coat, she was dressed in tight jeans, knee-high black leather boots, and an oversized navy woolen sweater. She wore no makeup, and as she glanced instinctively toward one of the restaurant's many mirrors, she saw there were circles under her eyes.

"What are you doing here?" Piotr sounded gruff as he opened the door, but Hanna recognized the tone for what it was hiding—the chef's pleasure at a personal visit from his old, unrequited flame.

Piotr was wearing a plain white T-shirt and had a tea towel tucked into the front pocket of his jeans. He hadn't shaved that morning.

"I couldn't sleep. And hello," Hanna said. "I forgot my phone here last night." She paused, aware that this statement, which had been distracting her from much else, might seem a little insensitive, given the circumstances.

"Also, I–I guess I needed some company. Can you believe what happened last night?" she added hastily and looked at the chef to gauge his reaction.

"It was not me, if that's what you're thinking," Piotr exclaimed as if she had just pointed a finger at him. "I didn't kill her. You mustn't blame the chef. Actually, according to the husband, you should blame the ambassador."

Hanna ignored the comment. Piotr didn't have the full story.

"I'm not blaming the chef," she said. "I'm just seeing how he's doing."

Piotr flushed a deep red and quickly turned to lead her to the kitchen, where some piles of herbs were stacked tidily on the countertop, and waved his hand to invite her to sit on an empty barstool by the fridge. He lifted up the last remnants of the angelica root Hanna knew he would have spent many hours foraging yesterday.

"This puny root has a reputation as a potential poison. But there was no way it could be responsible for last night's death. Watch this." Piotr picked up a stem, sniffed it, broke a piece off with his fingers, popped it in his mouth, and chewed. "This root was no murder weapon."

"Take it easy, Piotr. As I said, I'm not accusing you of anything. I'm just saying that I can't believe what happened." Hanna crossed her legs on the stool as she recalled the diplomat's final moments. "She looked so—desperate. Her eyes, they…" Her voice trailed off.

She watched as Piotr took out some containers and began filling them with leftover food.

"What are you doing? Are you allowed to move things around? Isn't this a potential crime scene?"

"No one died in the kitchen. If I don't get some of this properly stored, it will all be wrecked. We're not going to have any guests for the next several days. *Kurwa!*"

Hanna tried to see things from his point of view. Despite his tremendous efforts, curating a perfect menu to cater to innumerable dietary limitations, spending weeks pickling and curing and chopping and freezing, finding exactly the right quantity of angelica root that he needed, it was now all for naught after the disastrous evening.

As if reading her thoughts, Piotr said, "A death is sad, of course, especially at such a young age, especially so suddenly. I don't mean to make this all about me."

"No. Of course not," Hanna said dryly. "And let me guess, you're wondering, though, if the real tragedy might not be what could happen to the future of Skel. Your TikTok-friendly Flaming Viking will certainly become a thing of the past."

"That was just for the tourists anyway. But what will people make of the restaurant now? Will it be ruined by this one unfortunate incident?" Piotr was staring at Hanna, his eyes searching hers for reassurance.

"Piotr, you can say such things to me when we are alone, but you better not say that in front of the police, okay?"

As she spoke, Piotr washed and chopped and stacked in the area around her. The restaurant was going to be closed for the foreseeable future, and that meant rescheduling some deliveries, freezing some items, pickling others.

"I know," he replied. "But Skel is my life's work, and I need to make sure it survives this. That doesn't make me a horrible person. And that woman did not die from an allergic reaction—at least not from the drink I prepared for her. I never make errors like that."

"So do you think somebody put something into her drink?" Hanna asked him. "Something that would cause—"

"Death?" Piotr offered. "Of a diplomat?" His eyes lit up. "That would appeal to the macabre globe-trotters, the ones who trek from crime scene to crime scene to see and smell and touch the locations of infamous deaths." Piotr blinked. "Not that I would have wanted this event to take place at Skel," he hastened to add. "Or at all, of course. I wish it never happened."

"You're pretty good at looking at the bright side, aren't you?" Hanna said. "Seeing murder as a tourist boon."

"I'm not really. I'm just blowing off steam," Piotr said. "Did you know her, the woman who died? She called me endlessly the last few days, always questions about this or that detail. It was so annoying."

"Careful. Don't tell the cops that either. And for the record, I'd never met her in person until yesterday, but I'd heard she'd been helping some refugees travel to Canada via Iceland, or something like that. She was keen to get back to the mainland for some development on the program. Have the police talked to you yet?"

"No, not yet," Piotr replied. "But Jónas had someone put crime scene tape by the entrance to the main room. One of the search-and-rescue volunteers is making sure no one goes in there until a forensics team arrives from the capital. But who knows when that could be." He gestured to the room in which they had met last night, which now had a length of yellow tape across its entrance. "Jónas wants to get statements, and he should be here any minute now. I guess he'll go through that room too. You know, he's just a kid. He should probably have compiled witness accounts and removed samples last night, not waited until this morning. We've had ample time to get stories straight and destroy anything incriminating."

"Maybe it's part of some new age police procedure," Hanna said.

Piotr scoffed. "I think he only finished police academy training a couple of years ago. He can't have ever been responsible for more than fender benders and drunken brawls."

"Well, no one has spoken to me either," Hanna said. "Hence why I wanted to collect my phone. I thought the police might want to reach me."

"Where did you leave it?"

Hanna nodded toward the tape cordoning off the next room.

"You can't go in there," Piotr said.

"Oh." Her shoulders slumped. "I mean, I get it, I guess. But I really need my phone." Piotr had no idea how much. Now that she had learned who was footing the bill for her exhibition, the recording on her phone was crucial leverage, and although she didn't give any credence to Rahul's wild accusation, she was beginning to think she couldn't entirely trust Graeme. It was time to dial the persuasion up a notch. She opened her eyes wide and looked up at Piotr. She knew his emotions swung like a pendulum when he was around her. Regardless of the tattooed biceps and tough guy image, Piotr was vulnerable. She waited patiently.

"Listen, I can go over there, tell them I have to collect something I need for my work," Piotr suggested.

"Really? That would be so helpful. Thank you." Hanna hoped she didn't sound overly enthusiastic.

Piotr led Hanna away from the kitchen and to the entrance of the room where Kavita died. From that vantage, Hanna could see half-empty glasses on tables and crumpled napkins tossed here and there, some with lipstick marks, others with crumbs of food.

A burly member of Iceland's famed search-and-rescue crew stood at the room's entrance. He was wearing a thick black turtleneck, hiking boots, and a red jacket marked with the insignia of the local S&R division and his name. Former resident Hanna knew the young man had a reputation in these parts as a competitive soccer player and was a father, a community-minded individual. He must have been summoned by Jónas to watch the room and ensure that nothing was out of place.

Hanna watched as Piotr approached the volunteer. She flashed him an encouraging smile.

"I know I'm not supposed to go in there," the chef began. "But I left my paring knife on the table over there. I really need it to chop and process all this food that will otherwise go bad while my restaurant is forced to stay closed. Could I just step over and pick it up? You can watch me. I won't do anything more than that."

The man looked dubious.

"Sammi, it's one small paring knife," Piotr said. "No one was stabbed last night."

"*Já. Gjörðu svo vel.* Go ahead." The volunteer nodded his assent.

Hanna peered over the volunteer's shoulder as Piotr ducked under the police tape stretched across the entryway. She watched him head straight for the table where the components of the Flaming Viking still lay in disarray. At the moment she saw him pick up a knife, Hanna coughed loudly. Sammi looked at her just as she hoped, giving Piotr an instant to collect her phone.

Piotr smiled at the volunteer as he walked past him again. "Got what I needed, thanks."

"No problem."

"Well done," Hanna said quietly as Piotr returned to the kitchen and faced her across the bar.

"You have three missed calls from Graeme Shearer," he remarked, looking at the device.

She laughed nervously, then caught herself and shot him a cheeky glance.

"I have some secrets of my own, you know. You're not jealous, are you?"

Piotr returned her smile, though it seemed forced to Hanna. He took a bottle of local gin from the bar behind him and put it on the table.

"It's early, I know, but today seems to call for it. Can I interest you?"

Hanna sat down at the bar. "This is probably not the most mature way to tackle my shock." She paused, a thought returning that, in the early hours of this morning, she'd managed to dismiss as nonsense. "Do you think any of us is in danger now? If Kavita really was murdered, I mean, and there's a killer in our midst?"

Piotr shrugged. "I already know I have enemies. But I can look after myself. The real tragedy here is that this diplomat clearly couldn't."

"Well, I would like to protect myself too," Hanna said. "You know, I think we can scratch each other's backs a bit over the next little while. I'd love to have some eyes and ears at the restaurant, really get a sense of what the police have been looking for here."

Piotr puffed up his chest and radiated pride. "If you think it's important, I'd be happy to help." Their eyes lingered on each other for a beat longer than usual.

At that moment, Jónas entered without knocking. He appeared surprised to see both of them there, their heads together as if sharing a salacious secret, with two glasses of alcohol between them.

Piotr nodded at Jónas and pointed to a large silver thermos on the counter. "Coffee?"

"Please," said Jónas.

The trio sat together.

"I know it's early, but can I fix you something to eat?" the chef asked Jónas. Hanna smiled at him approvingly. It never hurt to be in the police's good books.

Jónas nodded enthusiastically. "That would be great, actually. You don't have something substantial by any chance? I haven't really eaten anything since before all this happened."

"Substantial?" asked Piotr. "I only make dishes that are the perfect balance of visually delightful and delectable in flavor." He opened his fridge and looked inside. "But it does seem that I can make you a burger. Okay?" Jónas nodded enthusiastically. The chef looked at Hanna.

"Far too early for me for that," she replied dryly, noting with irony the gin in the tumbler she clasped in her hand.

It took Piotr only a few moments to serve the officer a large cheese, mushroom, and bacon-topped burger, which Jónas dove into with gusto. The stress of his first murder investigation had not affected his appetite, Hanna noticed. She wanted to reach out and smudge out a dribble of sauce on his cheek with her thumb, but resisted.

"I know this is all raw," Jónas began, then looking at the bloody burger in front of him, he changed tack. "I know you are still in shock. But I'm getting a sense of what happened last night. No formal statements yet, just your initial impressions. Ready for some questions?" Piotr and Hanna nodded.

"Great, thanks. Piotr, I'll start with you. How did this dinner go for you last night? Was there anything out of the ordinary that you remember?"

Piotr provided a detailed explanation of everything that was served that evening, from the sea urchin to the arctic thyme sorbet. He included details of every item's preparation and presentation.

"All this I managed to do despite this woman's very strict dietary requirements," he concluded. "I mean, not that she was to blame for anything, obviously. We take these issues very seriously. And the customer is always right."

"What were those requirements?" the officer asked.

Wordlessly, Piotr pushed an oil-spattered piece of paper across the table. Jónas glanced at it. "May I keep this?"

"Be my guest."

"So as far as you can tell, there was nothing in the preparation of the meal or its contents that might have caused Kavita to react the way she did?" Jónas continued.

"Correct," confirmed Piotr. "We have some leftovers here too." He gestured to the food around him. "Test them if you want."

"Thanks, we will need to do that," said Jónas. "But what about the drink afterward, this Flaming Viking? How did that work?"

"You know we have important guests here," the chef began. "Dignitaries and VIPs whom fate has led to our island usually find an excuse to stop by."

Hanna rolled her eyes as he started reciting names.

"There was the crown prince of Norway, who took home a tiny jar of sea truffle. The prime minister of Spain sat over there with a much younger woman whom no one recognized as his wife. A Kazakh Instagram influencer flew in by helicopter for two hours, merely to try the guillemot eggs."

"The cocktail, Piotr?" Jónas repeated.

"It's a drink I make for special foreign guests," he explained. "And Kristján loves it. Or he loves the show of it. It's quite strong, so he likes it if I make one up for him and then he can make himself the big man a bit, you know, both adventurous and tough. I made the first one for Kristján. After he tried his, Graeme asked me to make one for everyone, so I did. Then I set them on fire, and everyone took one."

"Everyone?"

Piotr paused to think. "Maybe not everyone. Linda and Thór

don't drink it. They have tried it before, and they know how potent it is." He smiled.

"Could anyone have tampered with the cocktail?" Jónas asked him. "It was such a strong drink that the alcohol could potentially mask the flavor of anything that was not meant to be there."

"No, not that I noticed, though the lights were out when I set everything on fire. It takes a minute or so before they go back on while I'm preparing everything else," said Piotr. He added defensively, "But *I* didn't do anything to it! This woman, she must have had another allergic reaction to something that she didn't tell us about."

"We will be running tests, of course," Jónas repeated. "So, you say it was Graeme who asked you to mix the drink for everyone? What did he say exactly?"

"I don't remember specifically," said Piotr. "He just said something like 'That looks great. Can you make one for everyone?'"

"He said, 'We're all brave,'" corrected Hanna.

Jónas turned to her. "How can you remember his words so exactly?"

"Because it was such unusual phrasing. I guess he meant that we could all tolerate strong alcohol," she replied.

"We like to record dialogue as precisely as possible," replied Jónas. "Can you tell me about your own movements last night?"

"Of course. I was with everyone at dinner. Had a lovely chat with Jane at the table. I really enjoyed getting to know her. The food was delicious, as expected." Hanna gave a nod to Piotr, who blushed. "After dinner, I was talking to Ben, but by the time we reached the bar for a drink, he was off somewhere else. I was near the sofa."

Jónas nodded and appeared as if he were about to ask another question when Hanna's phone rang. They all looked as the name Graeme Shearer appeared on the illuminated screen.

Jónas raised his eyebrows. Piotr's nostrils flared, but he remained silent.

"Do you need to get that?" the officer asked pointedly.

What choice did she have? "Hello," she said politely, as she hoped the ambassador would not speak loudly enough for the others to hear through the device.

"The police are asking questions," Graeme said without preamble. "We need to meet. Jane's gone out. Can you come to my room now? Don't let anyone see you."

SEVENTEEN

THIRTY-FOUR HOURS BEFORE HE DIES

Kristján sat rigidly in his living room. A candle flickered on the table, and he focused all his energies on that blinking golden light. He was numb.

He was deep breathing, trying what that online shrink called "tools from the toolbox" to help him deal with stressful situations. His back straight, palms flat on each knee, he closed his eyes. Inhale through the nose—*one, two, three, four*. Exhale through the mouth—*one, two, three, four*. Focus on the rhythm of his breath, on the feeling of his hands against his knees. Slowing his heart rate.

He had barely slept the previous night and felt groggy. The image of Kavita's face, eyes open, her features contorted in a mask that proved the pain of her final earthly moments, was seared into his mind. When he finally managed to calm the chaos in his head, Ari's face flashed over Kavita's, taunting him to make sense of it all.

Kristján knew, of course. He felt it in his bones. Like his husband's, this death was no accident. And the two must be connected.

Coincidence could not explain both tragedies. Perhaps now the bureaucrats would begin listening to his doubts about Ari's official cause of death. It was not cardiac related. The letter he received yesterday morning confirmed that Ari had been looking into the activities of Vestmannaeyjar residents, and presumably he had made enemies doing so. There could now be no more postponing looking through Ari's files, the personal items he had been too grief-stricken to examine. Kristján suspected that through her work at the embassy, Kavita had discovered the same information Ari had. Maybe the same person who despised his husband despised her too. Was it also possible the ambassador was connected? Rahul had been convinced of that last night. Somehow, Kristján was going to prove that Ari's death was anything but natural, even if his cremation had made exhuming a body impossible.

Outside, the storm was subsiding, the wind diminishing. Under normal circumstances, the Canadians could have expected to return to the mainland once the weather warning was lifted. But calmer winds or not, life would never be back to normal again. And Kristján knew that the police would want the visitors to remain at least until they had all provided official statements. Maybe he should talk to some of the Canadians himself? Find out what hidden ties Kavita may have had to the Westman Islanders.

The phone rang, and the name of the chief operations officer for the *Herjólfur* ferry that ran between Vestmannaeyjar and the Icelandic mainland appeared on Kristján's screen.

"*Góðan daginn*," Kristján answered. "Any news?"

"We'll be running the ferry soon," the man assured him and

Kristján could hear the exhaustion in his voice. Even though it was not an uncommon occurrence, every time the ship was delayed or canceled it meant a flurry of messages, emails, and voicemails from irate passengers. Kristján was grateful that the man in charge never succumbed to pressure to send the ferry out when people's safety would be jeopardized.

This most recent stoppage, almost a full twenty-four hours, was unusually long for this time of year. "Thank you," he said into the phone. "I know you did your best to keep disruption to a minimum."

"That doesn't stop the calls, though," the man replied, his voice terse. "The woman who couldn't take her son to his chemotherapy appointment in the capital. The busy plumber who would not get back to his home village in time to bid his dying mother farewell. And of course the news of last night's death has already seeped into every crack and cranny of this community. One woman called me to ask if we were going to let the murderer get away this morning!"

"Thank you for letting me know about the ferry," Kristján said firmly and, without saying anything further, ended the call. He didn't have time for complaints.

Once given the go-ahead by the police, anyone on the island could return to the relative anonymity of a capital city. To hide, perhaps, from demons left back on Vestmannaeyjar.

The doorbell rang. Who could be visiting now?

The mayor got up and went to the door. He opened it to see the new widower, Rahul, face pale, eyes red, in the same clothes he had worn at dinner last night. His hair, normally as groomed as the mayor's, was equally disheveled.

Wordlessly, Kristján moved aside to allow Rahul to step in.

"I haven't slept," Rahul began. "I had to leave the hotel room. I think I paced ten kilometers in my socks last night. I just needed to change the view. I know the police, that kid, will want to talk to me. But I needed to talk to someone first, to help me get things straight in my head. I'm not sure why I'm here, but something told me you would understand." He shot Kristján a pleading look.

"I'm afraid I do." Kristján put his arm gently around Rahul's shoulder and guided him to the living room.

"Sit. You can wait here as long as you wish. Take some deep breaths."

Rahul sat with his palms on his knees. His shaky breathing began to slow. "I don't know what to say. Thank you for letting me in. In the middle of the night, I finally began to call people. Family. It was late in Toronto, where Kavita's parents are. I thought at first that I should wait, let them live a little longer in a world where they still believe their daughter is alive. But I had to channel my energies into something other than pacing."

He looked at the mayor apologetically. "I'm rambling."

"It's okay. I understand," Kristján replied.

"They were shattered, of course. In a brief ten minutes, they seemed to express almost all the stages of grief, from shock and disbelief to sadness, and even anger at me. They claimed I could not protect their daughter when she needed it most." Rahul's breaths grew rapid again.

"They were in shock, of course," Kristján said. What else could he offer Rahul but a little bit wider perspective?

"Then I called Kavi's younger sister in Vancouver," Rahul continued in a daze. "She was so distraught. I asked her to let her extended family know. This is not how things were meant to work out." Rahul pulled a tissue from his pocket and blew his nose delicately.

"I know there is nothing I can say right now," Kristján began. But he could see that Rahul was lost in his own pain and not really paying attention.

"I tried to pack her things again, just to keep occupied," Rahul continued. "I looked through what she'd brought for this trip. Her silk scarves still smell of her perfume." His eyes filled with tears. "She had a book on the bedside table—*Strategies for Multilateral Approaches to Global Conflicts*. That's the sort of book she reads… read." Rahul's face paled as he switched to the past tense. He looked at Kristján with an expression the mayor recognized. The widower's eyes were pleading with him, willing him to discover everything he knew about the woman Kavita had been. Because no one could be allowed to forget.

"She was such a good person," Rahul said. "She had so much unfinished work with refugees. It was unorthodox to have them in Iceland rather than in a refugee camp, but Kavita was willing to consider unorthodox solutions."

"She certainly seemed committed to her work," Kristján said.

"She was," Rahul agreed. "Kavi was always conscious about not sharing too many work secrets with me. She didn't want to break any confidences and took that part of her job seriously. Now look where that's got her."

He paused as if a thought had just occurred to him. Kristján knew immediately what that pause meant. He had often had similar dread creep into his own mind.

"If you have any suspicions about anything, raise them now," Kristján said. "You made a serious accusation last night. What was that based on? Don't let anyone talk you into some drivel about allergies if you don't believe that was the cause of…" He stopped.

"Of her death. It's okay. You can say it." Rahul blew his nose again, then continued. "It's my impression that Kavi didn't have a lot of regard for Bláhafid, but she was pushing for further cooperation between the embassy and that company. I can't tell you why specifically, but there are many immigrants—refugees too—working at Bláhafid," said Rahul. "I wasn't very happy with her friendship with that group, to be honest."

"Why not?"

"Because I don't trust them. Now I wonder if she was manipulated in some way."

"Last night it sounded like you had a different person in mind," Kristján commented.

"I know. I was angry. The ambassador just had an argument that really rattled Kavita. In fact, she told me he had threatened her. That's why I said what I said last night. What if he thought she was about to make public what she told him? Graeme ought to have known that Kavita was just blowing off steam. But I can't think of anyone else who would want to harm her. And, Kristján, he gave her the poisoned cocktail."

"Believe me when I tell you I understand," Kristján told him.

He tried to keep his voice from faltering as he continued. "Everyone told me that Ari died a natural death, but I know in my core that something suspicious happened. He was working on an important story, and I'm going to find out exactly what. Don't let anyone change your mind about what you know to be true. You must keep your focus if you want answers."

Rahul looked at him, his eyes wide and solemn.

"I'm trying to go over the evening in my mind. Kavi was upset about something. She didn't want to be here on the Westman Islands any longer than necessary. These visits weren't as glamorous as she liked, no offense. You know, she'd earned all these expensive degrees, lived all over the world. She was proud of how far she had been promoted in a short time, but she never cared about being in a local paper next to a nursing home resident's hundredth birthday celebration or the takings of the Women's Association bingo night."

"With all that overseas work, with all the vastly different people she encountered, was she popular or did she make any enemies?"

Rahul laughed cynically. "Enemies? Kavi was hard to like. But she meant well. She"—he stopped himself—"Do you know when we will be able to go back to Reykjavík?"

Kristján studied the distraught man's face. "Is there something you need to get back for?"

"No, I guess not. But there are…arrangements to be made. I need to go back to Canada as soon as I can."

Kristján could tell there was something Rahul wasn't saying. Was whatever that knowledge was making the widower concerned for his own safety?

"I understand," Kristján replied. "The short answer is that I don't know when we'll be able to leave. The weather has improved and the ferry is going to start running again, but the police will probably want to meet you in person, and they may want to wait until the more senior officers have arrived from the mainland."

Rahul nodded. He appeared deflated. His shoulders sagged. "I was hoping we could go back to Reykjavík sooner," he said.

Kristján's phone rang. "*Já, halló,*" he said briskly. He listened, nodded his head, and spoke rapidly in Icelandic.

"That was Jónas from the police," Kristján finally said after the call ended a minute later. "I am getting updates because I'm the mayor."

"Can you tell me something?"

Kristján looked at Rahul, a bereft version of the suave man he had appeared the night before, unshaven, rumpled shirt under the wrinkled Armani suit now partially untucked.

"I shouldn't tell you anything," he told Rahul. "You're a suspect."

Rahul nodded solemnly, apparently satisfied with this designation if it meant there was official recognition of his wife's cause of death. He stood and walked to the front door.

"They will want to talk to me in that case, and I have nothing to hide." Rahul stopped and faced Kristján. "But look, you just went through the same thing yourself, the challenge of having people believe you. If there is anything you can tell me about last night, confidentially, I would appreciate it."

Kristján couldn't help but feel sorry for Rahul. The pain he would be feeling now was unbearable, and, he reminded himself,

Rahul had witnessed his wife's final moments, not merely come across her body as he had discovered Ari's. Nothing Kristján could do now would bring Kavita back, but perhaps he could help supply some answers.

"First of all, don't believe anyone. Even the authorities." He looked directly into Rahul's eyes. "Trust your instincts. Everyone thinks Ari died from his heart condition, but I know he was murdered. Now I am on the way to proving what everyone else refuses to see."

Rahul looked at the mayor quizzically. Kristján wondered if he was not being believed. Was this man who was going through the same shock, the same grief, really just as skeptical as all the others? Did he think it was all in Kristján's mind?

"Kristján, I'm sorry about Ari. I really am," Rahul said. "But, please, what have you heard? About Kavi?"

"Fine, I'll tell you. But you haven't heard this from me."

Rahul nodded.

"It's not official because an autopsy is going to take time, and so are lab samples on the broken glass. But the doctor on duty said that it looked like Kavita may have been poisoned just as you thought. It seems that the blood coming from her nose was cherry red. This can in some instances indicate potassium cyanide poisoning. If that is indeed the case, then this is murder. Potassium cyanide is not a substance that appears accidentally in drinks or other food."

"Who has access to cyanide?" Rahul asked.

"I have no idea," Kristján admitted. "It can't be easy to find."

"Unless you have connections," said Rahul grimly. "Like an ambassador would."

EIGHTEEN

Hanna discreetly stashed her rain jacket behind a large potted plant in a quiet corner of the hotel lobby. People always clocked its bright color, but not the petite auburn-haired woman wearing it. Keeping her head down, she took the back stairs up two floors to where she knew Graeme and Jane's room was. She saw no one and in any case was confident that she could concoct a reason for her appearance, should anyone question why she was wandering the upper-floor hall of a hotel early in the morning.

She tapped lightly on the door and Graeme opened it immediately, ushering her inside with a furtive glance down the hall.

"No one saw me. Don't worry," she told him quietly after the door was closed. She took a seat in the single chair of the small room, and Graeme sat on the bed's edge facing her. "So, the police. Tell me," she instructed.

"It's not just the police," Graeme answered. "It's Jane. She's not happy with me—even more than usual. I think she might suspect something."

Hanna nodded. She had long ago decided she had nothing to be ashamed of, but for a relative stranger, Jane had seemed unusually friendly the night before. Hanna would have done the same thing in her shoes—ingratiate herself with someone from whom she needed to get information.

"Jane was being particularly candid with me last night," the artist acknowledged. "But she was quite entertaining. I thought she was very nice."

"She is. She's also smart. But you were shooting glances at me a lot at dinner, and she might have noticed."

Hanna stood and walked to the minibar, opening a bottle of fizzy water, choosing not to point out that it was Graeme himself who drew his wife's ire on the ferry over.

"Why don't you just tell her about us?" she asked him.

"You don't have everything on the line," he said sulkily. "I can't make any more mistakes." He put his hands to his forehand and rubbed his temples. "After what Rahul said last night, the way he looked at me." He stood to face Hanna. "Hanna, I can assure you that I had nothing to do with Kavita's death."

Hanna smiled kindly at him. "It never occurred to me." She put a hand on his shoulder. "Okay, well, until Rahul's accusation. But I know you well enough to trust you. Besides, if there was something suspicious about how she died, isn't it much more likely to be connected to Kavita's past? I mean, she's worked all over the world. Perhaps Rahul knows even more but was too shocked to mention it yesterday."

"I know she was not someone who you found particularly helpful," Graeme said.

Hanna felt herself bristle.

"You're right that I wasn't happy dealing with her. Can you blame me? You told me she always talked about being pushed aside because of her age and gender but had no sympathy for a fellow woman on that one occasion when I needed her help."

Graeme nodded and sat back down on the bed. "I recall," he said. "But that's also what brought you to me."

"And I'll always be grateful for that." Hanna put down her water glass. "I need to ask you some things, though. I heard you last night at the bar, heard your argument. From the outside, it did look like you threatened Kavita. What did you say to her?"

Graeme stared at her, clearly wondering why she was eavesdropping in the bar instead of introducing herself to the people she knew. But Hanna stood her ground; she had no need to defend herself. Right now, that was Graeme's job.

"Believe me when I tell you it was nothing to do with what happened last night. It was a personal matter. She was threatening to share some information about me that I would prefer is never made public." He sighed.

"And now, presumably, it won't be."

Graeme frowned. "What are you saying?"

"I'm saying it doesn't look great, Graeme! Everyone saw you hand a cocktail to Kavita."

Graeme didn't answer. After a moment, he said, "I'll talk to the police officer and clear everything up. Don't worry."

"Don't worry? Isn't that why you called me here?"

Graeme smiled at the young woman. "I knew it would make me feel better to talk things through with you face-to-face."

"Well, in that case, there is one more thing," added Hanna. "I found out yesterday that Bláhafid is the main sponsor of my exhibition. Is that your doing? Do you know whose bed you're climbing into?"

Graeme shifted awkwardly. "That's an uncomfortable metaphor. From what I've seen, they seem inventive and proactive. I'm here to learn more about this company. You know that. And I want to help you get on your feet in this new endeavor of yours. That's very important to me."

He gave Hanna a smile, and she forced herself to return it. It had been easy to trust Graeme from the beginning, and he'd been a huge support over the last weeks. Yet the more she spent time with him, the more she worried that tying her fortunes to Graeme Shearer was not necessarily in her best interests.

NINETEEN

Ben and Jane had decided to take a longer route to Kristján's house. The weather was clearing. The flat, grassy peaks and sheer cliffs of the islands surrounding Heimaey were more visible. Ben had suggested the route, via some steps off a road near the hotel. It would lead them to some gravel paths that lay over the lava from the 1973 volcanic eruption and would provide great views of the town.

"You don't really know where you're going, do you?" asked a somewhat breathless Jane as they trod uphill. Reddish pebbles lined the path on either side of them, lava that had sprouted moss in the intervening decades, but Jane knew that she and Ben also now stood several feet over family homes that had been covered in lava—homes filled with mementos, clothing, heirlooms as their inhabitants fled in the dead of a winter's night to escape a potentially lethal volcano.

"No." Ben smiled back. "I hate using map apps. There are no buildings here anyway. Let's walk for a bit and then head back down to the town center, but over in the direction of those houses."

Did the people whose homes were destroyed fifty years ago ever return? Did they live in fear of another surprise eruption, perhaps an even more devastating one? When Jane had faced her own proverbial eruption, her own domestic disaster, a few years ago, she had not needed to flee, but like the Eldfell mountain near which they now stood, that night loomed over her, crept into her dreams, reminded her that everything might fall apart again in an instant. She wanted desperately to prevent that.

There was still a breeze, stronger at this higher ground, the salty smell of the sea in the air. It must only be a few degrees above freezing, Jane thought with a shiver. But it was still an improvement on yesterday. They walked in silence, their feet crunching on the porous, rust-colored pebbles that marked the path.

"Do you know," Ben began. "Was Kavita happy in her marriage? What is Rahul like? I've barely spoken to him."

Jane considered. "He has always seemed very nice to me. He's quiet, but I took that as a healthy counterpoint to Kavita's more overt nature."

"Well, the quiet ones often have something to hide."

"Maybe in the mystery books. I find that hard to believe here." Jane sighed. "But I find everything about this hard to believe."

"What do you make of all the others?"

"Thór and Linda—Kavita only met them in person for the first time yesterday, though she was doing some due diligence on Bláhafid in case they went forward with that negotiation. She had been sort of hot and cold with that company; well, cold then hot, really. Graeme had been talking about it. He said she was wary first and by the time this trip was planned was keener on cooperation. I suppose she could have found some incriminating information on the company and tried to use it to her advantage and then threatened Thór. But why then would she be more interested in the partnership continuing?"

"Maybe she didn't threaten him. Maybe she was keeping the information in her back pocket, and he found out? It's a thought anyway," said Ben as they trod over the rocks.

"And the mayor?" Jane asked.

"Kristján? I can't think of any reason he would want to get rid of Kavita. The same goes for Piotr. The last thing a restaurant owner wants is a death in his establishment. Then there is Hanna. Again, she hardly knows Kavita. I can't imagine what her motive would be. But that just leaves Rahul—or…" He paused.

"Graeme," finished Jane. "It's okay. You can say it."

Ben had begun to articulate the worry that was intensifying in Jane's mind: not that Graeme's temper *had* got the better of him, surely that couldn't be so, but that others might think so.

"Ben, do you think the police know about Graeme's affair? And suspect him of something because of it? Thinking that he's manipulative or vengeful or something?"

Jane paused and studied Ben as the wind ruffled his wavy hair. Ben always seemed so stoic under pressure. He strode confidently, as if he had grown up in this community and knew all its secrets, as if he would never lose his way. How did one person have so much self-assurance? He would make an excellent poker player. Calm and able to take calculated risks. Or maybe his work, his writing, immersed him in dark worlds where he could grapple with murder more easily than she?

"How do you do it?"

"Do what?" Ben asked. They stopped walking.

"This," she said, gesturing at him. "You. Your confidence. Your calm. Your optimism. I'd love to take one of those pills."

"Funny you said that," Ben replied. "There actually are such pills. I take Saint John's wort to improve my mood and gabapentin to help me sleep. A good night's sleep makes all the difference, you know. Especially when you have an editor breathing down your neck for a manuscript due months ago. Especially when it's a sequel and expectations are sky-high."

Was Ben being flippant? Jane wasn't quite sure. Ben never seemed to have a care in the world, but if he was overdue with his next book, she could only imagine the tremendous strain that would put him under. She would want pharmaceutical help too. But she'd also want a friend's support. Perhaps she could also share something, help to strengthen their friendship with a confidence.

"There's more to the story of Graeme's affair," she began, and paused. Now that it came to it, she felt like she was cracking open her soul.

"Go on," Ben said. She looked up at him.

"When I found out about the cheating—not just some fling, but a full-blown affair, with a work colleague, with his *boss*, who had been to our home, who was friendly with our twins, who was supposed to be a trusted friend of ours—well, I lost control."

She kicked a stray pebble on the path in front of them, and it tumbled down the hill.

"I'm not trying to make excuses, but I grew up in an unstable family situation and I promised myself that I would never make the twins endure something similar. I didn't want them to grow up with parents who yelled and screamed at each other, who blamed each other for all of their own shortcomings and thwarted dreams.

"I was furious that Graeme had jeopardized our family. He forced me to choose: leave him, salvage my self-respect, and destroy our children's sense of safety and esteem or agree to his request for forgiveness, minimize the betrayal of this affair, and keep our family intact. I thought I would be stronger from it all, that my heart had the capacity for this compassion. But it turns out I'm not that good a person."

"Come on, don't be too hard on yourself. What happened?"

"I ended up making things worse. Graeme apologized, begged me to forgive him. I can remember it all so clearly. We were in the kitchen. There was a bottle of wine open on the counter. Some pasta boiling on the stove. Jazz playing. And I hit him, shoved him. Hard. He fell, broke his nose, had a mild concussion. They put two and two together at the hospital and then the police were in touch. They asked Graeme if he wanted to press charges of assault, but he declined. Then a few weeks later I heard from child protection services. They wondered if the children were living in a safe environment." Jane's eyes filled with tears.

"You were just showing that you're an imperfect human like the rest of us. You reacted out of anger on the spur of the moment. It could happen to anyone."

"Please, keep this quiet. I've never told anyone before. And I can't tell anyone else. But I just can't believe that Graeme would have done this to Kavita even if strangers may suspect it. It's just not who he is. *I* was the one who lost control. *I'm* the one who flies off the handle. Graeme never would. We need to find out something to prove that to others."

This sudden sense of conviction as she articulated it was a surprise and a relief to Jane. Yes, there was clearly something Graeme wasn't telling her, and Jane couldn't say their marriage would survive if whatever it was bubbled to the surface. But the idea that her placid husband was capable of murder? Suddenly it seemed ludicrous.

Ben looked at her doubtfully. "But you told him you were thinking of leaving him before Kavita died, right? Surely that concerned him, maybe even made him desperate. It's amazing what people are capable of in those circumstances."

Jane shook her head. "Murder is different. I just think there are people who are capable of it and those who aren't."

They were silent for a moment. Then Ben said softly, "You seem really convinced that he's a good man. Are you sure leaving him is what you want?"

Jane sighed.

"He's different from who he used to be. He used to have a confident poise, a swagger. As if he were born to do whatever he wished." She let out a cynical laugh. "White, heterosexual men of his background always feel entitled, I suppose. We've had so many good times and good years, but then somehow, recently, that sheen has faded. Parenthood bored him and arrived unexpectedly early for me. I didn't want to be a mom to twins at twenty-four!"

"I'm sure you're a great mom," countered Ben.

"You've never met them. How would you know? But a life of book clubs and mommy-and-me groups is not very fulfilling. And then Graeme's career turned out not to be as successful as he had expected. Sure, he's an ambassador, but to a tiny country. He's pla-teaued and he doesn't have much time left to do more. He seems so focused now on minutiae rather than the big picture. Then he gets frustrated when he makes a small error in those details. The glamour of this life faded for both of us, and I guess he fell prey to the usual temptations."

She paused and looked to the foggy mountains.

"And when he had brought our marriage to the precipice, I was the one who very nearly pushed it over. It's hanging on by a thread. I can't decide if his betrayal and my reaction cancel each other out in the ledger of marital sacrifice. I thought all I wanted was a stable family life. But maybe I just want happiness in whatever form."

"Jane, I wouldn't tell Jónas and the police all of this. It has nothing to do with what happened last night. Sharing this wouldn't help you, and it won't help Graeme either."

"What if they ask? They might hear about Graeme's affair and about Kavita threatening to report it. That's a motive for murder. I'm so scared for him."

Ben put his hand on her shoulder. "Think about it. An old

affair that is already sort of common knowledge? Doesn't seem like a motive for anything. But look, I'm here to help. Let me know what I can do."

"You can help me think through this, try and figure out what happened. I mean, what about a connection to the locals here? People in politics, people in business. Anyone in public life, really. People like Kavita, they all make enemies at some point, don't they? Especially in small communities like this? Hatred can run deep. Families have long memories."

"If there was a local connection, I'm sure the police would know it immediately," Ben pointed out.

"I doubt that. The locals are full of secrets, and they're good at keeping them."

"True." Ben stopped and turned to face Jane. Seagulls flew around them and the wind whistled around their heads.

"Jane." He looked at her with a serious expression. "Your husband. Who are his enemies?"

Jane returned his gaze, the implication dawning on her.

"Do you think someone at our dinner last night wants to frame Graeme for Kavita's murder?"

"It's a possibility," he answered gently. "Graeme has lived around the world. He's met people from all walks of life. He's been relatively successful, but at what price?"

She tried to invite the idea into her head, the thought that her husband could have an enemy who despised him so much that he—or she?—wanted him out of the picture and was willing to kill someone in the process.

"I know it's a difficult prospect to contemplate, Jane," Ben continued.

Jane shivered at the thought. It seemed so complicated—killing one person to settle a score with another. "I just can't imagine it. I really can't," she said. "No," she said with as much finality as she could muster. "This can't have anything to do with Graeme."

"Maybe you're right," Ben agreed. "But if the clues to this mystery are local, maybe we need to think more about it. Hanna has all of those connections; we could talk to her. Although she's a suspect too. Everyone who was at dinner last night is, including you and me."

"Hanna." Jane felt bitterness creeping into her voice. "Now there's someone who knows more than she's saying."

"What do you mean? She's terrific."

Jane rolled her eyes. It's true that Hanna was more vivacious, wittier, simply more *fun* than she had been expecting. But her intuition told her that the artist already knew her husband, and in some way that her husband did not want to reveal. No, Hanna was not someone she could trust to speak to about Kavita's death.

"Too bad Ari is no longer alive; he had his finger on the pulse of the town," commented Jane.

"Actually, that's exactly it," exclaimed Ben after a moment. "We can ask Ari—in a way. Hanna told me that Kristján is convinced Ari was murdered because of some big investigation he was undertaking before he died. Perhaps he had uncovered something that someone is desperate to keep hidden. Kristján still doesn't believe his death was natural, you know."

"Do you think it's possible Kavita's and Ari's deaths are related?"

"I have no idea, but we should ask a few questions, pull back the curtain on some of the big tensions in this town that aren't visible to outsiders like us. And what we need now is a way to understand who might have been motivated to harm Canada's deputy ambassador. We've got to get to know all the skeletons in this town's closet. Ari's research could be a place to start on that."

Jane wanted to be *doing* something, not just waiting for something to happen. It couldn't hurt, at least. And Ben did have this amazing knack for getting people to open up. Maybe he could turn on the charm with Kristján as well.

"All right. I'm up for keeping my mind busy. Since we're on our way there anyway."

The single-story detached home did not stand out in any way from its neighbors. On the front door was an oval-shaped silver plaque with the names Kristján Gunnarsson and Ari Jónsson carved in cursive writing.

"Okay, this is how it will work," Jane whispered to Ben as they approached. "We stick to the original plan: we're here to see how he's feeling today, given that two people he knew have died suddenly. *Then* we can ask about Ari and what he was working on."

"Right. I think we can find out more than that child cop can. It's not going to hurt, anyway. We just have to get him to trust us." Ben rapped on the door.

Kristján opened it within a few seconds. He was unshaven, his dark-brown hair somewhat ruffled. He was wearing khaki pants and a thin cardigan, gray woolen slippers on his feet. He appeared surprised to see them and rubbed his bleary eyes.

Ben spoke first. "Good morning. I hope you don't mind the imposition. Jane and I—" He looked at his friend. "We wanted to see how you were doing."

"It was becoming claustrophobic in the hotel," Jane said with a cautious smile. "We just wanted to come by and touch base. We're still in shock. I'm sure you are too."

"Right, yes. That's…that's really thoughtful." Kristján spoke as if he was having trouble recalling the foreigners standing in front of him. "I, yes. I'm totally in shock. It's shocking." He rubbed his temples and shook his head, continuing: "Did you see Rahul? He was just here. I hope someone is keeping an eye on him. I'm a bit worried about him."

"We didn't run into him," Ben said. "Maybe he just needs some time alone."

"I hope so. But come in, please." Kristján stepped aside to allow them in. "I was just going to make some coffee."

Out of habit and deference to the Icelandic tradition, both Jane and Ben immediately removed their shoes, placing them tidily on a low shelf next to the door. They padded along an ivory-colored hall and into a high-ceilinged living room that looked into an open concept dining area and kitchen.

Jane and Ben sat on opposite sides of a dark-brown leather sofa. In front of them was a Scandi-designed coffee table decked with tidily stacked glossy magazines and a few small candles on a circular tray. A shelf on the opposite wall prominently showcased framed photos of Kristján and Ari. There was one of the two of them smiling on a tropical beach, cocktails in hand. Another had been taken during a ski vacation.

Kristján busied himself in the kitchen, grinding coffee beans, pouring milk into a small porcelain pitcher. He opened his fridge door, taking out three varieties of cheese. Cutting generous wedges, he placed them on a decorative platter with four different kinds of crackers, adding a bunch of green grapes, a small dish of sweet chili jam, and some slices of imported smoked meats.

"Please don't go to any trouble," said Jane. "We don't want to impose."

"It's fine," replied Kristján. "I need to focus on something, to keep busy. I wasn't much help with Rahul, but I always have food on hand. Many people like to stop by and visit the mayor, and obviously I won't be going into the office today." He sighed as he walked over to the living room and placed the food in front of his guests. He sat opposite Jane and Ben in a leather chair that matched the sofa.

"We were thinking of you," began Jane. "We thought maybe you would want some company now." She glanced discreetly at the photos on the shelf. "I imagine everything is all very raw for you, that Kavita's death...brought up bad memories."

Kristján managed a smile for her. "Yes, exactly. And thank you. I appreciate your concern. But right now I am focused on last night and finding out what happened to that poor woman." He took a sip of his coffee, though Jane noticed that he didn't eat anything. "I'm in touch with the chief of police," he said. "She is hoping to return from Reykjavík later today to take charge; I'm told the ferry will restart services shortly."

Jane nodded. "We heard from Jónas that there might been foul play involved. Poison? It's all so unbelievable. Maybe Piotr accidentally gave Kavita something she was allergic to?"

Kristján shook his head. "No. You won't find a more fastidious chef than Piotr. He doesn't make careless mistakes like that. If anyone in that room last night was a murderer, I would have not put it past Thór, and I think he had been in touch with Kavita about her refugee project."

Jane wondered why the mayor was so quick to indulge in idle speculation with two relative strangers. In his grief, did he see potential criminals in many of those he knew? Was he deliberately planting seeds of suspicion in their minds? Something else niggled at her about his comments, but she couldn't put a finger on it.

"Why Thór?" asked Ben.

"His dubious business practices. Or that's what I hear at least. The police probably don't want us talking together so I shouldn't be telling you all this. I was trying to drop hints to Graeme about the company he seems so desperate to work with, but I'm in an awkward situation as the mayor. Actually, I think Ari was investigating Bláhafid. He never told me exactly what he was doing, but he said he was on the cusp of something big, something that would cement his reputation as a stellar investigative journalist—and we don't have many of those in Iceland."

"Where was Ari doing all this work?" Ben asked.

Kristján nodded toward a room down the hall. "Just here in

his home office. He used to spend hours in there but he never allowed me in. So there might be something quite damning behind that door. Something that made him enemies. And then I received a letter yesterday from some acquaintances in Norway that said Kavita might have known about questionable hiring practices at Bláhafid. There might be some connections."

He looked at the closed office door.

"That room, though. I haven't actually been there since…" His voice trailed off.

"I'm sure it must be very difficult, especially after everything that happened last night," Jane said gently.

"There are so many files and papers to go through, but Ari also hoarded all sorts of personal memories too. I'm just not sure I'm ready to feel the pain those will evoke," he said. "I need to at some point. I need to find proof of what I know to be true. Ari was murdered." He shot Jane a look of intense conviction. Suddenly he had an almost manic sheen in his eyes.

"Really?" asked Jane.

Kristján's eyes were wide, pleading. He nodded his head. "Yes," he said. "I'm certain he was working on something controversial. He texted me the word 'come' right before he died. I raced to the archives, where he had been doing research, but I was too late. The police say it was his heart giving out, that it could have happened any time or place, but I know better. Something—or someone—caused his heart to fail. Let me show you proof."

Kristján raced out of the room and returned with a piece of paper clutched in his hands. "Look," he said urgently to the duo.

"This printout is an email from the chief medical officer's office. I wrote them to direct them to some research I had conducted myself online and I received this about a week ago. Their answer shows that Ari may have been murdered."

"I can't read Icelandic," she said apologetically.

Kristján grabbed the document back. He jabbed a finger on the page. "It says that Ari's injuries might have been caused by trauma and not by a heart attack."

"But Hanna told me he hit his head on a marble floor. Isn't that trauma?" Ben asked.

Kristján shot him a look of deep disappointment. "It means that someone pushed him," he said slowly, as if speaking to a small child.

Jane was skeptical that the medical bureau could imply foul play was a possibility in Ari's death but fall short of opening an official investigation. Surely the mayor must have misunderstood the letter. Poor, grief-addled Kristján.

"And now someone else may have been killed. Those two events *must* be connected."

"Thank you for showing us this," Jane told him gently.

Kristján blinked twice and looked intently at Jane and Ben. Jane gently nudged Ben with her elbow. It was time.

"Kristján, not to be too blunt, but clearly officials are not taking you seriously when it comes to Ari's death," began Ben. "But let us help you discover the truth. I can read some Icelandic. Let me take a look at these documents in the office."

The mayor looked dubious. "Of course I want the truth. But

I don't know what's in that office. You're virtual strangers. This is something I should do myself." He exhaled a shaky breath. "Even if I don't want to."

This was not going to be easy, Jane realized. Kristján was distraught and vulnerable, but he was still shrewd. Clearly, a little deception was going to be necessary.

"I understand you're uncomfortable concerning what you might discover about your husband," Jane began gently. "I had a cousin once whose partner died suddenly. She was supposed to go through all his old things and found it incredibly difficult too. She could never bring herself to do it. Then two years later, when she was gone herself, her own family had to take the time to review all the documents and mementos she had kept. Not only was it stressful and time consuming, but they discovered insurance papers that would have given my cousin an impressive payout, had she submitted all the information on time."

She put her hand on the mayor's shoulder. "I know it's awful to think about. And I know that what happened last night has made everything worse. But we are here to help. Will you let us do that?"

Kristján looked from one to the other.

"Fine," Kristján relented. "After all these weeks of delay, it may just be best for you to get them started for me."

"Thank you." Jane smiled. "You try to relax. We'll let you know if anything turns up."

"Was that true, that stuff about your cousin's family finding the insurance details?" Ben asked once the mayor had shown them to the office.

Jane blushed. "No, but we'd come all the way here. I didn't want to back down because the mayor was getting jittery."

Ben grinned. "Look at you: Jane Shearer, ruthless investigator. All right, you start over in that corner, and I'll start in this one. How about that?"

TWENTY

THIRTY HOURS BEFORE HE DIES

Linda loved running in inclement weather. She was proud of the fact that she had completed a half marathon in under two hours, despite being in her late fifties. Accomplishments such as that were the result of determination, focus, and a willingness to push through pain to reap the ultimate rewards.

When it was windy, when the sleet was hitting her face and chilling her skin as it was now, she felt most alive. Her running shoes thudded along the pavement. Her one concession to the weather was that during these storms she didn't run along the narrow dirt trails by the cliffs. She would be no match for a gust of wind, and no one could survive a 100-meter fall to the chilly North Atlantic below.

Fighting the elements helped to focus her thoughts. That was what was needed now. When the unthinkable happened, as it had last night, the rhythm of running grounded her. So why did every gust of wind in her face feel like Kavita's last gasps for help? Someone in that room last night must know why the deputy ambassador ended up drinking a poisoned cocktail.

Linda turned a corner and headed up the hill past the golf course. In the distance, she could see the towering Eldfell volcano, seemingly so benign now, a dark shadow over the town. But Linda still vividly remembered the night of the eruption.

She was eight years old when her mother hastened into the bedroom she shared with her younger sister. She told them to dress warmly as they needed to rush to the harbor and from there to the mainland.

Gazing out the window, Linda saw a plume of molten lava spewing high into the night sky. She struggled into her snowsuit and helped her sister into hers. Within an hour, they were snuggling together onboard a fishing trawler, heading over the choppy waves to the mainland. Though they tried to conceal it, Linda could tell the adults around her were frightened. Yet all Linda could think about was the test she had studied so hard for that was to be the next day. Would she fail it if she didn't show up to write it? Would she retake it next week or whenever they returned?

Linda didn't know then that it would be over a year before her family would go back to Vestmannaeyjar, and then to a new house. Their old one, like every one of their possessions, was buried under meters of cooling lava.

In those days, there was no trauma counseling. People survived, and that itself was cause for thanks. Sure, the tax breaks and moral support helped. And a cousin put them up during the time they were away. But once they returned, it was their job to rebuild and get on with it. There was no suggestion that the aftereffects of the shock could last for decades.

For many years after, Linda would wake each night with a desperate need to escape, to flee. She promised herself that when she was an adult, she would never find herself in a circumstance when she would be caught unprepared. And for years, that promise had remained unbroken.

But watching Kavita die in front of her had been jarring, no doubt about it. And when bad things happened, people always tried to blame her husband. Linda could understand why: he was a successful businessman, and he'd done what was necessary to achieve that status. Thór needed to be protected, though. If he were backed into a corner, if he thought he had been falsely accused of something, he could be unpredictable. Linda had fallen out of love with her husband long ago, but his success had helped her too. It needed to be preserved.

Linda circled around the course and back toward the town. She had the streets to herself in this weather. She jogged past Skel. A search-and-rescue vehicle was parked out front and the lights were dimmed, but there was no other indication of last night's drama.

She jogged back up the hill toward her home. A few blocks up Illugagata Street, she saw two people knock on the front door of the mayor's house. Was that Ben and Jane? What could they be doing there?

Heart pumping, Linda turned and jogged toward home, her thoughts turning—as they always did—toward her husband. He wouldn't be very happy about the ambassador's wife paying a visit to his local nemesis.

TWENTY-ONE

TWENTY-NINE HOURS BEFORE HE DIES

"This will keep us busy," remarked Jane.

She and Ben stood in the inner sanctum of Kristján's house, in what had been Ari's study. The office was not small, but the amount of material it contained made it feel cramped. One window with a view of grassy hills had a minuscule pane that could open to let in fresh air, while the radiator underneath the window could be turned up to counteract any difference in temperature. The walls were painted a simple cream. A desk that looked to have been purchased from an upscale Danish designer was the primary piece of the room, along with a comfortable leather swivel chair. These were the only pieces of furniture, aside from a large lamp and stuffed, but organized, bookshelves.

Much of the remainder of the floor space was occupied by boxes. There were boxes of various shapes and sizes, boxes stacked on boxes, quite possibly boxes within boxes. Some looked so pristine as to have been recently unfolded from a bulk-buy purchase at

IKEA. Others were clearly older, dusty, ragged, faded, labeled with fountain pen in spidery Icelandic. There was more material here than Jane had expected, and she found it all quite daunting. She could see why Kristján hadn't yet managed to tackle it.

"I had pictured a tidy room with a filing cabinet and neatly organized folders," Jane said to Ben. "Perhaps even some that were helpfully marked 'top secret investigations.'" She looked around her and swept her hands in a wide gesture. "I was not expecting the chaotic hoardings of someone clearly unacquainted with a recycling bin."

"This chaos reminds me of last night. Could there really be something here that can explain what happened to Kavita?" Ben asked doubtfully.

Jane sighed. "There must be *something* here! But probably not what Kristján is expecting. He wants to find a motive for Ari's death and from that extrapolate a murder. But from what our briefing notes for the trip said, Ari died of a heart attack. I can't see how that could be wrong. Kristján thinks that letter from the chief medical officer supports his claim of murder, but my impression is they are trying to show compassion to a grieving widower. So where do we start, do you think?" She began to remove boxes from shelves. At least they could proceed in an orderly fashion, going through all the containers on the floor and placing them in the hall outside once they were done.

Ben was staring intently at all the boxes, as if his eyes were X-rays burrowing into the contents of each one.

They got to work with a box each, opening it up and peering inside.

"There aren't any papers here," grumbled Ben. "This is a bunch of old porcelain figurines." He lifted up a piece of an ashtray about the size of his hand. It was chipped in one corner. "Next!"

He moved that carton to the hall outside of the room and found another one. It was older and more tattered and contained handwritten papers.

Jane, meanwhile, was sitting cross-legged on the floor, an open filing box next to her. Seeing Ari's private space had surprised her more than she expected. Despite all his recent turmoil, Kristján seemed so put together. It seemed incongruous that his chosen partner was so haphazard. What else would surprise her about this dead man who she felt she was about to get to know very well?

Jane unboxed a pile of papers, mostly full of printed material.

"These documents are all in Icelandic," she said, disappointed.

Ben took his phone out of his pocket and showed Jane. "Here, you take a photo of the page, then put it into the app, and it works like an online translator. It's not perfect, especially for anything handwritten, but with technical documents it works surprisingly well. I guess there is less room for nuance in translation there. Using it has really improved my Icelandic comprehension."

Jane passed him the first page of the document and Ben took a photo, waiting for a moment as it processed the words.

"Right, so this logo at the top is for the Icelandic tax authorities—and, as you can also see, it's a letter addressed to Ari himself." He read on in silence. "Nah, this one isn't helpful. It's something about claiming back value-added taxes on business expenses and that he needs to submit the correct receipts. More of a form letter."

Jane sighed.

"Is this a lost cause? Are we looking for a needle in a haystack here? We ought to have known better."

"Let's not get discouraged. Even if we just open the tops of the boxes we might help with something. There'll be stuff here that can go right to the dump." He looked pointedly at the chipped porcelain figurines. "And other pieces that might have only sentimental value. That's fine. Keep those to show Kristján. But if we focus on the right items we might find some answers."

"Like this, you mean?" Jane had begun unpacking something else while Ben spoke, and now held aloft a mug plastered with 3D letters that spelled "I ♥ Dubrovnik."

"Yes, exactly! You're a natural at this!"

"Look at this one." Jane held up a faded newspaper clipping. "An English review of *Every Good Man*." She glanced through it. "Looks pretty middling, especially for a Booker winner."

"Thanks a lot," replied Ben sarcastically. He gave Jane's shoulder a friendly shove, and Jane looked down quickly, feeling her cheeks flush.

As they continued, the sun began to peek from the clouds. A ray of light shone straight into the window that Ben had opened and faded out only on the desk, the exact place, Jane imagined, where Ari had sat, had contemplated and googled and typed and organized and prepared whatever it was he was going to reveal to the world.

But as the minutes passed, Jane lost track of what time it was. Iceland's lingering sun could provide no proper indication, and she was beginning to feel some twinges in her stomach. But the hungrier and thirstier she became, the more discouraged she was about the purpose of this mission. They hardly understood anything and it was really difficult to tell what might be relevant, though there was plenty that was blatantly not so.

Ben seemed more focused. He was ruthlessly efficient in his perusal of the documents. He would open a box, grab whatever was inside, and make an assessment within a couple of seconds on whether or not he wanted to look further. He almost always didn't, and boxes were stacking up outside in the hall. Occasionally, Jane heard Ben sigh with frustration. No doubt he too was hungry. And tired.

"What if something vital was kept on Ari's computer?" Jane asked. "Wouldn't that have been a safer place to store delicate information?"

"Yes, possibly," replied Ben.

They continued in silence, sometimes with a sigh from Jane, a cough from Ben. There was dust, a few dead bugs.

"Hey, here's a fun-looking one!" exclaimed Jane. She peered inside the box in front of her. "Lots of handwritten stuff here, and it's pretty old. Couple of old photos too."

"Mind if I look?" Ben asked from across the room. "Maybe there's a photo of our common relative; maybe that's where I got my big ears."

"Oh yeah," Jane said, remembering how Kristján remarked on Ari's pride at being related to Ben yesterday at the museum. "But you don't have big ears. Sure, of course, have at it. There's plenty more."

She pushed the box over to Ben, who was now sitting on the floor himself, having cleared enough space for it.

As they unearthed an increasing diversity of material, Jane thought this was finally becoming more interesting. She was getting a glimpse into how another person saw things. Not through the modern gaze of highly curated social media posts that depicted only how someone wanted everyone else to see them. Instead, this was the assortment of what one person thought was salient about the world around him. That included sentimental mementos, as well as research on what Ari clearly believed had societal worth, papers and reports on organizations and people in the community. She had even seen an old menu from Skel, asterisks marking two different drinks. Next to them, someone had written $$$L? Did Ari disapprove of Skel's pricing structure? Here in these boxes, the public face he would have shown about his interests and priorities was removed. This was it. The raw truth about what Ari Jónsson kept closest to him.

Jane's gaze landed on a newer box. "Ben, this one is labeled Bláhafíd." She pulled back the flaps. "And the documents are mostly in English." She began to pick at them, her anticipation so great that it was a struggle to take in what was written there.

"Well…?" said Ben with a tone of impatience.

"Shit."

"What is it?"

"This is damning stuff, Ben. It looks like Thór Magnússon has some explaining to do."

Jane fanned a handful of papers in front of her, looking at them intently.

"It looks like emails, all from within the last couple of years. From a"—she shuffled some papers around—"company in Norway. It looks like Ari was writing to a personal contact there for some information on Bláhafid."

"What kind of information?"

"I'm getting to that. It seems that there was something unusual about the employees at Bláhafid and how they were compensated. Listen to this: 'It has come to our attention that your newest employees, three from Afghanistan and five from Yemen, have not been receiving sick pay and have had to work overtime at regular rates. Housing has not been provided as was negotiated according to the union contract.'"

Ben was silent for a moment. He left his boxes and moved toward Jane. "So there were some dodgy employment practices at Bláhafid," he remarked. "Do we know if Thór would have known about this? Did Kavita discover it while doing her due diligence?"

Jane looked at it. "Remember that Kavita was working on a project to temporarily match refugees with jobs in Iceland until all their paperwork came through to get to Canada. Graeme helped sometimes, although it was her initiative that she had built with the ministry of immigration. How would it have looked for Kavita if the workplaces where these people had been employed were operating more like Victorian workhouses, or worse?"

"Do you think she knew?"

Jane shrugged. "Graeme said she was desperate for this project to succeed. I can't imagine she wouldn't have said something if she had found out. But these are just a few documents. They don't prove enough, they're just incentive for us to keep looking."

"Do you think Kristján is aware of what Ari discovered?" asked Ben.

"We'll talk to him once we've looked at this a bit more. I'm not sure why this Norwegian company is the main source. Maybe there's something in these other files in Icelandic that I haven't figured out yet. Kristján already said that it was sensitive. If it got out that the mayor knew about this and did nothing, that may affect his electability. But if he was trying to do something about it, he can't have been the most popular person with Thór."

"We've seen that ourselves," said Ben. "They can't stand each other. But Bláhafid is also the town's biggest employer. Anything bad happening at the company will make the townspeople unhappy, and when people are unhappy, they often take it out on their politicians. That would be quite the journalistic scoop for Ari—although not the best situation for his husband."

Jane nodded. "If he knew, Kristján must have faced a dilemma."

She sat back and thought for a moment. "Let's consider this rationally. We have a company maybe cooking the books a bit, maybe not filing all the right paperwork for the people they hire. But they pay taxes, they employ a lot of people from the town. Their owner and CEO is a pillar of the community. Maybe he's not the nicest guy, sure, but this is a small town and people talk. Is this really a huge secret still?"

"Yes, I know what you mean. Would someone kill to cover up something like this?" Ben stared at her thoughtfully. His face had smears of grime and dust. "Ari would be the logical target, but he died of natural causes and all these documents are here to be examined. Meanwhile, Kavita's death is suspicious but I'm finding it hard to connect that to Ari's research. So what's the missing piece of this puzzle?"

TWENTY-TWO

TWENTY-EIGHT HOURS BEFORE HE DIES

"So why is the sky falling? Well, aside from the obvious."

Hanna was out of breath. She had dashed over to the folklore museum as soon as she saw Stella's text message: CAN U COME OVER RT NOW? SMTH BIG. ♥ She had rapped on the heavy museum door, her hair disheveled, her jeans scruffy, her Doc Martens plastered with old leaves.

Stella answered immediately and ushered her inside, into the room where they should have been earlier on that day anyway—for the grand opening of her exhibition. The launch had been postponed, of course, but Hanna was starting to worry that it might not happen at all.

"What's going to happen with all this?" Hanna looked around her. "I mean, I can't pose that question to anyone else right now. But between us, it would be a shame after all this hard work to shelve it all."

"Nah. We'll still display everything. We might just have to take a bit of time doing it, not have a splashy opening. And I don't really care whether the ambassador cuts the proverbial ribbon or not. For all you know, he's actually a murderer!"

"Stella!" Hanna chided her friend. "I know you want to know what happened, but why did you really call me here so urgently?"

"Well, given the events of last night, it's just strange…" began Stella. "Follow me."

She led Hanna up two floors, along the empty corridor, to the exhibition on Vestmannaeyjar during the Second World War. No one seemed to be in a museum-visiting mood that day and they were alone. As they walked, Stella told Hanna what she had heard through the grapevine about the fatal Flaming Viking at Skel. It was remarkably accurate intel.

Stella got straight to the point once they stopped walking. "Yesterday I showed the Canadians and Mayor Kristján around the museum. I talked about the history of the island during the war, about the American occupation, about what the soldiers did while they were here. I spent a while showing them this."

Stella pointed out the military uniform from the previous day.

"You've heard the story, I guess? We don't know who it belonged to, but the uniform was donated to us by old Lilja at the farmhouse."

Hanna nodded, curiosity etched on her face. "Everyone knows about this."

"Notice anything unusual about it?" Stella asked.

Hanna shook her head. "I'm no expert on military uniforms."

"Probably no one would notice, except for me."

Hanna was too tired for vague allusions to something dramatic. "Stella, what are you trying to tell me?"

"This uniform came with a satchel. In the satchel were personal effects. There was also a chain that we hung around the mannequin's neck. Attached to the chain was a small capsule. A cyanide capsule."

"Those lethal capsules were just lying around the museum?" Hanna raised her eyebrows. "I know you Icelanders are pretty laissez-faire about things, but isn't that kind of dangerous?"

"The capsule is decades old. I'm not sure it would even work, or maybe it wouldn't work so quickly. Whatever. I have no idea. I just know that the capsule that was on display with this uniform is gone."

Hanna paused. The text to drop everything and meet Stella at the museum somehow seemed to be more justified than she had initially thought. "Are you sure?"

"Yes, definitely!" Stella was firm. "Hanna, do you understand what this means? From what I've heard, this is exactly the kind of poison that could have killed Kavita."

Hanna looked at the uniform. If only regalia could talk.

"Even if that missing capsule wasn't used to kill Kavita," continued Stella, "it still means someone is walking around with a potentially deadly weapon."

"Wouldn't someone have noticed a person with it?" asked Hanna.

"No. They're small. You didn't even notice until I pointed it out. I only saw it coincidentally when I went to make sure everything was tidy after my talk yesterday. If I hadn't done that, we wouldn't be here now."

"So anyone could have taken it? Is that what you're saying?" said Hanna.

"Exactly. It's been here for ages, and now it's gone."

"Don't you have security cameras?"

"Hanna, this is a small-town museum. And you of all people ought to know that."

Hanna ignored the implication. She didn't want to become entangled in the case of the missing cyanide, but it seemed to her that someone was going to find out sooner or later.

"You need to tell the police," said Hanna.

"Wait. Will they file some report about lax security here? Will they blame this on us?" Stella looked worried.

"Of course not. That's not their remit. And Jónas is your second cousin! He'll understand. You need to tell them, though. Who could have taken the capsule is the more important concern than any mistakes you've made."

Stella raised questioning brows at her friend. Hanna knew what that meant. Stella wasn't referring just to her own lapses in judgment; she was referring to Hanna's.

TWENTY-THREE

TWENTY-SEVEN HOURS BEFORE HE DIES

Kristján sat in his immaculate kitchen with a cup of espresso. The mug was porcelain, painted with those popular Finnish children's characters that you could collect from airport duty-free shops that portended better days. Ari had liked this one in particular, the one with the Moomin father, probably because it reminded him of his rotund and much-loved grandfather from the northeast.

Kristján was relieved he had thought to ask others to be the first to investigate the inner workings of Ari's private space. Ari had not been the tidiest individual, and it promised to be burdensome work, so he was happy to share it. While Kristján was skeptical that they'd find anything relevant to Kavita's death last night, he was hopeful that they could begin to bring some order to the chaos and that it might prompt him to take the next step himself and continue the job.

It must have been almost two hours after they had entered that Jane and Ben, each marginally disheveled, emerged from Ari's office.

"Anything interesting?" Kristján inquired as he strode to the coffee machine. "Find anything fun about your common ancestor, Ben?"

"We found something far more interesting than that. Here." Ben's tone was serious. He and Jane were each holding a box full of notes and files, which they set on the kitchen table. Jane took the papers from the top of her pile and straightened them out, handing some to Kristján.

"Take a look at this." Jane gave Kristján some printed emails from the top. "These are in English, but there is a lot more in Icelandic. That didn't help me at all, but Ben glanced at everything. It seems to show a lot of dodgy business going on at Bláhafid, something that Thór was managing to cover up. Obviously, it doesn't prove anything and maybe doesn't relate to what happened, but you said yourself Ari admitted he was working on a huge story. This must be it. And regardless of yesterday, it seems to show that Thór Magnússon has dubious integrity."

Kristján put on his reading glasses to examine the papers. So these documents had been sitting in his home the whole time, all the fifty-seven days since Ari died, and who knows how many weeks before that. If only he had had the courage to look. In that drab room was potential proof that Thór had knowingly taken advantage of new refugees to the country by not paying them over-time or other benefits, much less union-negotiated wages. The documents also seemed to indicate that Thór was claiming tax deductions for which he was not eligible. At first glance, there was enough smoke to indicate a proverbial fire for Thór and for

Bláhafid. Was there more that could definitively prove this knowl-edge had led to Ari's death?

Kristján slowly put the papers down and looked at his guests.

"It looks like Thór has a lot to answer for." He sighed. "And clearly Ari made an enemy of Thór if he knew about this. But it's not likely related to Kavita's death, is it? She needed them for her refugee project."

Jane blinked at him. "What do you mean?" she asked incredulously.

Ben looked equally surprised. "We know Kavita had placed refugees at Bláhafid. What would Thór do to keep people from finding out about his corruption? Wouldn't he kill? Wouldn't this illegal activity be enough to take down his empire?"

Kristján paused. He thought about the letter he had received the morning of Kavita's death, which had suggested he needed to talk to the deputy ambassador about anything she may have been covering up for Bláhafid. Which he had wanted to do privately, and without involving officials.

"We need to take this to the police," Jane said. "Don't you agree?"

The mayor fiddled with the pen in his hand. "I can't," he replied. "Well, I don't want to, not right now. These are very important files, but this is a very delicate matter. If Thór gets wind that he is under suspicion for anything, if it becomes clear that we are looking into his business dealings, he could well close up shop and move his company elsewhere." He looked at Jane. "That would make your husband's efforts redundant, but more importantly, it would devastate this community. Bláhafid is the Westman Islands' biggest employer. And I am the mayor of this town."

"Maybe you're being a bit overdramatic," Ben said gently. "Thór might have an explanation. You can't know how he'll react, and it doesn't help anyone to second-guess something before it happens."

"Normally I would agree with you," replied Kristján. "But in this case, I know. I haven't seen these papers before, but they confirm something for me, something that I heard about several months ago. I was told that Thór was corrupt, that he was engaging in possibly illegal business practices. I even once confronted him about it. And he did exactly as I just said. He threatened to close the company and move its operations elsewhere. He knew that as mayor I would be held responsible for allowing our community to suffer such a blow."

"You mean he was blackmailing you?" asked Jane.

"No, not blackmailing, but he knew that the whole community would be devastated economically if I went public. So I waited." Kristján looked at the documents again. "But I didn't know that this was what Ari was working on. He never specified what he had been doing, other than to say it was big. You know, journalists get little credit for the risks they take when trying to uncover corruption and wrongdoing, nor does everyone recognize that in small communities they also risk being ostracized for their efforts." Kristján spat his next words out bitterly. "That made Ari an easier target for an attack, especially since he was considered by many to be an outsider with no long-term roots on the Westman Islands."

It had always been a source of shame to him that some residents of this town, his hometown, the one for which he cared so deeply and had devoted so much, also felt that his partner was not worthy of the same respect as they, simply because he was from another part of Iceland.

He glanced up at his companions. Were Jane and Ben looking at him with compassion or suspicion?

"Please, you must understand!" Kristján was almost pleading now. "Ben, you're a writer, you're a storyteller. You get it, don't you? You understand conflicts and secrets."

"We should go over everything in these files as soon as we can," said Ben. "I don't think you can avoid talking to the police either. This information has to come out one way or another."

"There's one other thing I'd like to know, though," said Jane. "If Ari hadn't told you he was looking into this, how *did* you know about Bláhafid's corruption?"

"Someone close to an employee told me. It's someone I trust and although I didn't see actual proof, when I spoke to Thór it was obvious from his reaction that my source was on the right track."

"But who was this person?" Ben repeated.

Kristján paused. He had promised to keep quiet. "I don't think that's relevant."

"It really is," pressed Jane. "Without a name, the police will think you did know everything that Ari was up to. You'll lose all credibility with them. And don't you need it more now that you need to prove your theories about your husband's death?"

Everything always came down to Ari and the lengths to which

Kristján was willing to go to make the truth come to light. The mayor's shoulders sagged. "Fine, but this is just one person of many who doesn't like Thór, and I'd appreciate your discretion. I don't want to make trouble for him."

"Who was it, Kristján?" Jane asked firmly.

"It was Piotr, the owner of Skel."

TWENTY-FOUR

TWENTY-SIX HOURS BEFORE HE DIES

Hanna stayed with Stella until Jónas arrived to learn more about the missing cyanide capsule. It would be helpful to her to make sure Stella didn't reveal any more than necessary about yesterday.

"Listen, Stella, I know Jónas is a distant relative," she began. "I know everyone was so proud of him when he graduated from police academy training at such a young age. I know you're so excited to encourage his success, that this is what he has always dreamed of doing."

"What are you saying, Hanna?"

"All I'm saying is that just because he is going to make a great investigator doesn't mean he is one yet. Just because he knows how to go through a checklist doesn't mean he is equipped to tackle a murder investigation. Don't muddy the waters by telling him anything irrelevant." She looked at her friend expectantly.

"Got it," Stella replied. "You know I'm always on your side."

She heard the creaking of a door. "Speak of the devil," she said.

Once Jónas arrived, Stella provided only the relevant details as she told him about the World War Two uniform and its missing treasure.

"Thank you for calling me," Jónas told Stella. "You may have heard that the initial medical findings last night indicated that poison was likely involved, and a neurotoxin such as potassium cyanide could well be the cause of death."

"So are you saying that this missing capsule, this *ancient* missing capsule, may have been what killed Kavita?" Hanna said. "It seems so unlikely."

"Perhaps not all that unlikely. Anyone who has read an old-school mystery knows that cyanide is a killer. And the existence of this uniform is widely known, at least here on the island."

"But why would someone poison a drink in such a dramatic fashion? It doesn't make sense."

"Right now, this is just one option we're investigating. Stella, is there somewhere we could sit and talk privately about this?"

"Mind if I tag along?" Hanna asked. She needed to hear their conversation. "I could be useful. Tell you more about my exhibition. That's why the diplomats were in town, after all." Stella shot her a quizzical look.

Jónas looked hesitant, but, as Hanna was sure he would, he agreed.

Stella showed Jónas to her office on the ground floor. The window looked onto the main entrance to the museum and the grassy slope in front of it.

The office was small. Its shelves were lined with hardcover

books, from photographic tomes on various museums to a biography of the elfin singer Björk. On the walls were a single framed print of a modern Icelandic painter and one of Hanna's own photographs that she'd signed. Numerous newspaper clippings in various languages were pinned to a bulletin board on one wall. The office still bore the signs of its previous middle-aged male inhabitants, not this up-and-coming curator who was shaking up the drab world of folklore. Hanna knew Stella had better things to do than redesign her office.

Hanna wondered if Jónas would lecture Stella about lax safety procedures at the museum. But it was often the Icelandic way: progress first, fix problems later. Stella was succeeding in attracting younger and more diverse crowds to this obscure museum on Vestmannaeyjar. Surely she could be forgiven for having forgotten to cross a few *t*'s along the way.

"We don't know for sure whether this missing capsule is relevant to our investigation," began Jónas as he unpacked his iPad. "But it would be quite the coincidence for this to have disappeared on the same day as a poisoning."

"But was it definitely taken?" Hanna asked. "Could it have fallen off the mannequin or been lost in some accidental way?"

Stella shook her blond head, long earrings dangling against her cheeks. "No way. You would need to deliberately tug on the chain to detach it. And we've looked around on the floor. Nothing there. Nothing anywhere."

"What about security cameras?" asked Jónas.

"I was planning on getting to those early next year."

None of this made things look good for her friend, Hanna thought.

"So, you pointed out the capsule during the museum tour yesterday morning? From that time to Kavita's death, who could have had access to steal it?"

"I suppose anyone could have. The front door is open during regular hours, and I told the story of this soldier and his poison capsule to all the visitors."

"So everyone at dinner last night knows about this poison?" clarified Jónas.

"Yes. Well, Hanna wasn't with the group yesterday, although she knew the story already. And neither were Thór and Linda, but I would think they know it too. It's legendary on this island. But I never thought it would still be lethal, so many decades later."

"Could anyone from that group have taken it during their visit?" Jónas asked.

Stella considered this. She rubbed her thumb against her forefinger as if removing a smudge.

"I didn't notice. But maybe, I guess. The mayor disappeared to talk on the phone. The ambassador asked questions but seemed distracted."

"What about later in the day? Did any of that group return to the museum?"

Hanna could see Stella thinking. She knew the museum director wanted to be helpful but also wouldn't want to muddy the investigative waters. Hanna willed her friend not to put her foot into it anymore. She already appeared unprofessional for not properly securing museum property or installing the right safety equipment. No one would be the wiser if she stayed quiet about any visitors, especially the ones she trusted.

"Let's see. Well, Kavita called in the afternoon to ask a detail about the exhibition for the report she was writing. Hanna and I spent some time here setting up the exhibition."

Stella paused. "Even later than that, as I was about to go home for the day, Piotr came by too. He wanted to talk to Hanna, but she had already left."

"Did he stay long?" asked Jónas.

"No, I don't think so."

"Don't *think* so?"

Stella faced them again, a sheepish look on her face.

"You know how it is here. We are all friends in this town, or at least we are all acquaintances. I had been socializing with Hanna, I was going to meet another friend for a drink, and I just wanted to leave. And Piotr said he needed to use the bathroom."

"And?"

Stella looked even more awkward. "And so I just said okay and could he pull the door behind him when he left."

"You mean you left him alone in the museum?"

"I guess I did." Stella looked at the stern cop. "When I returned this morning, I didn't initially notice anything out of place, nor did I expect to. We do that sort of thing all the time. Send people to pick something up in our homes, leave our keys in our car. It's why we live in a small community. Because you can trust people. And it's Piotr. I mean, what on earth was he going to do?"

Jónas's face was impassive. Hanna could tell what he was thinking: Who else would know how to disguise poison but a talented chef?

TWENTY-FIVE

TWELVE HOURS BEFORE HE DIES

The next morning, the sun was bright and the breeze was pleasant. The salty sea air wafted across the town, and gulls chirped hungrily in the harbor as they awaited the arrival of trawlers ready to unload their catches.

Jane pushed her eggs around her plate. She was feeling antsy and disturbed. Had it only been forty-eight hours since they were on their way to the ferry to travel to this island? Her foundations had been so shaken in that short period that it felt like a lifetime ago.

It wasn't just the ultimatum she had given Graeme. There was something else bothering her, something she couldn't quite put her finger on. Kavita had clearly been an unpopular person, even on occasion with her husband, but from what Jane's instincts told her, no one truly hated the diplomat. So many of the people at dinner last night hardly even knew Kavita. Aside from Rahul and her own husband, Thór was probably the most familiar with the deputy ambassador, but would he have been so concerned she was about to reveal Bláhafid secrets that he could kill her? Kavita was so intent on her refugee scheme that she would never have sacrificed Bláhafid. None of it made any sense.

Sitting opposite Jane at breakfast, Graeme was staring at his coffee mug and had hardly touched his food.

"Do you think some of this town's secrets had anything to do with Kavita's death?" Jane mused aloud. "Did she really wield so much influence that someone wanted her to die before she revealed something? If that secret is still discoverable, does that mean someone else is in danger?"

"Well, no one else drank a poisoned cocktail." Graeme replied. "If you're asking me, I think we should let Jónas and his colleagues do their jobs. The more they know, the sooner we'll all get out of here. The ferry is running again, but I suppose we need to stay here until told otherwise."

"Why don't you make some phone calls and see if Kavita's refugee plan can still be salvaged?" Jane asked. "She would have wanted that. Meanwhile, I'm going to tell Rahul the latest news about what we saw at Kristján's. I have hardly spoken to him since everything happened."

"He probably wants to be alone," Graeme said. "And I'm not sure we're the people he wants to speak to right now. But do what you want. What is Ben up to?"

"He is going back to Kristján's this morning to finish going through the last folders with him. There's something you should know about what we were doing at the mayor's house yesterday."

Jane explained their search in brief terms. "We tried to go

through as much as possible in such a short time, and we did come across a lot about Bláhafid. It seems that the company, specifically its owner, has not been engaging in very desirable practices."

"What?" Graeme put down his coffee cup so forcefully that it splashed hot coffee over the tablecloth. "That can't be right. Kavita would have done due diligence. She never mentioned anything to me."

Jane wasn't surprised; she'd expected Graeme to be upset. He'd been resting all his hopes on having a big Canadian deal under his belt. "I'm sorry, I know this meant a lot to you. But I don't think that this is the kind of company you want to be associated with. We don't need them expanding into Canada with their exploitative practices. Imagine if that became public knowledge in the press!"

"That must be what Hanna mentioned," Graeme murmured to himself.

Jane looked at him sharply. "Hanna? What has she got to do with Bláhafid?"

"Hanna? Nothing, I'm sure," Graeme said hastily and unconvincingly. "But I'm surprised Kavita hadn't told me if there was truth to this. Some of the refugees she brought over were working for a Bláhafid-related company in Ólafsvík."

Jane nodded. Kavita hadn't wanted to jeopardize her refugee program, even if conditions weren't ideal. She understood why the deputy wouldn't have told Graeme anything negative about the company. It would have reflected badly on her professional judgment. But what would Rahul have made of that?

"Should we do something with this information?" asked Graeme.

"I don't know, to be honest. Kristján may have to turn everything over to the police, find out if any laws were actually broken rather than bent."

"He won't be gaining any votes from doing that," Graeme said.

"No, but he'll be doing the right thing, and that's what lets you sleep at night."

Graeme put down his knife and fork and looked intently at Jane. His focus was so sharp that she felt herself blushing.

"Speaking of sleeping at night, Jane," he began. "I can't. I haven't. There has been this horrible, awful death, but I can't stop thinking about what you said to me on the boat two days ago. About how the foundations of our marriage are crumbling." His eyes bored into Jane's with every syllable. "Do you believe that, really? Because I don't."

Was Graeme finally trying to have a serious conversation about this? Without getting defensive?

"There's something fundamentally wrong in our marriage, Graeme, yes," Jane said, as gently as she could.

"Jane, I love you. You must know that. Please. I know I don't say it often. I don't show it much. But I feel it and I mean it. I don't know how I could go on without you. I'm sorry for my part in all of this." He reached forward and took her hand.

Jane couldn't remember the last time Graeme had said he loved her, other than a quick way of ending a phone call when he was traveling. So why was he doing it now? It was all too neat and tidy.

Why would he start wooing her at this moment unless there was something else he was trying to hide?

"Thank you," she replied. "But, to be honest, I'm just not sure I believe you."

She pulled her hand away from his, stood up, and left the restaurant, using all her will not to turn around.

TWENTY-SIX

ELEVEN HOURS BEFORE HE DIES

Inside the stark walls of Skel, Kristján sat opposite Piotr. The chef had stored as much food as he could in anticipation of an extended forced closure and seemed grudgingly prepared to adjust to what this would mean for the momentum of his business. When Piotr had called the mayor at eight that morning and asked him to come to the restaurant as soon as he could, Kristján agreed.

After all, he felt indebted to Piotr. It had been good of him to give him those points on the fishing baron all those weeks ago. Then again, he knew why: Piotr's stepfather, who had so supported him as he built up his business, had died on the job as a line operator at Bláhafid.

Perhaps he ought to warn the chef that he had told Jane and Ben about Piotr's whistleblowing effort for Skel. But Piotr did not seem interested in hearing what Kristján had to say. He was focused on himself now.

"I know that in the short term there will be disgruntled

customers, some even scared off by the tarnish of death," Piotr told the mayor as he finished wiping off a countertop. "But after a few months, especially once this crime has been solved and a criminal brought to justice, Skel will have enhanced its culinary reputation with an extra serving of fame."

He paused and gazed skyward. "The B+-list celebrities will reappear. The social media posts now tagged with #Iceland and #bestcocktails will also be marked #truecrime and #reallifemystery."

"You really know how to look on the bright side," Kristján said wryly.

"I'm not really thinking about *how* the crime will be solved," Piotr continued, unabashed. "Jónas may be too juvenile to figure anything out, but there must be other officers who have their heads screwed on right. They'll solve it. And if they have any trouble, I can always point them gently in the right direction."

Kristján raised his eyebrows.

"Well, the solution to this crime seems perfectly obvious to me. But my area is food and entertainment, and I don't want to step out of my lane unless it's necessary." The chef looked more seriously at the mayor. "Actually, there is something I wanted to talk to you about. That's why I called you over here. It's, um, rather personal."

Kristján cringed. Piotr had a habit of oversharing. Three months ago, after saying the words "I need to share something personal," Piotr had removed his shirt to show a clearly infected and festering tattoo on his upper shoulder. Kristján was in no mood to witness any more medical crises. But perhaps it would be more information on Thór and Bláhafid. He needed to discuss that with Piotr in any case, make sure their stories were straight.

"It's about a woman," Piotr confessed. "About Hanna."

"Do you think she had something to do with what happened to Kavita?" Kristján asked.

"Of course not! No. It's more of a—romantic question."

Relief washed over Kristján. He could counsel on problems of the heart. He had been happily married for decades, after all.

"Go on," he encouraged.

"It's been a couple of years since I've seen her. And we had only hooked up two—well, maybe two and a half—times when she lived here, but they left a lasting impression," he began.

"There have been quite a few other women," he continued with a swagger in his voice, "and they were fine for passing the time but didn't fill me with the same delight that Hanna managed effortlessly."

"Right," Kristján said, hoping to dissuade the chef from providing more detail.

"It was only when I saw her again yesterday that I realized how much I still thought about her. I played it cool, of course. She doesn't suspect a thing. She's a big shot now, about to travel the world and forget all about tiny Vestmannaeyjar and its inhabitants. So I tried to ignore her during the dinner."

Kristján was not sure Hanna would have described the dynamic with Piotr in quite the same manner. Nevertheless, he added: "Well, it seems that you have avoided a potential crisis, then."

"Not at all," replied Piotr earnestly. "After the Flaming Viking.

After the death. After the shock, there she was at this doorstep yesterday morning. That same red jacket I remembered from before.
The sparkle in her eyes. The faint scent of citrus in her perfume.
We shared a drink together," he said with significance. "Kristján, do
you think that my newfound fame when the restaurant becomes a
global phenomenon will ingratiate me with her?"

There was a strong rap at the door before the mayor had time
to reply.

"Piotr? Are you here?"

It was Jónas's voice, curious but firm.

"In the kitchen!"

"Can I have a word with you?"

"Is he being more formal than usual?" whispered the chef to
Kristján. The chef gestured to a barstool overlooking the kitchen
area.

"I can stand, thanks," replied Jónas. Piotr looked quizzically
at the officer.

"I was speaking with Stella at the folklore museum as part of
the investigation."

"Stella?" asked Piotr. "She wasn't at the dinner the other night.
What could she help with?"

Jónas kept his even gaze on Piotr, but his pale face began to
redden. "I understand from Stella that you stopped by the museum
on the day of the murder."

Piotr paused before he answered. "Yes, that's right. I stopped
by. I"—he shifted his feet—"I was close by and wanted to say hello
to Hanna. I thought she'd be working on the exhibition, but no one

was there. Only Stella, who let me in. I looked around for Hanna. Then I left. I had to go and forage some herbs for dinner, and the weather was getting really bad."

"Is that really what you did?"

Kristján wondered why the officer's tone was so confrontational.

"Yes. I got the herbs. I went back here. I ran into Hanna and Ben on the way, gave them a drink to warm up from the weather. Does any of this matter?"

"Well, yes. It gave you an opportunity to swipe the cyanide capsule from the museum," asserted Jónas.

Kristján cringed. Jónas could not have sounded more triumphant if he had pointed a long finger at the chef and proclaimed "*J'accuse!*"

"Cyanide capsule? What are you talking about?" Piotr looked confused.

"Jónas. Officer." Kristján thought tensions were beginning to get a bit high. "We all want the same thing here, to find Kavita's killer. You've been put in charge of the first murder this island has seen in recent memory. Certainly none of your colleagues will have been given the same responsibility that was thrust upon you two nights ago during the storm. To make it more stressful, your suspects include a mayor, an influential pillar of the business community, a literary celebrity, and a senior foreign official whose passport grants him diplomatic immunity. But you must recognize that we are surprised when you show up here nearly attacking Piotr and talking about cyanide. Maybe we should wait for Chief Margrét. She got back last night."

Jónas flushed a deep shade of red that matched his hair. "Chief Margrét has asked me to continue the investigation and report back to her. It's possible, even probable, that Kavita was poisoned by cyanide," the officer explained. "And it turns out that an ancient cyanide capsule was stolen from an exhibition at the museum. And you were there yesterday. Alone."

Piotr scoffed. "You think *I* poisoned that foreigner with some stolen pill? Why on earth would I do that?"

"You had been complaining about her all day," countered Jónas. "Perhaps she would destroy the reputation of your beloved restaurant. Perhaps you would never work in your dream job again."

Piotr clenched his hands.

Kristján stepped in. "If Piotr wanted to poison someone, which of course he wouldn't, he would have done so with something else, some sort of obscure ingredient whose powers he had discovered in one of those dog-eared books of his long-dead grandmother's. This accusation is ridiculous."

"You know yourself that that suggestion is absurd," Piotr added, emboldened by the mayor's support, his voice rising ever higher. "Look at you, red in the face, virtually quaking next to me. You're pathetic."

Jónas slammed his hand on the counter in front of them. "Enough!" he hollered. "When I charge you with impeding an investigation, you'll have plenty of time in jail to think about how else to insult me. What do you think? That because I blush easily, I somehow don't care what people say about me? That because I'm still young enough to have a full head of hair, it means I know nothing? My mother told me that you can't control what other people think of you or how they treat you, but you can control how you react. Well, I have had enough."

His speech was so forceful that both Piotr and Kristján stood mutely before him.

"I know my skills. I know that I'm a good judge of character, that I have a clear mind. Chief Margrét trusts me, and you need to as well. This is clearly the most serious crime I have investigated. But there is a first time for everything, whether that be committing murder or investigating it. You can either help me catch a killer or hinder this investigation. Which is it going to be?"

Kristján was impressed. Perhaps Jónas was the right person for this challenging task after all. Perhaps he had just enough distance, just the right balance of cynicism and compassion to sort the truth from the lies. Perhaps he just knew how to exploit the fact that many people, murder suspects included, underestimated him.

"I'm sorry," Kristján said. "We haven't been fair to you. We want the same things you want." The mayor looked to the chef, but Piotr remained silent.

"Thank you. I'm glad to hear it," Jónas replied. "We are all in uncharted waters now. And I hope you're prepared to look at possibly unorthodox approaches. I've been talking with my colleagues, brainstorming about what could have happened. Everything was chaotic that night. We don't know where anyone was standing, although the photos people took help. So, we were thinking, since everyone is still here and what happened is fresh in people's minds, why not try a reenactment?"

"What do you mean 'reenactment?'" Piotr asked skeptically.

"We are asking everyone who was at dinner to return to Skel, to sit in the same places first at the dinner table, and then as they were near the bar. Stella can come too and stand in place of Kavita. I will observe. It might remind someone of something they forgot to tell us."

Piotr looked a bit confused. Kristján was petrified at the thought of reproducing everything, of shaking loose even more shards of grief from his heart, but he understood the logic behind it. "Of course, anything that will help," he said weakly.

"But Jónas, there is something more relevant I'd like to discuss with you," Kristján continued. Piotr had stuck his neck out by telling the mayor the rumors about Bláhafid. Now Kristján could take a risk too. Especially because this proof would also help vindicate his assumptions about Ari's passing.

"Can I walk out with you? I assume you're finished here."

The officer stood and allowed Kristján to escort him from the premises, as Piotr mouthed his thanks to the mayor from behind Jónas's back.

"Listen, I wanted to tell you about something that Jane and Ben discovered in my home yesterday," Kristján began. He told the officer about the documents found in Ari's office and about why he hadn't told anyone about his suspicions before, that Thór had threatened to close the factory and therefore devastate the community.

Jónas listened silently until Kristján had finished. When he spoke, the officer's brow was furrowed with concern. Clearly, he'd understood as well as Kristján the implications for the community if Bláhafid were to go under. For the second time that day, Kristján suspected that Chief Margrét's faith in the young officer was not misplaced.

"How much evidence do you have?" Jónas asked. "We have to be absolutely certain before making a move against Thór Magnússon. Are you sure this isn't Piotr pretending to know more than he does or spreading vicious rumors?"

Kristján shook his head. "I trust Piotr implicitly. He holds a grudge, sure, but he's a teddy bear at heart. He only told me about this information because he wanted to do the right thing. Besides, it's not just his word we're reliant on. There is likely enough evidence to charge Thór and Bláhafid with something. I have everything in my car. Come and take a look."

TWENTY-SEVEN

TEN HOURS BEFORE HE DIES

Jane tapped gently at the door of Rahul's hotel room.

She knew she was probably one of the last people the grieving man wanted to see now, after his accusation on the night of the murder. But it was exactly for this reason that she needed to speak to him. She needed to find out what he knew: about Kavita and Bláhafid and about Graeme.

As she waited for Rahul to answer, Jane thought back to Graeme's remark at breakfast, that nobody else had drunk a poisoned cocktail. Now that she considered it, wasn't it peculiar that, amid all the confusion of the Flaming Viking performance, the killer had managed to target Kavita so accurately?

The door opened slightly, revealing Rahul's drawn face in the crack. Jane saw the wariness appear in his eyes the moment he ascertained who it was.

"May I come in?"

"Why?"

"I want to talk to you. I have some questions." Jane sighed. "Please, Rahul. I'm just trying to understand."

Jane could feel Rahul sizing her up but then, to her relief and surprise, he opened the door wider and stood back to admit her. He gestured for her to sit in one of the two small hotel armchairs before taking the other.

Jane leaned toward Rahul, her elbows resting on her knees, her eyes not leaving his. "I also wanted to check on you," she began. "Have the police been in touch?"

Rahul sniffed and shrugged. "Yesterday morning. That officer asked me a few questions. I visited the mayor. I thought he'd understand what I was going through, and he was nice, but he can't see past his own grief and paranoia about his husband's accidental death. By all other accounts, that death was tragic but natural."

Jane wondered why the police hadn't been keeping a closer eye on Kavita's husband. Surely he was considered a suspect as the person closest to the victim? "I imagine the police have been rather busy with the most urgent inquiries, and it's pretty clear they are short-staffed. But I'm not making excuses. To be honest, I think you should have someone with you all the time, ready to answer any queries you have. It would be helpful to have an official, someone whose job it was to look out for you, to talk you through what is happening and what will happen next."

"You're probably right," admitted Rahul. He spoke in clipped tones, his body weary-looking but tense, his eyes still narrowed in suspicion.

"Look, Rahul, about Graeme—"

At her husband's name, Rahul stiffened, but Jane pressed ahead.

"Of course it's understandable that you want someone to blame. But I can honestly tell you it wasn't him. I know him better than anyone; he isn't capable of murder."

Rahul's eyes were scanning her furiously, searching for signs of an agenda.

"But I'm also curious to know why you were so convinced it was him."

Rahul stared at her a moment longer, then, to Jane's surprise, he slumped forward.

"They'd had that huge argument: Kavi was in a real state about it. Then I saw him hand her the cocktail from the table. It all seemed to fit."

"But now you're not sure?"

"I'm not sure of anything anymore." Rahul put his head in his hands. He looked exhausted. "At the moment, all I know is that I want to leave this island and never return. I think I want to leave Iceland altogether."

Jane felt a surge of sympathy for the shrunken man in front of her. She couldn't imagine what it would be like to be in his shoes, nor did she want to.

Rahul's phone pinged, and he glanced down at it.

"People were sending me notes all day yesterday. Mostly bull-shit expressions of sympathy." He handed Jane the phone. "Look at these heartfelt messages," he said, sarcasm dripping.

Jane began to scroll through the texts. The first one read: "I can't believe it! K was the best. Wish I'd been able to see her more since university. Sending you so many hugs! <3." Each one was seemingly more disingenuous than the next, each focused more on how the sender themselves had responded to the shock, or were poorly disguised efforts to elicit gory details, rather than offering any genuine concern for the man who had seen his wife die in front of his eyes. These notes, and the ones putting the onus on Rahul to get in touch "if you need anything," made up almost the entirety of all the messages Jane saw.

"I just can't believe how quickly news has reached people," she commented.

"I know," said Rahul darkly. "Friends often claim to have been drowning in work if they miss a birthday or are late for a get-together, but when the news is associated with scandal, it blows through like a hurricane."

Jane handed the phone back to him.

"But there was nothing else. About Graeme I mean, nothing…I should know?"

Rahul hesitated, and Jane could see the thoughts whirring behind his wide eyes. Then he sighed. "I guess, now that Kavi is… It can't hurt. She confessed something to me about that refugee project. There were problems, evidence of exploitation. She was trying to keep it from the ambassador to keep the project afloat while she figured out a solution."

Suddenly, Rahul was overcome by a wave of tears. He gulped for air. "She really only wanted the best. She was desperate to help."

"She was an amazing person," Jane said, getting up to put her arm around Rahul. "I think she had a very warm heart. I'm sorry I didn't get to know her better while you were here."

The coil of tension in Jane's stomach that had been growing tighter over the last two days had eased, as though somebody had loosened a knot there. So this was why Rahul suspected Graeme: he feared Graeme had discovered Kavita's secret and thought she'd jeopardized the embassy's reputation and reacted in fury. But it was obvious from Graeme's horror at breakfast that the revelations about Bláhafid had come as a genuine shock to him.

Rahul blinked at her. "What will you do with what I've just told you? About Bláhafid?"

Jane paused, remembering her promise to the mayor to be discreet. But if Rahul was already aware of it, what was the harm?

"Actually, I already knew. It turns out that Ari was looking into it before he died. We found evidence in his study."

"We?" asked Rahul.

"Ben and I. We stopped by yesterday after you were there. To help the mayor go through some of Ari's papers."

Rahul nodded in understanding. "He and Ben were distant cousins apparently, so it must have been interesting."

"Did you know that too?" Jane asked. "I only heard the mayor mention it once we arrived here."

Rahul nodded. "Kavi told me Ari had tried to get Ben's details through the embassy because of the connection. I guess Icelanders think they can just call an embassy to reach anyone well-known with that citizenship. She told him she couldn't share contact information for private individuals." He smiled wistfully. "She was such a stickler for the rules."

"Shame," Jane answered. "Ben probably would have enjoyed meeting Ari if he'd known about the family connection. He had tracked down a few other relatives of his in just a few months. He used to tell me about some of them, real characters. And then one time he lost his passport in a hot spring." Jane chuckled to herself. "He should tell you himself. It's actually a really funny story. Standing closer to the steam than he should have, naturally."

"You know, I think I heard about that misadventure," mused Rahul. "Passport lost in a hot spring means embassy contact for a replacement. I'm pretty sure Kavi dealt with that too." He stood up, filled two glass tumblers with water and handed one to Jane.

"She dealt with so many different people, both locals and expats, but nobody knew Kavi," he said with conviction. "No one in this town knew her or even all the other colleagues and expats; they just saw her abrasiveness, not the woman who was so passionate about justice, about giving people a better chance in life. That's why I don't understand this at all. Someone did this to her. Someone wanted her to die..." His voice trailed off.

They were interrupted by a firm knock at the door. "Rahul, it's Officer Jónas," came a voice from the other side.

Rahul looked nervously at Jane.

"I'll stay if you want," she whispered.

Jónas looked surprised to see Jane as Rahul led him in. Understandably, Jane thought, given that the last he'd heard, Rahul suspected her husband of murder.

"Jane just arrived to check on me," Rahul explained. "Are you here with news?"

"We are making progress."

Jane recognized the tone of Jónas's statement: noncommittal, reassuring yet giving nothing away. She'd heard Graeme use something similar many times before.

"The reason for my visit," he continued, "is to let you know our next steps. I just got back from the restaurant, and I asked Piotr and the mayor if they could return later to reenact when happened two nights ago."

Jane and Rahul stared at him.

"Is that really necessary?" Rahul asked.

"I think it would be helpful to think of this case from a different direction," Jónas said firmly. "I'd like to establish what else is going on here, what other duplicity might exist between the parties."

Jane flushed, immediately thinking of her husband and his connection to Hanna. But if Jónas knew nothing of that, she wasn't going to enlighten him now.

"And we need to start with what exactly happened that night. What people saw or didn't see. I'm confident we're going to be in for some surprises."

TWENTY-EIGHT

EIGHT HOURS BEFORE HE DIES

Linda and Thór's home was one block down the road from the mayor's and was also built of concrete but with larger bay windows and a big extension toward the back. Two black Land Rovers were parked in the double driveway, and a basketball hoop was affixed above the built-in garage. The lawn was professionally manicured. Near the front of the large expanse of grass, a massive anchor weighing hundreds of kilograms rested on its side in a bed of pebbles, an arrangement that indicated that a fishing captain once lived at the premises.

Inside, Linda and Thór were embroiled in a loud argument.

"This isn't actually about you!" Linda was shouting. They stood in their living room, facing each other like bulls about to charge, nostrils flared, tempers fired. "Someone has died. Yet all you seem to care about is how that affects your company's bottom line."

Thór shot his wife a look dripping with condescension. "Even you cannot be so naive as to believe that. If there is even a whiff of impropriety around Bláhafid, any potential projects in Canada will be stopped." He lowered his voice a notch. "You know as well as I do what that would mean for the company and for us personally. I had Kavita on my side. She finally realized that refugees working for a bit less money was better than refugees suffering in a war zone. Better the devil you know, after all. And she was helping speed up the process for us and Canada. So actually, her death is quite inconvenient."

Linda shot her husband a withering look.

"Yes, I'm sure that's how Rahul would describe it. And as for the Canadian deal, I'd say there's plenty to jeopardize that already. Hanna, for instance. I saw her with her phone out after dinner. It won't have been for selfies. I only hope you weren't saying anything incriminating."

"I'm not worried about her," Thór scoffed. "We are sponsoring her exhibition, not only here but in seven cities around the world. She's put her lot in with us. Doesn't matter what she was doing with her phone that night; I didn't say anything about anything important, just reinforced to the ambassador what great business we would do in Canada."

"What about Rahul?"

"What about him?"

"We had a lovely chat at the dinner. He told me about his misgivings with how Kavita was dealing with you and what that meant for the Canadian deal; probably thought I actually held some clout in this marriage. But you, you've never even taken a moment to consider any ethical implications of the choices you make. It's about the bottom line and your reputation as a tough guy."

Thór took a step toward Linda, ready to lunge at her, then stopped, breathing heavily.

Linda had seen it too. Outside the window, a police car had pulled up.

While Thór went to the door, Linda did a last sweep of the kitchen floor. She had dusted earlier in the morning, of course, but she found any spec of dirt intolerable. Linda also knew that officers, even inexperienced ones such as Jónas, were human just like the rest of us. They were prone to unconscious bias and prejudice.

She'd already selected two framed photographs and placed them in obvious view in the living room. One of her and Thór looking tanned on a beach holiday, the other of the whole family taken ten years ago at their son's confirmation. One big happy, successful family with nothing to hide.

"Lovely to see you, as usual," Thór enthused to Jónas as he ushered him toward the kitchen table. Linda sat opposite the officer, but her husband remained standing behind her. "Though I admit I'm a bit surprised. Isn't Chief Margrét back yet?"

"She and the others arrived on the first ferry that ran yesterday afternoon," Jónas agreed. "But the chief has asked me to lead up the routine inquiries for the time being." He spoke the last line with a note of pride.

"Well, son, she must think you are very diligent in your work." Thór smiled at the man who had been a year behind his and Linda's own son at the local elementary school. Their progeny was long departed for the big city and living in his parents' spare condo in Copenhagen.

"Anything more we can do to help?" Linda asked innocently. "I think we've told you everything we can from that night. I didn't know that woman at all, and Thór had hardly met her." Thór shook his head in a sympathetic way.

"What a tragedy it is," he murmured.

Jónas's face remained impassive. "You've been helpful so far, thank you. But now I want to ask you about something more general. From before."

Just then, Thór's phone rang. "Pardon me for a moment," he said, standing to leave the room.

Jónas looked like he was about to object, but before he could say anything, Linda glanced at her husband's departing figure and added: "I am sure he'll return very soon. What is it I can help with?"

"We've received some information, some printed material, about Bláhafid employees with foreign citizenship. The documents show evidence of poor business practices, corruption, tax avoidance, and more."

As Jónas ran through the litany of accusations, Linda remained erect in her seat, her hands clasped in front of her. She could feel herself begin to blush and hoped that Jónas did not notice.

"I haven't seen these documents," she began hastily. "But the accusations sound to me like gossip and hearsay from cynical locals rather than actual evidence."

"The documents are right here." Jónas pulled them out of his briefcase. "But perhaps we should wait until Thór returns to look at them?" Linda picked them up and flipped through them with the nonchalance of perusing the IKEA catalog, ignoring the glare he shot her as she took his papers.

"This? Is it this that you're talking about?" Her voice was rising more than she had intended it to. "There's nothing here. Take this, for instance." She flipped through some pages and jabbed her finger against a chart full of figures. "You'll probably try and tell me that this chart shows that Bláhafid was not declaring its full income for the last five years. That's ridiculous. All companies are required to file this paperwork. This one shows that Bláhafid was supposed to do that in the spring but filed a month later. So sue them."

She picked up another sheet. "And this. Is this supposed to indicate that those workers were exploited? Maybe if someone who knows nothing about business saw this, they would find something suspicious, but it's just how things are done around here. Besides, none of this is new." She paused and gave the officer a "we're among friends, aren't we?" look. "Jónas, you know Rúna down the road. She wrote a long Facebook post about factory conditions six months ago. Nobody cared then. Piotr has been complaining for months too, though you didn't hear a peep from him when his stepfather was still alive and earning a decent wage with us. Even Kavita at the embassy knew, and she…" Linda stopped herself.

As her voice had risen, Thór strode back into the kitchen. He towered over the seated officer and his wife.

"Things getting a little heated?" he asked.

Thór had operated in the world of cutthroat capitalism for several decades and he often complained to Linda that every few years, some well-intentioned champagne socialist from the city arrived to file earnest reports on working conditions and best practices. Thór thought of himself as the heart and soul of this community and ignored outsider criticism. This was but another small bump in the road.

Jónas spoke up. "Can you explain what these documents mean?" He handed him the selection of papers he had brought with him.

Thór remained standing directly in front of the duo, commanding the space, looming over the youthful officer. "Young man, aren't you meant to be investigating a murder right now? I think this can wait until that is solved, no?"

"Ari thought this couldn't wait," Jónas said.

"Ari? The man who is *dead*?" Thór couldn't help but keep the disdain out of his voice. "Are you saying that you got these documents from him? Or Kristján got them from him?"

"Not only is this unimportant," Linda said, "but it has nothing to do with finding out who killed that diplomat." She rose to stand next to Thór, the duo now towering over the officer.

Jónas stood. He collected the papers and put them under his arm. "As you can see, there are a lot of loose ends here and a lot of rumors circulating. This is unorthodox, but murder is unorthodox. I'd like you both to meet me back at Skel this evening. I'm gathering the dinner party there again. I want to dispel some rumors. And I hope that reproducing the events of that evening might help to jog your memories."

"Fine," Thór said. "Is that everything?"

"For now, yes," said Jónas.

Saying nothing further, he made for the door. Linda hurried after him. It wouldn't do to leave things on a sour note.

"Thank you for coming," she said, reaching ahead of him for the door and holding it open for him, giving the younger officer what she hoped was a charming grin.

But back in the kitchen, neither she nor Thór was smiling. Thór brought his fist crashing down on the table, unable to hide his frustration.

"This ridiculous kid is going to ruin everything," he complained.

Linda desperately hoped he wasn't right.

TWENTY-NINE

SIX HOURS BEFORE HE DIES

Jane's breakfast with Graeme hadn't gone as she had expected. Graeme had been so vulnerable, so raw. Perhaps he really was willing to try, really did realize that she had been serious with her threats on the ferry. Yet until he could be fully honest with her, she wasn't prepared to cut him any more slack. The choice was in her hands, though, and Jane liked that control.

As she walked back to Kristján's house to continue their work, she wondered what Jónas thought about the documents they had uncovered. The officer seemed so well intentioned that he was probably being underestimated by everyone and knew to use that to his advantage. But it couldn't hurt to have someone behind the scenes to discreetly guide him in the right direction. Jónas could claim all the credit for any successful outcome, naturally. Jane had long ago given up expecting any acknowledgment for her valuable work.

She wondered, too, what exactly the officer had in mind with this reenactment. Was it possible that the same doubt that had been bothering Jane was also troubling Jónas? That, even given everything that had been uncovered about Bláhafid and Kavita's knowledge of it, none of it added up to a plausible motive?

Kristján looked exhausted when he let her into the house, and Jane's heart went out to him. First Ari, then Kavita, then evidence of a major corruption scandal that could have unthinkable implications for his community. The mayor certainly wasn't having an easy time of it.

"Coffee?" he asked, as he led her into the kitchen.

"Thanks."

"So Jónas has already told you about the reenactment?"

"Yes." Jane waited as Kristján poured steaming black coffee into her cup. "What do you make of it?"

The mayor considered. "I think he's a capable kid, and he'll have his reasoning. But I can't say I'm looking forward to it."

"I wondered if he thinks it'll show that things didn't pan out as they were meant to for the killer."

Kristján, taking the seat opposite Jane, stared at her. "What do you mean?"

Jane was about to answer when Ben strode into the room from down the hall, phone glued to his ear.

"I know, yes," he was insisting. "I had this chance to go away for a couple of days, but it's almost done. I'll get it to you next week, I'm sure." He was pacing the hall and did not acknowledge Jane's and Kristján's presence.

"Yes, I know. That part's all worked out, yes. Second book

syndrome, I know. I get it. You'll have it soon." He ended the call and stared at the phone before Jane interrupted his reverie.

"Sequel stress?" she joked weakly.

Ben seemed surprised to see her. "Stress? Me? Of course not," he said unconvincingly. "My editors are on my back to get the manuscript submitted, but I have a process. I don't want them to know anything until the whole thing is handed in. And that's going to be very soon. Very soon. As soon as we get out of here probably."

Jane raised an eyebrow. "That quickly?"

Ben shrugged, his familiar swagger returning. "It's basically done. I've just been waiting to dot a few *i*'s. This whole business has actually provided a bit of authorly inspiration."

Kristján put down his coffee cup with an audible clunk and shot the writer a look. "This isn't your next novel, Ben."

"He's right, Ben," said Jane. "This is his life."

Ben looked contrite for a moment. "You're right, of course. Sorry. I do realize how serious this is."

Jane sometimes wondered whether he did. It had surely been a shock to everyone to witness a violent death. But otherwise, Ben didn't have much connection to what was going on. He hardly knew Kavita. He had never been to Vestmannaeyjar before. He had no partner to worry about and whether trust or vows had been broken between them.

"Jane, what were you saying?" Kristján said, his brow furrowed. "About the killer?"

"Well, it has struck me as odd that the killer was able to accurately target Kavita's glass. They all looked the same, and there was so much confusion with the lights going out. And then I wondered, what if they weren't accurate at all? In fact, what if that glass was meant for somebody else?"

Across the room, Ben snorted.

"That's ridiculous. It's really starting to sound like a game of Clue. 'Who poisoned the drink in the restaurant?'"

While on occasion Jane found herself caught up in Ben's orbit, she was also old enough to disengage from it when needed. And in those moments, she resented his cavalier nature, his insensitive remarks.

"Ben, would you give it a rest?" she said, a little more sharply than she intended.

"What?" Ben asked in surprise. "I'm just being honest. You don't think that there is some big plot to murder someone and then they messed it up? It's so far-fetched. Jane, you know I'm fond of you, but you're getting a little bit emotional here."

"The man who was just quaking in his boots while talking to an editor across the ocean is calling *me* emotional?"

Ben flushed, and when he spoke again, there was genuine anger in his voice. "I know you think you can come out with bullshit theories and everyone will take you seriously just because of who your husband is. But *come on*."

"Excuse me?" Jane couldn't believe what she was hearing. She'd confessed to Ben how it felt being Graeme's shadow, and now he was throwing it back in her face. But then, she thought, wasn't that what he did? Take other people's worries, their insecurities, and use them for his own ends? Didn't he squeeze people for inspiration, then leave them in his wake? Before she knew it, she was on her feet.

"How dare you speak to me like that? Just because you're frustrated with your work doesn't mean you can take it out on me, Graeme." The anger was surging up: her fingers found the pearls around her neck. She pulled them loose and flung them.

"Graeme?" sneered Ben as the pearls clattered across the floor. "I'm not your husband, Jane. I'm not someone you can hit just because you've found out about a tawdry affair."

Jane felt like she'd just been slapped. Kristján stared intently at his coffee mug.

And in an instant all the anger seemed to escape Ben. There was no longer a hardness in his eyes, and he looked at her with contrition. "Jane, I'm sorry. It was just an offhand comment."

Jane stared at him. "Get away from me," she said. "I don't need 'friends' like you."

"Maybe you should take a walk, Ben," Kristján said, finding his voice.

Ben looked from one to the other. He glanced back at Ari's office, as if to see whether that was a possible escape route. But as both Jane and the mayor continued to look pointedly at his flushed face, the writer nodded curtly, shoved his feet into his shoes, and strode out the door.

Kristján's intervention had diffused the situation and Jane felt herself coming back down to earth, still simmering just underneath.

"I'm so sorry about that, Kristján," she said, and her voice was once again hers. Calm, soothing, diplomatic. "Should I have another look through Ari's things? See if there's anything else I can dig up?"

The mayor, no doubt reeling from the last twenty-four hours, nodded wordlessly, and Jane returned to Ari's office.

But alone, surrounded by the muddle of documents, Jane found she couldn't concentrate. Her thoughts kept returning to Ben, to their argument. She looked about her. There was still a lot to review, and they would have to return to Reykjavík soon. Without pausing to overthink her impulse, Jane stuffed the contents of the nearest box—several folders and an old-looking notebook into her backpack. She'd review them back at the hotel, once she was calmer, and then she'd return everything to the mayor with no one the wiser.

"Actually, you know what?" Jane called to Kristján as she reemerged from the office a few minutes later. "I should go and talk to Graeme, tell him about the latest developments. I can help more later if you want."

She dashed out the door, leaving the bemused mayor of Vestmannaeyjabær behind.

THIRTY

Hanna puckered her mouth and applied a coat of power-red lip-stick. She was in the small one-bedroom apartment she had rented for the week from an old friend. Her cell phone, rescued by Piotr yesterday, lay on the duvet next to her. What a relief to have it returned to her, with all its secrets. When she had discovered earlier that it had been lost, there was no question in her mind that she was willing to do whatever it took to get it back. In the end, "what it took" wasn't much, just a glance of the right warmth in Piotr's direction.

What Hanna was reluctant to admit was that her morning drink yesterday with Piotr had sparked more joy than she had felt in a long time. She tried never to be emotionally entangled with men who were in her life primarily to serve her physical needs, but Piotr was a bit different. He was so malleable, yet so simplistic about his desires. She knew he would do anything for her. The chef was rough around the edges, but that made him more authentic than Ben, whom she had correctly clocked immediately as a kindred spirit when it came to no-strings-attached romps in the hay.

As to the phone, she had listened to all her recordings and looked at the photos, and there was nothing incriminating there concerning her dealings with Thór Magnússon.

Hanna would need to figure out what to do with that phone when they made this strange reenactment of the serving of the cocktail soon at Skel. She knew that anything she had captured could potentially be beneficial to the investigation but did not want anyone to find out the real reason she'd been recording anything. It was definitely best to let sleeping dogs lie. She would send a few images to Jónas to show she was being helpful, but the rest could stay with her.

They were all in shock, of course. But Hanna was a pragmatist. She could enjoy herself a little, even while under suspicion, so she felt she could make time for one more quick assignation. There was a knock at the door, and Hanna raced to it. She opened the door of the flat. Her jaw dropped open when she saw who was there. This was not the person who had just texted to say he'd be by in ten minutes.

"Hello," said Piotr awkwardly. He had removed his warm hat and was holding it in his hands in front of him, tiny beads of sweat forming on his bald head despite the chill outside. "May I come in?"

Hanna did a quick calculation. The last thing she was in the mood for right now was soothing Piotr's ego. Still, he was looking at her with those deep brown eyes. Something was worrying him beyond the superficial.

She nodded and moved aside, gesturing to a small chair by the kitchen table. She didn't offer him anything to drink. Piotr had hardly sat down before he began speaking breathlessly: "Jónas just came to visit me. He seems to suspect me of something. Hanna, apparently there is poison missing from a display at the museum, and I was there alone yesterday afternoon."

"Why were you there?" she asked him, wondering why she hadn't run into him herself, given how long she had lingered there two days ago. But as soon as the words escaped her lips, she knew. It was to see her, of course. Was there another reason too?

"Now the police think I am a murderer!" Piotr exclaimed, ignoring her question. "I went to the place where the poison is missing, and they have discovered that I had told the mayor about Bláhafíd and everything they get up to there. Now Jónas thinks I have poisoned someone because I hate Bláhafíd, I hate Thór Magnússon."

Hanna thought that there was an inordinate amount of focus on who had visited the museum and archive and when. She hoped that Stella was still staying quiet about Hanna's own off-the-record visit.

"Piotr, I'm sure Jónas won't be jumping to conclusions. Think about it: hating Thór Magnússon isn't a reason for you to poison the deputy ambassador. Besides, who *doesn't* hate Thór Magnússon?"

Piotr considered this. "True." He sighed. He looked at Hanna a moment longer, then he said: "Have I ever told you how Skel got its name?"

"Piotr, is this relevant?"

"It was an old school friend who took a chance on me, offered me the money to set up on my own. I'd spent years on the mainland by then: learning from the best, honing my craft. I'd also worked in Berlin, Stockholm, Copenhagen—"

"Piotr. Can you stick to the point?" Hanna looked pointedly at her watch. Her next guest would be arriving soon.

"Right. Anyway, the night I got the funding, I went to my mother and stepfather's flat. They were so proud: everything I'd fought for. My stepfather took out a frosted bottle of Sobieski, one of his home country's finest vodkas, from the freezer. He poured three shots and handed two silently to me and my mother. As he lifted his own glass, my stepfather's face finally cracked into a wide grin, and his eyes seemed to glisten with pride.

"'Cheers, my son,' he toasted. '*Skál.*'"

"The next morning," Piotr continued after a brief pause, "my stepfather, the man who had raised me as long as I could remember, awoke feeling unwell. Indigestion again, he muttered, and departed for work at Bláhafid at 7:45 a.m. on the dot as usual. At 11:23 a.m., my mother received the call. Her husband was dead. A massive heart attack took him just as he sat down to his morning coffee break. He was gone before he hit the ground, she was told."

Hanna shuffled. "I'm sorry, Piotr, but I don't see—"

"I named the restaurant Skel not just because the word so closely resembles that last toast of my stepfather's but also because it's the Icelandic word for 'shell': a dedication to the man who raised me and his maritime profession. I'm telling you this because of what it says about Bláhafid. My stepfather had a heart attack though he was only in his fifties. He was always overworked, never encouraged to take time off. Wouldn't even stay home that day when he felt sick because he feared repercussions. People think our community would be lost with Bláhafid, but I'm telling you we would be far, far better off without Thór Magnússon. He cares nothing for the people of these islands, only for the profit they might make him."

Hanna didn't know what to say. Piotr's obvious love for his stepfather, his outrage at the social injustice of this company. It was moving and, she wanted to admit, a bit attractive? Before she could respond, however, there was another knock at the door. This time, she knew who it would be. Things were about to get awkward.

"Ben!" exclaimed Piotr when he saw who Hanna had just let into the apartment. His eyes narrowed. "What are you doing here?"

"That's my business, Piotr," Hanna answered. "Ben and I have something to discuss. I'm afraid we'll have to finish our conversation later."

Piotr glowered at the writer. "You hardly know him," he hissed in Hanna's ear as he grabbed his coat and slouched out the door, letting it bang behind him.

"I guess you enjoyed our post-pool adventure the other day as much as I did," Ben said coyly after the chef had left.

Hanna returned his enticing gaze. "I don't usually engage in those activities in such possibly public spaces. But now you're here." Hanna gestured to a Nespresso machine on a side counter. "Coffee?" she asked the visitor with faux professionalism. Opening a cabinet above the machine, she took out a bottle of vodka and two glasses. "Or perhaps something stronger?"

"I think you know what I'd like—a healthy dose of distraction." Ben was very good at this, thought Hanna. Damn him.

"Thanks for the message," she began after pouring two straight shots of vodka for them. "I thought you were over at the mayor's going through papers?"

Ben downed his shot in one go.

"I was there yesterday and again this morning, but then… It doesn't matter. There are *a lot* of boxes there. Jane and I found quite a bit of information on Bláhafið. Plenty of corruption there; no surprise."

"No," agreed Hanna. "No surprise."

"We've let the police know about the documents we found. You know," he mused, "this might work out quite well in the end. It's endless inspiration for my next novel, really has provided me with a newfound creativity. Soon, we will all be headed back to Reykjavík, where I can take a break from all this domestic travel, settle down and finish the novel, and return to Canada just in time for the accolades to pour in." Ben smiled. "I might even make a brief return to the only pub in Gimli. Local boy done good and all that."

"Did you hear…" interrupted Hanna, who was losing patience with Ben's dreams of grandeur. "The police think Kavita was poisoned with an old cyanide capsule stolen from the museum?"

Ben raised his eyebrows as she explained how they discovered this.

"And by the way, Jónas called earlier," she continued. "He is asking us all to go to Skel this evening. A reenactment."

Ben grinned. "So I've heard." He looked at his watch. "But that doesn't give us much time here."

"Just enough." Hanna smiled back at him.

THIRTY-ONE

FOUR HOURS BEFORE HE DIES

Jane had not completely lied to Kristján. She had genuinely wanted to speak to her husband and find out if he had talked more to the police and to calm herself down. A brief text had revealed that Graeme was in a quiet bakery near the harbor. Trust him to calm his nerves with sweetened carbs, uncaring who saw him or what people thought of his eating habits.

At this time of day, the bakery was empty except for a wizened elderly gentleman in one corner who was nursing a cup of coffee and biting into a roll. Graeme was scribbling in a small spiral notebook, a large cinnamon bun nearly untouched in front of him. His gray hair was unwashed, stubble sprouting on his face.

Jane couldn't help but smile. She knew of no one else who could consume so much sugar with no adverse effects. Graeme's results for his annual physicals regularly showed he was in peak condition, all the figures on cholesterol, blood pressure, and vitamin levels just where they should be. Jane, on the other hand, had already been warned that she needed to monitor her sodium intake. At least pinot gris was low in salt.

She sat opposite Graeme without a word. Her husband finished a note before putting his pen down and looking up at his wife.

"You look tired," he said.

"Thanks a lot," Jane answered.

Graeme removed his reading glasses. Folded his hands on the table in front of him. Jane couldn't recall when he had last really focused his full attention on her.

"Jane," he began. "I didn't mean to insult you. I was—am—concerned about you. I'm trying, Jane."

Jane stayed silent. She wanted to see where this was heading and wasn't prepared to cut him any slack by throwing him conversational bones.

"I came to this island with one goal: to set up something with Bláhafid. Then you blindsided me with your talk of ultimatums and leaving me, right when I was trying to focus."

If he's trying to apologize, putting the blame on me is not the way to do it, thought Jane.

"I talked about you looking tired because I notice you. You're beautiful. I love the intelligence in your eyes, the silver in your hair. I love the fact that you are proudly entering your forties, and that you don't let others around you dictate how you should dress."

There he was, her husband, a man she recognized from long ago. He was clumsy perhaps, but Graeme was also endearing. He really was trying, and it shocked her.

"Thank you for saying those things," Jane replied. She touched Graeme's hand and sighed. Saying sorry in the throes of a tragedy was not enough to make up for years of ignoring and patronizing her. Still, she could recall the fun-loving, adventurous man she knew back at university. He must still be somewhere underneath the bureaucratic layers he had accumulated over the years.

"I mean it, Jane. I want to spend more time with you, with the twins. I've wanted that for a while but, well, you're so self-sufficient, you don't seem like you need me in any way. So it's been really easy to concentrate on my career."

He picked up Jane's hands and held them in his. She let him.

"I want to do better. I want to be a great husband and father. I don't know what I would do without you. I want to work on our marriage together. That's the most important thing to me."

There was real honesty in his eyes. How easy it would be to accept what he said, not voice what was still on her mind, go home to Reykjavík, and continue as they always had. But Jane knew that she needed to speak her fears out loud, or Graeme would never realize what was bothering her.

"Graeme, I'm going to ask you something, and I want you to be completely honest with me," she said.

"Of course," her husband answered. "I always am."

Jane took a deep breath. "Is there something going on with you and Hanna?"

Graeme looked stunned. He let go of Jane's hands. "What makes you ask that?"

"Come on, it's glaringly obvious that you've known each other for some time, long before this trip, and she's certainly your type. I can tell that you two have a connection."

Graeme was silent for a moment and looked down at his plate. "Something going on? Like an affair? Of course not. How many times do I need to tell you that I will never make a mistake like that again?"

She waited for Graeme to elaborate.

"But your intuition is right," he admitted after a long silence. "I do know Hanna better than I have let on."

"Care to tell me how?"

"She used to live here on the Westman Islands when she was doing scientific research on Surtsey Island. That was several years ago, before you and I were here. But there was a scandal and she left suddenly."

"What kind of scandal?"

"The typical kind: sexual harassment. The department manager, who was also Canadian, as luck would have it. Hanna chose to leave and start afresh in Canada rather than fight what she thought might be a losing battle, or at least a time-consuming and costly one."

Jane grimaced. The same old story. Over the last two days, she'd resented Hanna so much—the attention she attracted from men, the way she seemed so at ease with Graeme. She'd never stopped to consider how things might look from her point of view.

"What does this have to do with you?"

"Hanna had tried to pursue formal complaints via the embassy, but the previous ambassador didn't follow it up much. Once there was a change, she tried again. I gather that Kavita was surprisingly unsympathetic. I suppose she was used to such difficult behavior and thought Hanna should be figuring things out for herself. Or at least she didn't think an embassy could or should be involved."

Graeme paused and took a sip of his coffee. "Then Hanna contacted me directly. Something about her story struck a chord. I suppose because it was not so long after you and I had had our difficulties. Or maybe it was because she seems to have such a promising future ahead of her. In any case, I said I would try to help her, maybe atone for my past sins, though I didn't tell her that. It was going to be too complicated to press charges against her former boss, but I did say I'd help her get on her feet in the art world. So I found her main sponsor, not just for the exhibition here but globally."

Jane paused. "Why didn't you just tell me about this? It's not a big deal."

"I didn't want you to get the wrong idea, and Hanna wanted it kept under wraps too. That's the other spanner in the works: the main sponsor is Bláhafid. I didn't tell Hanna that. They seemed like the perfect partner to me. Plenty of cash, locally based, and I knew Kavita had been doing some work with them in Ólafsvík. But Hanna found out once we were here, and she was furious with me. I guess it has something to do with their corporate ethics—or lack of them, as we are discovering. She said she was going to take matters into her own hands."

Jane didn't respond.

The last twenty-four hours had torn her heart. All the worry about what Graeme might be hiding, about what could happen to him if the police really did suspect him of murder. And once again, when she blamed her husband for all his faults, she acted like someone she didn't want to be: lying to Kristján, shouting at Ben, acting disloyal to Graeme.

"Also, you've been quite the detective with all this sleuthing, Jane," he said.

Was that admiration she heard in her husband's voice? "All I really want is to help. But, you know, it's interesting to try and piece it together."

"You are very good at noticing things that everyone here, who are so interconnected, will not." He took a sip of his coffee. "By the way, where is Ben? Didn't you say you were looking at documents with him?"

Jane nodded. She couldn't bring herself to share the details of their argument. Secrets could be poison in a marriage—but on the very day when it seemed they had finally made progress in their relationship, she could not threaten it again by admitting she had exploded at Ben and then "borrowed" a dead journalist's personal files. "I didn't think we needed to keep poring over papers right away, so he's taken a walk. But there's one more thing. I heard the police want us all to meet at Skel soon. Will you go?"

Graeme nodded. "Yes. But no cocktails."

THIRTY-TWO

"Not a word about what I'm wearing this time," warned Linda. She had had enough of Thór's machinations. "We're supposed to be wearing the same clothing as we did the first night, and that's what I'm going to do."

Thór grunted. "This whole exercise of replaying that evening is ridiculous. I'm in no mood to humor an incompetent officer with this playacting."

"You don't have much of a choice, though."

Thór gave her a sour look. "What do they think they can possibly achieve with this?"

She shrugged. "Now is not the time to question. Now is the time to be helpful, to be confident, to show that we have nothing to hide." They exchanged a glance. "And stick to the routine. Remember, the whole purpose of the ambassador's trip was to give us, to give Bláhafid, a chance to expand into the Canadian market. This is a hurdle, but it shouldn't necessarily be the end of things.

Show the ambassador that you're a helpful, compassionate professional." She snorted to herself. "Or fake it at least."

"You don't need to lecture me," retorted Thór. "I know how to play this game, and I know it's a long one. This is but a bend in the road, and we'll get through it like we do with everything else."

Thór walked over and pecked his wife on the cheek.

Linda was surprised by the uncharacteristic burst of sentimental affection. "What was that for?"

"For being a team player," he answered, leaving the bedroom for the front hall.

THIRTY-THREE

ONE HOUR BEFORE HE DIES

Jane and Graeme arrived early at Skel. Wearing a white T-shirt and flour-dusted smock, Piotr greeted them wordlessly, ushering them to the private dining room where they had eaten only two nights before.

He gestured on the way to the main area, still cordoned off by police tape. "The police are apparently finishing up a couple of things and are going to take that off for us to replicate the evening." He shrugged. "I don't know what this is about, really. It's not going to help anything."

Jane was more encouraging. "I think it might do some good. In times of trauma, we often bury our most intimate reactions. Recreating conditions might jolt us out of our own versions. Or scare someone else from theirs. And then people do things they regret, say things they may not otherwise."

Did *she* regret having just pilfered personal files from the mayor of Vestmannaeyjabær? Not yet. They could be of benefit to everyone; it wasn't a selfish crime. She hoped. Instinctively, Jane put her hand to her neck. She did regret destroying that gift of Graeme's. Her anger at her own overblown sentimentality over a few pearls didn't help her mood either. She wasn't sure she would have the maturity to be the first to speak to Ben when he arrived. Actually, it wasn't a matter of maturity, she reminded herself. After what he'd said, he could damn well make the first move.

Graeme was silent. He had brought his notebook with him, and for once, Jane found his scribbling oddly endearing. It meant he was really making an effort to figure things out, to keep track of all the threads.

She gently glanced over his shoulder. His writing was barely legible, but she could make out words like *timings, flavor, regret.*

"Sleuthing?" she asked playfully.

"It helps me to focus," he replied.

"Me too," she said. "Although I keep it all up here." She tapped her head in a not-unkind way. As someone who was used to wearing many hats in her life—mother, wife, traveler, companion, featureless spouse—Jane was adept at following the trails of many projects and concerns at once. She didn't need a physical notebook for that mental organization. But if Graeme wanted to write to create order in his chaotic world, she was fine with it. "I think this was an interesting idea of Jónas's, to have us all re-create things. Don't you agree?" she said to her husband.

Graeme looked up from his note-taking. "It was his idea? That kid?"

"He's not a kid," Jane said. "He's a man who may perhaps have just the eccentric ideas that are required to solve an unorthodox case."

Graeme shrugged. "This all happened the day before yesterday, not months or years ago. I think everything is all too raw in our minds."

"Perhaps, but there was so much confusion, it might help to set things straight. And I hope after we finish we're at least allowed to take the ferry home."

"So we'll just stand in the same places as last night?" Graeme asked.

"Yes, I think that's essentially it. Stella will stand in for Kavita. With Jónas watching our every move, I suppose. It might jog some- one's memory, someone might see something that is different than before if someone stands in a different spot or something."

"So where is everyone?"

"We were early," Jane responded soothingly. "The others should be here any minute now."

Half an hour later, Jane observed the group around her. Graeme and Jane, Ben, Rahul, Hanna, Thór and Linda sat assem- bled around the table. Stella sat where Kavita had been and Piotr stood in the corner. Next to him, a pitcher of water and a carafe of coffee had been placed on a table which also had familiar cocktail components. Understandably, the group was less congenial than two nights ago.

Graeme held his notebook in front of him, while Jane sat patiently. On her other side, Ben was swinging his crossed leg somewhat zealously, his eyes darting around the room. He and

Jane hadn't yet spoken. Rahul appeared to have shrunk more into himself. His arms were crossed in front of him, feet crossed likewise at the ankles. He looked down, avoiding eye contact. Hanna was typing something on her cell phone, while next to her, Linda tapped her manicured nails nervously on the table. Thór looked like he was about to give the entire experiment thirty more seconds before he stormed out.

At that moment, Jónas entered. He gave them all a polite smile, tossing his jacket onto the back of a chair and crossing to Piotr and the coffee.

Was it unusually warm in the room? The air had been circulating better two nights ago, thought Jane. She had a bad feeling about this group gathering here, again, so soon. She looked from those faded old photos on the wall to the guests collected around the table. Their faces showed little of the emotion that was churning inside. But small twitches and movements belied the truth.

Jónas poured himself a cup of coffee, adding a generous stream of milk and equally large spoonful of sugar. All eyes watched him. As he finished, he lifted up the cup.

"Anyone else?" he asked. His offer was met with silence.

After a while, Graeme spoke. "Could we perhaps begin whatever it is we are here to do?"

"We're still waiting for Kristján," Jónas answered.

Graeme looked pointedly at his watch, and the officer added, "While we do so, I can review the plan for tonight. We're going to re-create everything, every detail that we remember. Not just who sat next to whom but also who walked where and when. What did you talk about? What was your mood? The moods of those around you? There might be just a small thing that you may not have considered yet or have been looking at in the wrong light. This is all to jog our memories. And to help discover what really happened to Kavita. Understood?"

There were a few nods and murmurs of approval.

"So you want to know everything, starting from when we sat in here eating two nights ago?" asked Jane.

"Yes, exactly," the officer agreed.

"Rahul and I were talking about the portraits on the wall here. How we are all related," offered Linda.

"The ambassador and I had a good dialogue about potential cooperation," added Thór, while Graeme looked on awkwardly.

Ben said, "Yes, we heard all of that. It was about halfway through the meal."

"Yeah, and then you spilled something on my skirt," said Hanna to Piotr. "I think you did it on purpose."

"Hardly. I treat all my customers with the utmost respect," Piotr scoffed.

Suddenly, the room became quite animated. "All right, guests, please let's not talk over each other." Jónas glanced again at his watch. "After dinner, Piotr set a drink on fire, right?"

"He set several drinks on fire and that was in the other room," Jane corrected. "Kristján tried the first one, then the lights went out while the other drinks were finished."

"What happened once they were ready?" the officer asked the group.

"The lights went back on, and we all tried it," Ben said.

"And Graeme handed my wife a poisoned cocktail," shot Rahul.

"I didn't do anything wrong. I just grabbed a glass and handed it to her," exclaimed the ambassador.

"All right, all right!" Jónas's voice rose above the din. "Piotr, can you mix the Flaming Viking for us again now? You don't have to set it alight—we'll wait for later for that—but just so we can see how it's done."

"Yes, of course," shrugged Piotr. He began assembling ingredients, mixing and chopping and garnishing each with a sprig of angelica.

"Wait!" exclaimed Jane. "I don't like angelica."

"We know," muttered Ben darkly.

"I can't stand the flavor of it," Jane continued. "I would have noticed if you'd put it in the cocktail the other night. You didn't."

There was a confused silence.

"But there was a sprig of angelica on the floor by Kavita's shattered glass," said Jónas. He took out his notebook, flipping back a few pages and squinting at his writing. "Yes, that's in the report. The poisoned drink must have been garnished with angelica."

Piotr slowly put down his shaker. "You know, you are right. I usually garnish them with angelica, but I didn't have enough. So I sprinkled chopped chervil on them instead. I only used angelica on the first sample drink." He looked grim. "The one meant for Kristján."

There was another silence, as everybody took in the implications of this.

"But he tasted that cocktail in front of all of us," said Graeme. "It couldn't have been poisoned."

"Yet the poison ended up in that glass," said Jónas. "How?"

"The lights went out," said Jane slowly. "Someone must have slipped the poison into it then, presuming that the mayor would pick up the same glass once all the drinks were ready." Her pulse was racing. She had been right.

Graeme's face paled. "I just grabbed what was in front of me and handed them out. I had no idea. But does that mean that no one wanted Kavita dead? They wanted—"

Graeme was interrupted by a ringtone of a Bach fugue. Jónas flushed as he reached into his pocket. Jane saw the name that appeared on his screen—Mayor Kristján. "Excuse me a moment," he told the group.

"Hello. Jónas," the officer said in clipped tones as he walked to the corner of the room for some privacy. Jane caught what sounded like a volley of coughing from the receiver.

"What is it? What's wrong?" Jónas demanded. He paused for a moment, then, his voice rising a notch, said: "I'm on my way." He took the phone from his ear and announced, "There's a fire at the mayor's. Can someone call emergency services?" Then the officer dashed out the door.

THIRTY-FOUR

Kristján's lips were tinged with soot. He was doubled over, coughing. How desperately he wanted to run out of his house, to escape. But there was a wall of fire in front of him, and he couldn't summon the energy. He was fiercely trying to suck in air that couldn't seem to reach his lungs. He had managed to call Jónas, and now surely the community's single fire truck would be here within a few minutes.

For an instant, he had a flash of the dramatic volcanic eruption near that very spot in 1973. He was an infant then, but his parents had ingrained in him the story of their hurried escape from the island in the middle of a winter's night in a tiny fishing vessel.

His thoughts were unclear, flashing in his head. Something had happened in almost the blink of an eye—a fire, somewhere in his house. What had he been doing? Yes, getting ready for the meeting at Skel. He had put on the same tie. But then, suddenly, he was surrounded by smoke, choking for air.

It seemed to be coming from Ari's office, but he couldn't be sure. Could he? Kristján found it hard to think. Whatever was in the office was clearly destroyed now, would be a pile of ash by morning. This fire must have spread more quickly due to all the dust and papers there.

But no one else had been here since Jane left earlier today. He had been alone in the house…hadn't he?

It was not supposed to end like this. He was not meant to be here, on the verge of death, before he had completed what he needed to do.

Kristján could feel himself slipping away. Were those flashing lights somewhere? A voice, coming to him as if through a fog.

"Kristján! It's the search-and-rescue. Help is on the way, hang on. We will get you out. There is a helicopter on its way from Reykjavík."

Heat was radiating from all directions. Embers crackled. It was becoming nearly impossible to breathe. Perhaps if he just closed his eyes, he could rest a while. Kristján could feel someone shaking his shoulders, but at this moment he didn't feel it was worth opening his eyes again. It would be so simple to let himself slip away… Then he could be reunited with the one person he was missing.

"Ari…Ari," he gasped, and then fell silent.

PART THREE

SIX MONTHS LATER

THIRTY-FIVE

Jane was seasick. She sighed, sucking on a mint. This affliction never improved, no matter how experienced she was on the waves. It was worse when she had to make journeys such as this one—a trip that would entail reopening painful wounds.

The *Herjólfur* lurched to the right and Jane gripped the side of her chair, staring fiercely out the window, her eyes focused on the island of Heimaey looming ever closer to them. Had it really been half a year? They were returning for the much-delayed official opening of Hanna's exhibition, a perfect excuse to gather the group on the island and for the police to provide an in person update on the investigation; they had all been given permission to return to Reykjavík immediately after Kristján's death if they promised to keep police abreast of any international travel. Now Jane found herself returning to the exact place that had brought so much sadness, raised so many questions, and awoken so many of her own demons.

It was Graeme who had really convinced her, insisted almost. He did much, but he rarely insisted.

"I need you next to me," he had urged her sincerely at their Reykjavík home when the idea had first come up. "It will send an important message."

"What? That I'm still by your side? I don't think my presence is that valued."

"I think it's more that life goes on. And Rahul will appreciate it." Graeme played his trump card. That clinched it.

Jane had spent a lot of time with Rahul over the first couple of months after they returned to the capital, preparing homemade soups and stews and other healthy foods for the widower. They went on bike trips to Heiðmörk wood and chatted together at the swimming pool, all part of Jane's plan to keep Rahul from staying at home like a hermit and to ensure there was no lingering resentment of her husband. Then once his affairs in the country were completed, he had moved back to Canada (with the blessing of the police) and she hadn't seen him in person since.

Now they were here, on the *Herjólfur*, Jane gazing stolidly out the window. Graeme in the seat opposite, endlessly note-taking. Rahul was to Jane's right, tailored shirt tucked in neatly, hair trimmed, face grim. He had lost weight since she last saw him in person. Become gaunt. The trauma of the last months was etched onto his face, the uncertainty of the as-yet-unsolved death of his wife still an open wound. He looked worse than she felt.

"Can I get you anything?" she asked him, feeling responsible for his grudging presence here.

"No thanks, I'm fine with this." Rahul glanced at the plastic bottle of sparkling water in front of him.

Even though he had moved back to his home country only one month ago, Rahul had returned from Canada for this occasion. Not exactly for closure, as he told Jane earlier, for how could there be closure when so many questions still surrounded that stormy fall evening at Skel? But to help draw a line under what had happened so he could finally begin afresh.

"I'm nervous, and I'm surprised we've all been invited back," Rahul confessed. "The island isn't safe, and I'm not talking about natural disasters. There's still a murderer on the loose." He took a sip of his drink and looked at Jane.

"But I do appreciate all your help over the past few months. It was good to focus on some of what Iceland has to offer before I went back to Canada. Not let what happened to Kavi stain all my memories of this place. I meant to ask you, by the way, what's happened to Ben? You used to do all that stuff with him, you said, but seems like he hasn't been around much. Was he too busy with his work?"

"Honestly, we haven't spoken since we were last here together. We had an argument, and I've been pretty stubborn about getting in touch again. But clearly so has he. Plus I suppose he's busy promoting that book, as you say," she added with a tinge of bitterness. Ben's new book, a continuation of his Booker-winning novel, fast-tracked to publication in the wake of the author's presence at an unsolved death, had been topping bestseller lists, praised for its authentic and insightful exploration of the Icelandic psyche. There was talk of a big-budget movie, even a line of clothing to support the distinctive pattern in the Icelandic *lopapeysa* sweater that the book's hero Daníel always wore.

Expectations were already sky-high for an as yet unconfirmed third installment of the series. Jane, however, had only managed to skim the novel so far. It felt too personal to read Ben's words.

The truth was that the memory of their argument was still raw and painful, and part of what had made Jane so reluctant to agree to come back was the idea of facing Ben again. But she didn't tell Rahul this part. Jane was determined that this trip would be different, that she would channel the hurt and anger of the last months into something constructive, not by losing control of her rage yet again but by harnessing it like Iceland's plentiful natural energy.

Since her return to the capital six months ago she had been tirelessly working to see if she could figure out what the police couldn't. As much as she liked Jónas, Jane had to admit that no significant progress had been made in finding Kavita's killer, aside from forensic tests confirming what they had all by then figured out: that Kavita had died from acute potassium cyanide poisoning. That traces of such cyanide had been found in one shattered glass and it was the one Kristján had first drunk from, the only one garnished with angelica. Given that Kristján was unaffected by sampling the drink, that meant the poison had been audaciously added during the cocktail-mixing process, when the lights were out. So far all indicators were that the cyanide had been sourced through the missing capsule in the exhibition at the museum.

The police had been so optimistic that these murders would be solved quickly. Perhaps that's why the chief of police had been so willing to let an inexperienced officer lead the investigation. They were clearly both spontaneous acts of violence, which ought to have left behind many clues to the killer's identity. But it was their sheer daring that made solutions elusive.

Jane's hope that further clues might surface was futile. Even Kristján's murder and the destruction of his home had elicited no further information. According to the neighbors' statements, anyone could have snuck in to set the fire and then escaped before it was noticed.

Then there were Ari's old files. She had pored over what she had stolen from his office and managed to smuggle back to Reykjavík without anyone's knowledge, even Graeme's. Unfortunately, none of it appeared to have anything to do with Bláhafid or with anything that might shed light on Kristján's death. The only noteworthy item was an old leather-bound notebook belonging to Ari's great-grandfather, his name written neatly in fading ink on the inside page. Jane had kept it because it seemed like something that someone in the family would want. The Icelandic was written in small cursive script, although she had a hard time making out more than the occasional first name.

Graeme looked up from his notes. "You have supper plans for tonight, don't you?"

Her husband's repetitive questions bothered her less than they used to. Jane used to interpret them as insincere small talk. She would be more patient now. Somehow, two unsolved murders had led Jane to cling to stability, however imperfect. Her ultimatum of the last journey had mellowed into a truce. Jane was willing to leave it at that for the time being.

"Yes, I'm having dinner with Hanna, remember?" Now that she knew the truth behind Hanna's friendship with her husband, Jane had exchanged occasional texts with the artist as she traveled the world with her exhibition. The trauma of two murders in three days had bonded them in a bittersweet friendship. When Hanna had asked her to dinner the night before the exhibition opening, Jane thought it would be a good moment to review in person what had happened in the intervening months since the delegation had returned to the mainland one diplomat short.

"And who else will be at the opening tomorrow?"

"Thór and Linda, I believe, even though Bláhafid is no longer involved in sponsoring the exhibition. Piotr. He's catering. Jónas is coming to provide an in person review of the investigation since we'll all be there. And I hear that Ben is taking the early morning ferry tomorrow and will be present too." Jane could picture him now, his eyes sparkling, his charm working overtime.

"It will be good to hear from the police directly," commented Graeme. "Nothing seems to be progressing. It's as if all the avenues they were pursuing have dried up."

Jane focused on the islands, fluffy clouds dabbing the treeless, grassy peaks. She sighed deeply. If only she could solve the mystery of Ari's research and what it really meant. If only she could be sure they would all be safe again here on this small island, now in the never-ending daylight of an Icelandic summer. If only she could piece all the clues together before it was too late.

THIRTY-SIX

Hanna was looking forward to her girls' night out with Jane. She had come to appreciate their text exchanges more than she'd anticipated, having a person who understood the strangeness of it all. This summer evening was unusually warm, and the storms of half a year earlier now felt like a distant memory. The awareness that the days were stretching longer provided its own encouragement. Their view from a trendy new eatery in the harbor area was stunning on a night like this, the sun glistening off the peaks of the nearby islands across the harbor. As she had walked from the hotel, Hanna had passed Skel, its newly installed outdoor area heated by lamps and warm woolen blankets (it was an Icelandic summer, after all) and full of clusters of dining patrons.

Murder had done little to damage Skel's reputation or that of its savvy owner. Bookings had skyrocketed; the Flaming Viking had undergone a rebirth and was now part of a "Taste of Iceland" special menu described on Skel's website in nine languages. No one complained about the drink's taste. And no townsfolk, it seemed, minded the development. After all, each new booking at Skel meant new tickets on *Herjólfur*, hotel reservations, breakfasts at the bakery, admission tickets to the folklore museum or the excursion boats that plied the sea caves dotting the islands that surrounded the main community.

Hanna was aware that Piotr knew better than to overtly exploit a tragedy as part of his marketing plan. But she was sure he never objected when people posted social media comments or recorded TikTok videos outside his establishment. Murder, quite frankly, had been good for business. Perhaps a group of murder suspects returning to the island would be even better.

At this other, quieter restaurant, Jane and Hanna began with Manhattans while they waited for appetizers to arrive.

"I'll never try a drink again with components I don't recognize," Jane told Hanna. "Cheers."

"Cheers," Hanna replied and took a sip of her drink, enjoying the bitter fizzle of it on her tongue. It felt a bit disorienting to be on the island again, drinking with Jane. Over the last six months it had been so easy to forget the autumn's events. Their friendship now struck her as unlikely, in a way it hadn't in Reykjavík. "Do you ever find it odd," Hanna said tentatively, "to think that we are both suspects in an ongoing double murder investigation?"

Jane grimaced. "Of course." Then, with a hint of a smile she said, "Why, are you suddenly thinking you ought to be more wary of me?"

Hanna laughed. "No, you're pretty far down my list. You don't have any doubts about me?"

Jane paused. "I'd be lying if I said I hadn't considered it as an outside possibility. But I can't see it somehow. I guess the police can't either, since Jónas didn't blink an eye at you going on tour with your art. These were spur-of-the-moment crimes, and you don't strike me as the impulsive type."

"You're right." Hanna paused. "I mean, if pushed past my limits, I think I could kill. But I'd stab in the night—smoothly, discreetly, effectively. Nothing so showy as what had happened over at Skel."

Jane looked at her thoughtfully.

"Speaking of which, how is Piotr? Have you seen him since you arrived?"

"Not yet. Piotr's just a lovesick puppy," Hanna replied. "Those tattoos, the rugged chef look are just an act. He's fine. He can be lovely, actually. You know, back when I lived here before, I got to know him a little bit. He's always been so focused on that restaurant. It's his dream, running a place like that. Always has been."

"What does he make of its newfound fame then?"

Hanna laughed. "Oh, I don't think he's too bothered about *how* Skel has earned a reputation, as long as the tables are filled and the TripAdvisor reviews are positive. That's what his emails say anyway." She took a sip of her drink. "But that's not necessarily a bad thing. He's not a bad guy, just a realist. And I kind of admire that." She lifted her glass. "To being yourself."

"Cheers," answered Jane. She put her drink down. "Listen, Hanna. I'm sorry if I wasn't all that friendly the last time we met in person."

Hanna waved the comment away. "Don't think about it. I would probably have acted the same in your situation. Why these guys can't just be honest when they should be, I'll never understand."

"Very true," Jane agreed. "But it's fun to catch up now. You know how it is in Iceland. It can be really hard to make friends here."

"I know all about that," agreed Hanna.

"It was easier in other countries," said Jane. "But the diplomatic community here is so small, and many of the foreign women my age are the ambassadors themselves and are very busy—or they're the spouses of ambassadors of more patriarchal countries, demure hostess types." She cringed. "That's not really my thing, if you hadn't noticed."

"Well, I'll be moving around a lot with the exhibition, but next time I'm in Reykjavík I will definitely look you up." Hanna took a bite of her starter and said, as casually as she could: "So, will Ben be there tomorrow?"

Jane raised her eyebrows questioningly.

Hanna kept her voice light, even though she was more interested in the answer than she cared to admit. "We, uh, had a couple of 'moments' during the last trip," she confessed. "He paid me a visit at the folklore museum."

"What?" Jane sounded surprised. "We were only here for three days and there were two murders in that time. How does he find the time? Even at a *museum*."

"He's an appealing guy, your Ben."

"He's not 'my Ben.' He's a friend; that's all."

"Sure, it's an expression."

"Well, he's a grown-up."

Hanna took another sip of her drink and leaned in conspiratorially to her dinner companion. "Do you have any theories about what might have happened that night? I've been thinking about it a lot, probably like everyone else," she said. "I wondered whether any of this had anything to do with Thór and Bláhafid after all."

"It's been on my mind too," agreed Jane. "What's given you that idea?"

Hanna paused a moment to look around. In Icelandic restaurants, the walls always had ears. "That night, when everything happened, I took a video on my phone."

"A video?"

Hanna sighed. "You know that Bláhafid was the main sponsor of my exhibition. Not only on the Westman Islands but in other cities and countries too. And we all know the rumors about them. They wouldn't have been my favorite company to work with, but Graeme hadn't shared the details with me. He just said he'd secured funding for the project and, naively, I didn't ask more questions. Beggars can't be choosers."

"They can, actually," Jane said. "Lots of people avoid association with corporations that don't align with their own values."

"Well, I'm practical," Hanna replied. "I wanted to get my work out there and their pockets are deep. Anyway, it's a long story, but suffice to say that I had this harebrained idea that if I could get some sort of proof about Bláhafid's questionable dealings, then I could maybe use that to encourage them to stop their treatment of immigrant labor and dodgy workplace safety. When I found out they were my main sponsors, I thought I'd made a deal with the devil. But then I decided I would continue with my plan to find the proof, keep quiet until my show was a huge success, and then by that point maybe they would need me more than I needed them, and everything I collected could be some sort of leverage."

"You mean to blackmail them?" Jane asked.

"Well, *blackmail* seems a little harsh," Hanna said casually. "This wasn't really for my own benefit. It was to highlight their criminal activity. But I didn't have many chances to meet or inter-act with Thór so I thought that dinner at Skel would be perfect. Everyone was relaxed. So after dinner when we were mingling more, I discreetly turned on my phone's video recorder in the hopes of catching some incriminating conversation."

"That's all very cloak-and-dagger."

"I know. I just set it on the bar. I knew Piotr would never ques-tion anything I did. At some point when the drinks were being handed out, it must have got knocked over. But obviously I didn't want anyone else to find out what I had been doing. I certainly didn't want the police to know. So the next day, I went back to Skel and got Piotr to collect it for me."

"How did you manage that? Wasn't it all sealed off?"

"Feminine charm," Hanna answered coyly. "The method doesn't matter, though. The point is that I got it back. And after all that effort, there was nothing to show for it." She sighed. "I managed to get it so that Thór was in full view of the camera the whole time. The picture admittedly isn't great, but there's no way he put any-thing in the drinks. His hands are firmly by his side the whole time."

"Are you sure?" Jane asked. "Did you give it to Jónas and let him decide what might be relevant?"

"Honestly, I'll show you." Hanna took out her phone and began scrolling through her videos. "Look." She held the phone out for Jane to see and tapped the play button. She watched as Jane peered at the video Hanna herself had already viewed countless times. "You'll see in a sec, when the lights go out. Thór is nowhere near the cocktails. That's why it occurred to me that maybe Bláhafid has nothing to do with all this."

The video got darker when the lights went out. Hanna's was an old phone, without the technology to adjust. Jane leaned closer and squinted her eyes at the screen as the Flaming Viking was assembled in a blur of blue flame.

"*Gerið þið svo vel.* Be my guest," floated a voice from the distance. There was a smattering of cheering and clapping.

"See? There's nothing of interest." Hanna took her phone from Jane's hand and put it back in her purse.

Jane's face had paled. "Hanna, I'm not so sure about that. You need to show this to the police. Can you send this to me?"

"Jane, I'd rather not have to explain to the police that I snuck back to a crime scene to get my phone. Why do you need it?"

Jane took some banknotes out of her purse and put them on the table.

"I can't explain right now. But I promise discretion. I have to go and check something out. Thanks for meeting me. And thanks in advance for sending me that video. Let's talk tomorrow."

Hanna watched, stunned, as the ambassador's wife gathered up her purse and her jacket from the back of her chair and almost ran out of the restaurant. Hanna took out her phone again and stared at it, confused. What had Jane seen that she had missed?

THIRTY-SEVEN

"Of course we're going," Thór said to Linda as they stacked dishes in their kitchen on the afternoon of the art opening. They had eaten an early dinner, seated together at their kitchen table, a half-decent bottle of Côte du Rhône split between them. Thór had a new corker for opening wine in one deft move and he seemed keen to show it off, even to Linda. Linda wasn't happy about Thór's return to drinking since the night of the Flaming Viking, but she had bigger issues to deal with. It didn't take them too long to finish the drinks, and the alcohol relaxed them both.

"All I'm saying is that I'm not sure we are welcome," Linda answered as she rinsed serving bowls and put them in the dishwasher.

"Jónas asked us to be there, asked everyone who was at dinner that night at Skel. So we'll be there."

"I know," she answered. "But think about it. Is this really the moment to make our big new public appearance?"

Thór shrugged and began looking in the cupboard for a second bottle. "The ambassador will be there. We can start afresh."

"Aren't you still concerned about Ari's research being made public?" she asked Thór as she wiped down a countertop, tidying up after herself as she felt the near-constant need to do. He watched her clean.

"Kristján's out of the picture. No one will take whatever Piotr says seriously if he chooses to file a complaint."

It could not be denied that Bláhafid had undergone a rapid transformation of its image since the events of the previous fall. Ari's papers had not been made public. Linda never saw them all but assumed that the most damning ones had been destroyed in the fire. Rumors had nevertheless begun to circulate. Yet only two weeks after the Canadian delegation left the island, just as minute-by-minute updates on the fallout from the mayor's tragic death began to diminish, Bláhafid announced the opening of a slick new corporate social responsibility division, headed up by a well-coiffed, well-tailored fortysomething man with shining teeth. The new CSR team promised donations to support "sustainability," "diversity," and "multistakeholder engagement." Soon after, glowing interviews with senior staff peppered industry magazines. Thór Magnússon was named *Ethical Fish Farming Monthly*'s CEO of the Year. In Vestmannaeyjabær itself, well-pruned beds of flowers in Bláhafid colors sprouted in public parks. The local junior soccer teams sported new uniforms with the Bláhafid logo.

A charming public relations blitz featuring an ad with a happy multicultural staff had been unleashed on the Icelandic public, and they lapped it up. By now, if anyone dared to sully the reputation of one of the nation's leading fisheries companies, they would never be taken seriously. And if any documents were somehow revealed to the public to back up any outrageous claims, then a team of expensive legal experts was waiting in the wings. The police would be focusing their limited resources on more pressing issues.

"No," Thór continued. "I'm not worried. Ari is dead. Kavita is dead. The Canadian government hasn't officially made a decision on the tax incentives we'll be offered to move there, but I'm optimistic. Things are getting back to normal and all is well with the world. Just relax. Have some more wine. Hanna's exhibition is riding on our coattails."

Things were hardly back to normal with two unsolved murders, Linda thought. Although she tried not to let it distract her too much, there was a great deal about the ongoing mystery that she questioned.

"I'm thinking about the Canadian connection," she answered. "If Graeme has been swayed by our PR campaign, then this might be our last chance to finalize this expansion deal into Canada. Think about it. We could leave these puny islands, build a new life in a country with a brighter future."

And I can finally leave you for good, she thought. *All my sacrifices will come to fruition.*

Linda's new guiding mantra was to make hay from last year's events. Hanna's launch was an opportunity to rekindle professional relationships and to chat with the artist herself, to thank her for her help in solving Kavita's immigration project issues.

Linda reached out and put a hand over the bottle just as Thór was about to uncork it.

"Why don't we leave that?" she suggested. "Keep our heads clear for later. There will be plenty of time to celebrate at the end of the evening if it all goes as we want it to." She flashed her most enticing smile at her husband.

"Fine," Thór grunted. He gave his wife a quick glance up and down. Linda was familiar with the look. He was calculating her value to him for achieving the evening's objectives.

"Put on that purple top," he commanded. "And those silver earrings. It'll send the message that you're modern, professional, but supportive."

Linda swallowed the bile that rose within her. *Success tonight helps me too,* she reminded herself. She could easily put on her game face and work the room. Tonight would be like any other night in that sense. But also, it wouldn't. The pall of suspicion still hung over the group.

If she could get through the evening, if this kicked things off the way she wanted, maybe this time next year she'd be home free in her new life. That would be worth celebrating.

THIRTY-EIGHT

Jane paced the small square of their hotel room. She was sure she had done the right thing but was dreading how things might play out at the exhibition launch. But she had reached the right conclusion, hadn't she?

She had woken early with a headache the morning after her dinner with Hanna—a middle-aged badge of honor but a frustrating one. She had enjoyed the night out, at least until her horrifying discovery. It had been a long time since she had enjoyed the nourishment of female friendship.

She padded slowly to the bathroom, applied a thick coat of moisturizer to her dry skin, and swallowed two Advils with a tumbler of cold tap water. Graeme was still sleeping soundly in the king-sized bed, a rarity for an Icelandic hotel room.

Hanna obviously hadn't noticed what Jane had on that video. She had been trying in vain to find something to pin on Thór, and that had caused her to miss what Jane had spotted straightaway.

Although, admittedly, she'd had to put the video on her laptop and brighten all the images to be certain. If only Jane could talk through her swirling thoughts aloud with someone. Perhaps she ought to trust her husband more, confide in him. She continued to mourn the dissipation of that communication. She was, as she had so often been, on her own.

Jane went for a long walk instead. The sun was already high in the sky, reflecting off an unusually calm sea. The gulls chirped. The golf course was full by 10:00 a.m. The squeals of delighted children were emanating from the swimming pool. By lunchtime, the hangover was gone, her mind clear and focused. She sat down to review everything she knew, or thought she knew, scribbling notes in a spiral notebook back in the hotel room about everything she could think of: Piotr's obsession with the artist. Hanna's dalliances. Bláhafid's PR strategy. The contents of the documents she stole from Ari. And, most importantly, the damning video on Hanna's phone. Slowly, a pattern emerged.

She made a call. The phone was answered on the second ring. "Jónas." A crisp voice.

Jane told him everything.

THIRTY-NINE

Hanna gazed approvingly around her. The exhibition was ready. Her paintings that had garnered the biggest raves on her tour hung on the walls of the folklore museum, the same venue where they had been ready half a year before. The arrangement was nearly identical, with the addition of some new portraits that had more local relevance, close-up images with clusters of the area's plentiful angelica. A visitor ignorant of the events of the previous year would have noticed nothing amiss about the setup. Only regular patrons may have spotted the new security cameras in all the corners, the glass cases that surrounded other exhibits, the movable barriers erected across one or two spaces.

In the far corner, a table was laid with wineglasses. A dozen bottles of hard-to-procure-in-Iceland Niagara Valley whites and reds stood ready to be opened, though only in the presence of witnesses. Another table had an assortment of crudités provided at a discount rate by the culinary team at Skel. At the entrance to the venue, Stella had placed a stand with small cards that described each work of art, included a legend that explained the images, and listed their prices. Everything was for sale, naturally, even if a piece was to finish traveling the world before being relinquished into the home or office of a deep-pocketed art lover.

Hanna was dressed in a navy-blue pencil skirt and red blouse. She didn't usually wear skirts, but this was an upscale occasion. She felt both relief and, to her surprise, a slight nervousness. She'd toured northern Europe, but somehow being back here was different. It was both completely familiar and eerily alien. Would people really look at the art? Would they perceive the nuance, the emotion that had gone into every piece of work?

She walked over to Stella, who was busy placing a leather-bound guest book and fountain pen near the cards at the entrance.

"Thanks for seeing this through," Hanna told her friend.

Stella squeezed Hanna's arm. "Of course. It's important, not just for you, but for all of us."

In his dress uniform, Officer Jónas Jónasson stood tall. "How many are you expecting overall?"

"We have an open invitation to the townspeople to stop by," Stella answered. "There's a notice in the paper and a Facebook event. But the formal ceremony is half an hour earlier, just for the Canadian delegation and Bláhafið representatives."

They began arriving at seven o'clock on the dot. First was a dapper-looking Thór along with Linda, her hair glossy and well-coiffed. They appeared relaxed and happy, shaking hands heartily with Hanna and the others and beginning with small talk on the weather, the popularity of the museum, and upcoming vacation plans. Hanna's stomach turned. She'd read all about the success of Thór's new PR campaign, and it sickened her.

Piotr was the next to arrive, this time in a crisp pale-blue shirt that still bore the telltale creases of being unwrapped and worn for the first time. He kissed Hanna on both cheeks, shook Jónas's and Stella's hands warmly, and pointedly ignored Thór and Linda.

"Where is everyone else?" he asked no one in particular.

"The Canadians should be here in a few minutes," answered Stella. "We invited just a few for the first half hour, to give us a chance to talk before everyone else arrives."

Stella nudged Hanna and said quietly, "That shirt was ordered online, I'm sure, and it's for you. I've never seen Piotr in something he needs to button up before!"

Hanna smiled. "That's actually a little sweet, but don't tell him I said so."

The front door swung open again and Ben strode inside, kissing both women on the cheeks and shaking the officer's hand. "Wonderful to be back here again," he said, as if he had just returned to a childhood home or from the beachfront of his favorite sun vacation. "Thank you for this invite, Hanna. What a great excuse to get back to the Westman Islands."

"Welcome back," said Stella. "And congrats on another bestseller!"

"Thank you, thank you." Ben smiled demurely, but Hanna noted that he was sporting a new and expensive-looking watch. Clearly, the success of his second book was paying dividends.

"Where are the others?" Ben asked at the precise moment that

Graeme, Jane, and Rahul entered as if on cue. Hanna watched as the group exchanged greetings, although Ben and Jane made a point of ignoring each other.

The group clustered near the refreshments, and a waiter appeared to pour drinks. Hanna noticed that the eyes of the guests never left the bottle or the glass they each accepted. There were a few more minutes of forced small talk, Jónas and Jane exchanging some glances. What were they trying to communicate? Hanna had attempted to interrogate Jane more about the video since their dinner, but she had been peculiarly reticent.

Hanna moved toward Piotr. "Nice shirt," she commented. Piotr looked down at the sleeves, creases still sharp. "I just bought it," he offered.

Finally, Stella began. "Welcome, dear ambassador, dear guests and friends. I am so glad that you have decided to return to the folklore museum for this happy occasion. It's been a long journey, but we are here finally to celebrate my dear friend Hanna Kovacic and her exhibition on the—"

She was interrupted by a blushing Jónas, who stepped forward.

"May I?" he asked, in a tone that implied he was not seeking permission.

Stella stepped aside with a bemused expression on her face and the officer took her place.

"Apologies to Stella and Hanna. We are here to celebrate this art today, but before the general public arrive, I also want to use this opportunity to update you all on the status of the investigations into Kavita's and Kristján's murders."

There was some slight shuffling and murmurs among the group.

"Of course that's fine," Hanna said in a conciliatory tone.

"Thank you," said Rahul with relief. "I don't care when or how, but I want to know as much as possible."

"Thank you all for coming. As you all know, these tragic deaths have gripped the island. We can't believe that events this shocking would take place here. But they did.

"These were audacious crimes. The first happened right under the noses of a room full of important diplomatic guests. The second was one of stealth. Somebody slipped into the mayor's home and deliberately started the fire that killed him. Both appeared to be opportunistic, fairly spontaneous, and risky in execution.

"We now know that Kavita accidentally drank from the mayor's glass. That he was the intended victim. The mayor, who, of course, was recently bereaved himself."

The officer scanned the room, trying to catch everyone's eyes and, Hanna suspected, assure himself that he had not lost their trust. Jane smiled back at him encouragingly and kept a reassuring hand on Rahul's elbow.

"I also wanted to examine the poison itself," Jónas continued. "Who had the opportunity to take the cyanide and an intention to kill? Stella told us that the cyanide capsule wasn't a secret. It had always been a part of the display of the uniform. And, of course, all the visiting guests from that day heard a special lecture that drew attention to it.

"There were no security cameras in that room and the museum

was open to the public. The members of the tour group had opportunity, but so did Piotr, who also visited the museum that day, after
the others."

"That proves nothing," said the chef, with a tinge of indignation.

"You have made tremendous financial gains from Kavita's
death, not least because it is an unsolved crime," Jónas continued.
"Even once we realized Kristján was the likely target, you were not
absolved. You were known to hate Bláhafid. In fact, Kristján told
Jane that you were a whistleblower for Ari before the journalist
had died."

"So why would I want to kill Kristján?" demanded Piotr.

"Your hatred of Bláhafid may have driven you to other lengths
when Kristján didn't immediately use your information to bring
down the company. But of course, you were not the only person
who visited the museum after the delegation's tour. And the two
visitors to whom I am referring did not disclose their movements."
He looked pointedly toward Ben. The author gazed back. Hanna
felt a chill creep up her back. Where was Jónas going with this?
And how did he know?

"Me?" asked Ben placidly. "Yes, I was there. I met Hanna there.
I don't think you'll hear her complaining about it. Sorry I didn't
mention it earlier. I didn't want to add any fuel to the gossip fire."

Jónas looked at the curator. "When we interviewed you that
day, you told us about Piotr but didn't mention Ben and Hanna. Yet
you must have known. So why not say something?"

Stella reddened but spoke defiantly. "Perhaps I should have,
but Ben was just visiting. He has never been here before and has no

connection to Bláhafid, and Hanna is the most trustworthy person I know." Hanna smiled gratefully at her friend.

Stella paused and her eyes narrowed. "How did you know about that?"

Jónas shrugged. "Jane told me."

"And Hanna told me last night," Jane continued.

"And what about motive?" Jónas asked. "Ari was in possession of many documents in connection with a secretive, but potentially explosive story he was working on when he died. Despite the controversial nature of the work, Kristján said he had not been able to look at any of the papers, he was so overcome by grief. He was just getting ready to go through everything when Kavita's murder brought back the pain and turmoil of Ari's death. But Jane convinced him to continue with the plan to examine Ari's things.

"It didn't take Jane and Ben long to come across some valuable information. Documents on the goings-on at Bláhafid, on corruption that involved worker exploitation, unpaid overtime, even possible tax fraud."

"Exactly," said Piotr with a satisfied tone.

"No, not exactly!" Linda burst in. "None of those documents prove anything. And none of them is any worse than what international companies must undertake in a competitive marketplace."

Thór turned to his wife. "Thank you," he said quietly to her. "But everyone knows this. No need to get emotional." She glared at him.

"Regardless, there was much animosity between Kristján and Thór," continued Jónas. "The documents only confirmed this, even if Kristján hadn't reviewed them before and only knew in very vague terms what they might have contained."

"I didn't set a fire at Kristján's home! I wasn't even anywhere near there when it happened!" exclaimed Thór. "This is ridiculous."

Hanna thought back to the video. As much as she was loath to admit it, she really couldn't see that Thór was guilty, at least not of these murders.

"We pursued all avenues of inquiry," continued Jónas, ignoring the fishing baron. "The documents that Ari had been storing had been almost entirely destroyed by the fire, a convenient development for Bláhafid."

Thór snorted in disgust.

"Did any of you look into any motive for killing the mayor aside from immediately assuming I or my company were involved?" Thór looked accusingly at Jónas. "He was a politician, for God's sake. Of course he would have enemies. In a small place, people take slights even more personally. I should know."

"That's a fair comment," Jónas acknowledged. "And of course there were also others who, to one degree or another, had made their bed with Bláhafid. Kavita herself had ignored rumors because she was moving 'her' refugees to Canada. And Hanna had allowed Bláhafid to be crucial backers for her foray into the art world."

"That's no motive," scoffed Hanna. "And besides, I didn't even know about that until the day Kavita died."

"The point I'm trying to make is that those papers are the key." He paused for a moment. "And someone in this room is guilty of another crime in relation to them."

Hanna looked around her and wondered what the officer could be referring to.

Jane stepped slowly forward, distancing herself from Graeme, Rahul, and Ben, who gave her bemused looks as she joined the young officer.

"It was me," she said. "I stole something from Kristján. But I'm not sorry. It was something I felt I needed to do to help in the investigation, something I knew I could do best alone. Ben and I had been going through all of Ari's old files. There was so much material. So when I left, I took a few folders at random. I thought I could tinker away by reviewing them in due course."

Ben looked at her sharply. "You never told me that."

"We haven't exactly been in touch lately," she responded sadly.

"I think all of us, or most of us"—Jane looked at Thór and Linda—"initially thought the key to these murders was documents that implicated Bláhafid in shady business. It seemed to be even more the case after those documents were destroyed. Whatever our criminal wanted was now out of reach, with no one the wiser."

"And we were no closer to a solution," said Jónas. "Until Jane got in touch with me this morning. She made the excellent point that perhaps we had never found the right proof of murder in those documents about Bláhafid because those files weren't the bombshell secrets that Ari was storing. Maybe the missing piece of the puzzle was something else entirely."

FORTY

Jane felt all eyes trained on her, as if waiting for her to make a mistake. She was good at small talk, good when conversations were on an even keel, not at this public speaking. She could relate to Jónas's impostor syndrome but knew she needed to push through it.

"When Ben and I began to examine Ari's old files, the theory that his papers would provide a final clue was reinforced," she continued. "He had been working on something that, according to his husband, was of vital importance to the whole community. Something that might shake the status quo so much that even the mayor himself could not bring himself to find out. Bláhafid felt like the obvious connection. Yet the necessary evidence to connect the murders to Thór Magnússon didn't materialize."

"Of course not!" snarled Thór, and Hanna noted his cheeks were dangerously flushed. "Because I didn't commit them!"

"Then," Jane continued, as if he hadn't spoken, "last night

Hanna and I went out for dinner. During the meal she showed me a video that she had taken on her phone the night of Kavita's death."

Several pairs of eyes turned to Hanna curiously, but she kept her gaze pointedly on Jane.

"Hanna looked back at the footage and was able to establish that there was no opportunity for Thór to slip anything into the drinks as they were being prepared. But I'd already started to wonder whether this mystery needed looking at from a different angle, and so when I watched the video, I was looking at the other people in the frame. It was very dark and the quality was not good, so I couldn't be sure about what I'd seen. But when I got home I used some software to brighten the images. I'm going to show it to you all now."

Jónas walked to the wall and turned on a screen. It took him almost a minute to connect to the network to be able to call up the video, and the tension in the room seemed to swell with every second of delay.

"All right, we're ready," announced Jane. She tapped on her phone, and the film began to play in eerie silence.

"That's so much sharper than it was on my phone," said Hanna in awe.

"There, right there!" Jane cried suddenly and froze the image. "Look down here, in the lower right-hand corner. Watch as I play it again."

Jane pointed to an area of the screen. It was only the slightest movement in the corner of the footage, but it was clear. A hand tipped something quickly into a cocktail and swirled the liquid around with a finger.

"How could I miss that?" Hanna said to the group in an astonished tone.

"It's not your fault," Jane reassured her. "I've edited this to make it brighter and zoomed in on this single section."

"Wait, is that someone poisoning the drink?" exclaimed Rahul with urgency. "Who? Who is that?"

"I'm afraid I need to drag this on another moment, Rahul," Jane answered. "Let me take a step back and explain one more vital clue. You'll remember how I grabbed several documents when I left the mayor's house. I didn't tell anyone else I had done it. Once I opened them, I noticed that much of the writing was in Icelandic, which I don't read, so I didn't know what they contained."

Jane removed a battered leather notebook from her handbag and held it up.

"Here is one of the items I took. This was Ari's. Well, it was his great-grandfather's. I thought I would share a short passage from it that I had translated online."

Jane began reading aloud. It was a text about the dreary weather, a story about a local boy who had nearly been killed trying to collect sheep during an unexpected storm, about the patterned *lopapeysa* he wore that protected him so well against the elements. The phrasing was lyrical, and the crowd was spellbound. Jane finished the last line. There were several seconds of silence.

"It's beautiful," acknowledged Graeme. "But the description of that boy, his appearance, that's Daníel from *Every Good Man*, Ben's Booker-winning novel. Ben's famous for imagery exactly like what you just read."

Jane sighed shakily. "That's just the problem. *Every Good Man* is not Ben's writing. It's his great-grandfather's. And Ari's great-grandfather's. Ben Rafdal is a plagiarist."

The group turned to look at the writer. He drained the drink in his hand.

"What?" he asked the group. "You're asking if I had inspiration from my ancestors? Of course I did. Don't we all?"

"We're talking about more than inspiration, Ben," said Jónas, picking up the thread. "This book, this novel manuscript that Jane took from Ari's office, is clearly meant to be the third part of a trilogy. *Every Good Man* was a massive international bestseller, and we were all so excited it helped bring positive attention to Iceland. Presumably Jón the Learned had a few manuscripts and one obviously ended up back in Gimli, where his descendants emigrated. But once you cribbed that and published it as your own, the clock began ticking to find the next two manuscripts.

"With your Icelandic skills, it would have been easy for you to realize what you'd found in Ari's office and grab the second book. No wonder you had been so worried about deadlines… You hadn't even found the document yet, so not a single word of 'your' manuscript would have been written. I can't imagine your relief once you did see it and could take it without the mayor ever knowing."

"This is bullshit," Ben protested. "I write about crimes; I don't commit them."

Jane faced her erstwhile friend directly. "You may claim that plagiarizing proves nothing criminal but the video we just saw?

That's your hand. I recognize your watch on the wrist. That's *you* poisoning a drink."

Ben's face grew white. "Watch?" he asked, a slight quaver in this voice. "Look. This is not that watch." He held up his wrist and pulled the sleeve up.

Jane shrugged. "Success has afforded you more luxuries. And a chance to shed any ties, even sentimental ones, with your relatives."

"Ari had figured it all out," explained Jónas. "He was trying to find further proof of Ben's plagiarism by contacting his relatives around the country and then Ben himself."

"And yet when Kristján told Ben about the familial connection, he pretended he didn't know," added Jane. "Rahul told me a story about the times Ari tried to reach Ben but the requests never got to him."

"But Ben wasn't here when Ari died," said Stella. "He can't have had anything to do with that."

"True," agreed Jónas. "Kristján was nearly out of his mind with grief, and he was fixated on the idea that Ari's death was murder. But Ari's death was a tragic yet natural event, as the medical authorities have always said. As to the other deaths, it was only once Ben arrived here and learned about his relationship to Ari that he realized for sure that the other two books might be right here on the Westman Islands and that the mayor might imminently discover them."

"What happens to the books now?" asked Hanna.

"We'll let his publisher know," said Jónas. "They might yank copies from stores. And Jón's descendants can sue Ben for their rightful share of the royalties. Regardless, Ben's reputation will be worthless."

"So Ben really killed to protect his literary reputation? To prevent the mayor from finding out and revealing him as a fraud?" asked Piotr.

Jónas nodded. "That's exactly what he did."

FORTY-ONE

"Hang on a second," Ben said slowly as he put his empty glass down and faced an antagonistic crowd. "You're all here accusing me of *murder*? I'm a writer, for God's sake!"

Jane couldn't speak more. She had invested so much energy in her speech to the group, in revealing what she knew about the manuscript she stole, that she had nothing left to give. She stepped away from the front of the group and stood next to Graeme to observe quietly.

"Writers are capable of evil acts, just like the rest of us," Jónas said sternly. "With this video from Hanna's phone, showing you put something into the cocktail, and this original copy of the third part of the trilogy that Jane took from Ari's office, we have enough to charge you with two premeditated murders."

Suddenly, Ben lurched for Jane and for the notebook in her hands. She jumped and moved aside.

"This is mine! He was *my* great-grandfather. I am only helping him get his stories to a wide audience!"

"You are a fraud, a cheat, a coward, and a murderer," said Jane.

Jónas gestured to the two uniformed officers who had been standing silently by the door. They approached and began to handcuff Ben. The group watched wordlessly.

"All right, all right, my books are really my great-grandfather's," Ben said almost plaintively as the police began to lead him away. "But I *earned* this. I have been searching the country for the remaining two after I discovered the first one among my great-grandfather's belongings back home in Gimli. But I didn't kill Kavita, I swear it."

"How do you explain what I saw on the video then?" Jane had found her voice again.

Ben shot her a desperate glance. "That was a sleeping tablet, two of them. Jane, you know I've been taking them. I discovered that Ari was related to me, that he might be the person who had the last two books. Then I found out that the mayor was going to go through Ari's old things. I panicked. I thought if I could sneak into his house while he was out for the count, I could find what I needed. I just put prescription meds in the drink, not poison."

"Lies!" Piotr's face was suffused with rage. "Not only was it poison, but you had plenty of chance to steal it from the museum when you met with Hanna to fuck her," he spat. "And all this time, the police thought I was a suspect because I had been there earlier that day."

Hanna blushed and shot Piotr an angry look. "Be quiet, Piotr. Don't be so melodramatic."

"I'm afraid nobody is going to believe that, Ben," said Jónas sternly. "We know you started the fire at the mayor's. We've gone back through the timing of everyone's arrival at the reenactment, looking at who would have the opportunity to go there first, and yours fits exactly. You needed to destroy the evidence."

Ben's shoulders slumped. "I found the second book when I was looking with Jane," he said. "And took it with me. I knew I wouldn't have time to find the third one. We had to return to the mainland." He looked around him with a desperate look in his eyes. "I thought—I thought if I returned and burned the rest, then no one would find anything. I could somehow postpone news of the third volume, make an excuse why it wouldn't be published. I didn't know the fire would spread so quickly and that Kristján would die too!"

"Two deaths already for your precious literary career. And what would have happened if you'd discovered that Jane had the manuscript? Would you have come after her too?" Graeme shouted. Jane felt a pang of pleasure at watching her husband's protective id take over. But he was right.

Ben looked at Jane. "I would never, I couldn't… Jane, you must believe me."

Jane took two steps toward the writer. His hands were handcuffed behind him. This man who she thought exuded confidence and charisma, who felt and behaved as if the world were his oyster, as if he were entitled to whatever he wished. Here he was, thanks to his own greed and pathos, reduced to an insecure, sniveling wreck. Perhaps he had always been that way under the sheen.

Jane approached him, her face mere inches from his, and put her hands on his shoulders. "Ben," she whispered, so quietly that only he could hear. "That is quite the tale you spun for us just now. Maybe you wouldn't be heading to jail if you'd only told your own stories from the start."

PART FOUR

ONE WEEK LATER

FORTY-TWO

Much to her own surprise, Hanna was still in Vestmannaeyjar. She had thought that after the launch of her exhibition, she would have a chance to relax in Reykjavík for a few days before flying on to her next event in London.

Fate, however, seemed to have more in store for her than a criminal development hijacking her Icelandic art debut—again. She was still mad at herself that she hadn't noticed Ben's hand in the video. Notwithstanding that detail, Hanna was thankful for Jane. If she hadn't figured everything out, there would still be a killer on the loose.

Hanna straightened her skirt and applied a thick coat of her signature red lipstick, fluffing up her curly hair with her hands.

It was also shocking that she had had sex with a murderer. Not that she regretted it. In fact, the thought titillated her. She had sailed close to the wind of danger without being at risk of anything herself.

Hanna sprayed her favorite perfume over her neck and then glanced quickly at her watch. Almost time to go. What she was about to do was perhaps the most surprising development of this whole roller coaster. She had postponed London for it, after all. For despite all her nerves about her exhibition, despite all the agency she had shown in her love life, she was finding herself entranced by the banality of an old-fashioned romantic.

There was a knock at the door and Hanna strode briskly to open it, grabbing her coat and handbag on the way.

Piotr stood in the hallway with a small bouquet of roses in his hand, a tiny price tag still on the plastic in the corner.

"Ready?" he asked her.

Hanna grabbed the front of his shirt and pulled him to her in a lingering kiss.

"More than ever," she answered as they drew apart.

FORTY-THREE

Linda returned panting and sweaty from a run up to the Stórhöfði lookout point and back. She always felt exhilarated after the challenging 15-kilometer circuit, but this day was a special high point.

Her bags were packed. Her paperwork was ready. Her flight to Canada was due to depart the next day. A ticket for one. The cards had fallen in her favor, albeit after some deliberate shuffling. The Canadian government had offered the tax breaks Bláhafid had requested, but only if Thór resigned as CEO. He had grudgingly agreed, and only after Linda was once again able to placate him by assuring him that, as interim CEO of Bláhafid Canada, she'd be able to offer him some board positions among friendly colleagues back in Iceland. She didn't tell him she wasn't planning to follow up on any of it.

Linda traipsed to the bedroom, boxes stacked tidily in the corner, and began stretching her hamstrings and quads. To some degree, she couldn't believe her own luck that she was finally escaping this island. The icing on the cake was that she could move away knowing how the recent murders had been solved satisfactorily. Watching that video Hanna had taken the night of Kavita's death had been the final piece of the puzzle. She almost felt a bit sorry for poor, hapless Ben, destined to spend years behind bars because he had had to rely on someone else's ingenuity to quench his thirst for fame.

Thór entered the bedroom from their en suite, a towel wrapped around his waist. He ignored his wife and began to put on a dark suit and shirt. Linda recalled that he had mentioned something about a meeting with a potential contact for a new project, overseeing the import of fresh foods for the local elementary school and elderly care home.

She couldn't resist. "Is that the tie you're wearing?"

Thór turned around as if he hadn't noticed she'd been in the same room. "What's wrong with this tie? I wear it all the time."

"That was back when you ran the biggest company in the country," she said with faux kindness. "You're no longer in the driver's seat. Now bingo night at the old-age home is a networking event."

She picked up a striped azure tie from the closet, walked to face her husband, and draped it around his neck. "This one brings out the blue of your eyes, *elskan*." She tapped one hand on his chest and smiled disingenuously.

"Play your cards right, and you might even get a contract to cater the sports hall too."

FORTY-FOUR

The doorbell rang at the Canadian ambassador's residence in an exclusive part of Reykjavík. Jane greeted Jónas, who stood in uniform outside. She showed him into the living room, with its soapstone carvings, throw pillows, and paintings by up-and-coming artists, including a watercolor by one Hanna Kovacic.

"It's all meant to showcase Canadian design," Jane explained as she gestured for her guest to sit.

"Ben has been formally charged with both murders," Jónas told Jane. "I wanted to tell you in person."

"That was quick," she said dryly.

"He's still claiming he had nothing to do with Kavita's death and that Kristján's death in the fire was an accident. But the justice system will show otherwise." Jónas took a sip of water. "I'm here to thank you. If it weren't for you, I don't think this would have been solved."

Jane leaned back in her armchair. Naturally she was glad it had been wrapped up, that the perpetrator was about to be brought to justice. But the feeling of betrayal was nearly overwhelming. How could she have been taken in by Ben's charisma, like an insecure adolescent? To trust him with her secrets? For all she knew, they would appear in some self-published piece he composed from prison. The thought both terrified and enraged her.

"Ben completely distracted me from the real reason we were looking at those papers," Jane said to Jónas. "He kept saying we'd find something that implicated Thór in the murder, but really he was desperate to find those two books. But why do you think he returned to the islands last week?"

"I think he thought he'd gotten away with it," Jónas answered. "His new book—his great-grandfather's book—was a huge bestseller. He was pretty sure that the third book had been destroyed. So he had nothing to lose. In fact, he could show off how successful he was."

"Why do you think Ben's great-grandfather never published his novels during his lifetime?" Jane asked.

Jónas shrugged. "I think over the last years there has been a renewed interest in local tradition, but at the time perhaps they seemed unfashionable. Or perhaps he never had confidence in them. Lots of people in Iceland like to write, but many don't publish, and of course there was far less money to release books at that time."

"I guess you're right," Jane agreed. "If there's one thing Ben can't be accused of, it's that he lacks confidence."

There was something else about that evening at Skel that

was dancing in the back of her mind. She hadn't believed Ben's protests—not exactly—but something about what she had seen on the video nagged at her. Something that didn't feel right, though she couldn't put her finger on what it was. Perhaps it was simply that there was some part of her that was reluctant to believe the man she'd considered a friend was capable of such awful things.

"Have you told Rahul about Ben being charged?"

"Yes, I had a video call with him last night," Jónas said. "He sends his best wishes and thanks from Toronto." He paused a moment and the tips of his ears reddened. Jane smiled at Jónas's involuntary physiological response to insecurity.

"You look like there's something else you want to tell me," she prodded gently.

The officer nodded. "Yes, well, it's nothing to do with this case really, but I thought you'd like to know. Chief Margrét was very happy with my handling of the case." He looked down at his feet and toyed with his wrist cuff as the red of his ears crept across his face. "She suggested a promotion for me. I'm getting transferred here…to the big city."

"Jónas, that's well deserved!" exclaimed Jane. "I'm very happy for you."

"Thanks. It's just a temporary placement, but if it goes well, I might be able to stay longer. And perhaps here I'll be known as the officer who caught a double murderer, not 'little Jónsi.'"

Jane was genuinely happy for Jónas, who seemed to have grown in confidence during the course of the few months she had known him. Perhaps something good had come from this tragedy after all.

Perhaps something else too. She still wasn't sure how much true romance had ever existed between her and Graeme. But the saplings were worth cultivating. It wasn't too late. Graeme genuinely seemed to be doing his part. So she could tackle this like she had tackled so much else. Ensure that she and her husband had more than habit and children keeping them together.

"The new deputy ambassador is going to continue with the refugee project placement by the way," she said to Jónas. "At least some of them will work for Piotr at Skel."

"They're desperate for more staff," agreed Jónas.

The subject reminded Jane that she wanted to keep her mind challenged too. She should be doing more than filling the fridge for her ravenous teenagers and surreptitiously trying to shadow their social media accounts. Maybe she could help with the refugee project too or perhaps get to know more locals. One of the parents at the twins' school had mentioned something about a choir nearby. That might help to quell her doubts about her purpose here, or at least distract her.

Jane smiled at Jónas as he sat opposite her. She was nearly old enough to be his mother, yet she was just discovering for herself the power of humility and learning to trust that she had all the tools she needed to forge her own destiny. Now was the time to build the future she wanted.

FORTY-FIVE

She leaned her seat back and gazed out of the window over a cloudless ocean. She couldn't recall the last time she felt so utterly relaxed and able to look forward to a bright future, one that she knew she had earned. One that she had paid the price for.

A flight attendant stopped to offer her a refill on her gin and tonic, and she assented.

"Can you put some extra lemon in it, please?" she asked sweetly. "Garnishes are kind of a lucky charm."

The flight attendant looked at her curiously. "I can't say anyone has ever told me that before," he said with a smile.

It was, of course, more luck than charm. That Hanna's video had cut off before anybody could see who had taken which glasses. That nobody had noticed that crucial detail in the video, the one that would have validated Ben's otherwise preposterous story.

In truth, it was a little surprising that neither the ambassador's wife nor the police officer had registered the absence of the garnish in the glass in the video. That telltale sprig of angelica that had been vital in confirming that Kavita had drunk from the glass intended for Kristján. Whatever Ben had put into the ungarnished cocktail—and who knew if they really were sleeping tablets—it was not what killed Kavita. She had drunk from the garnished glass.

Of course, she regretted the diplomat's death. It was unfortunate that she'd been distracted in the moment, unable to ensure the mayor picked up his original glass again. But then, there was a cost to everything. She'd been alarmed, too, to think she'd have to try again to ensure the mayor would be permanently silenced, unable to stop her from fulfilling her well-laid plan. But how neatly Ben Radfal had resolved that for her.

Yes, it had all worked out remarkably well. And even if the discrepancy was noticed, she'd be long gone by then.

"Here you go." The flight attendant handed her the gin and tonic, and she allowed herself the smallest of sips, savoring the juniper tang on her tongue, the bitterness of the lemon. So much nicer than angelica.

EPILOGUE

BEFORE ANYONE DIED

Ari was waiting right where he said he would be at the museum—down the hall with the exhibition of the old fisherman photographs, just off the entrance to the archive, where there were no security cameras and would be no unexpected visitors.

"Why the cloak-and-dagger assignation?" she asked the journalist without preamble. "Want to brag more about your latest investigative discovery?"

"Nice to see you too," Ari answered dryly. "But that's why I called you here today. Our arrangement is no longer working for me. I've earned quite a bit from you the last few years. I've even enjoyed digging up the dirtiest secrets on this town's power brokers and letting you silence or manipulate them as you wish. But now all my hard work has paid off and I've hit the jackpot of discoveries. I won't need your money after this becomes public."

She looked at him coldly and raised a questioning eyebrow. "Is that so?"

"It's about Bláhafid Seafood Products," Ari said slyly. "I've uncovered proof of all kinds of illegal acts. The company will be finished. I can get far more fame and influence from breaking that story than from our amateur transactions over town gossip."

Linda's face paled. She never expected Ari would turn on her like this after the money he had made off her over the years.

"What do you want from me?"

Ari smirked. "To see you squirm. Thór is a despicable human. He deserves to lose everything. So do you."

Linda shot him a pleading look. "Do you think I don't know that? I live with the man. But, please, just wait. I haven't seen this proof, but I believe you. I'm sure it's bad. If you can just hold off a while, we are about to finalize an agreement to relocate to Canada. We'll move over there and I can finally be free. I'll even help you take Thór down if the company stays afloat. We can work together. It means more money for you. When I'm running Bláhafid from Canada on my own, I'm sure there will be ways I can help further your fame and career."

"You think I believe that? You're just as bad as he is. No, this is happening now. I've just texted Kristján. He can witness this. And I have all the proof back in my office at home."

Linda felt anger well up inside her. The years she had spent keeping Thór's crimes quiet, blackmailing erstwhile whistleblowers with information she had bought from Ari. All so that she could one day control the narrative, allowing Thór to take the fall for corporate misdeeds while keeping a very profitable business intact. So that she could then escape and build a new life for herself. She had worked so hard for it. It was within her grasp. And now this hack was trying to take it all down, just for a byline on some white-collar crime that would garner headlines for a day or two. It was too much.

"You can't do this. Please. It will ruin everything."

Ari scoffed. "Maybe you should have thought of that before you and your husband exploited workers and filled your own coffers."

His phone vibrated. "Ah, Kristján's on his way. This is going to be quite the scene," he added gleefully.

Linda reached out to grab Ari's phone, but he sidestepped her nimbly. He slapped her across the face. "You have no choice in this."

Linda felt her rage erupt. All the years of grinning and bearing the humiliations and the slights, and now her dreams of escape were vanishing. Before she knew what she was doing, her hands were on Ari's shoulders and she was pushing him with all her might. "No one hits me! No one ruins me!"

Ari cascaded backward. His head hit the floor, his skull cracking audibly.

"Ari!" What had she done? Ari lay on the ground, seemingly unable to move, his eyes blinking pleadingly. His fingers were twitching, but he didn't seem to be able to get up. He uttered some slurred sounds.

She had to think quickly, to stay calm. Kristján would be here any moment. Stella might emerge from her office at any time. She hadn't intended this to happen, but like everything else, she could tackle it. Nothing was going to stop her from completing her plan when it was so close to fruition.

Besides, Ari had brought this upon himself, with this blatant self-promotion and utter lack of principles.

Quickly, quietly, Linda removed her fluffy jacket. Efficiently rolling it into a ball, she knelt gently on the journalist's chest, restricting the ability of his lungs to expand.

"I hadn't planned on doing this, but you and I are cut from the same cloth. I'll keep an eye on Kristján for you." She pushed the coat over his nose and mouth and held it there firmly.

Ari squirmed. His eyes bulged. His arms and legs flailed weakly. She persisted. It only took a minute.

How convenient—and now ironic—that she had previously paid Ari for dirt on the town doctor's early career negligence in a case. That had helped to eliminate any health and safety inquiries after a couple of unfortunate accidents at the factory. But now it would also be easy to ensure Ari's death was recorded as a tragic but natural accident, some cardiac event connected to his heart condition, perhaps.

Linda did not turn back to look at the body, its eyes open and glassy, its lips turning blue, as she rushed down the hall and out of the museum. The location, with its World War Two display, provided inspiration to formulate her next steps. Ari had told her that all the valuable evidence was at his and Kristján's home, so there was only one solution. Kristján would have to be stopped too, before he discovered what information he had. When to do it? She probably had some time, given how devastated she knew the mayor would be at what he was about to discover on the floor of the museum. And it would be easy to disguise. After all, the world was full of deadly hazards and peril. It would be so easy to find a moment to slip him some poison that all the town had access to.

Yes, this could all end up quite well after all.

Never underestimate the wife, Linda thought as she strode away through the ocher leaves.

ACKNOWLEDGMENTS

Some of you may have visited Vestmannaeyjar already, but if not, I hope reading this book has sparked a desire to do so. This work of fiction is based in a real community but is peopled with completely fictional characters and sometimes fictional places. The *Herjólfur* ferry does indeed transport people from the mainland to Heimaey and back, and it can indeed be delayed or canceled due to weather. There is also a well-known museum that talks about the 1973 volcanic eruption on the island, details of which I hope I have accurately recounted in the story. On the other hand, the museum and archive that the ambassador and his delegation visit is not a real place, although it is roughly in the same spot as a real folk museum, which does feature a fascinating mural about the Algerian pirate raid. (The World War II display is a fabrication. For exhibitions from that era, the best place to visit in Iceland is the Icelandic Wartime Museum in the Eastfjords community of Reyðarfjörður.) Likewise, the Hotel Heimaey is not real. Finally, the restaurant Skel is fictionalized, although some of its description does bear a close resemblance to a deservedly popular eatery on the islands.

This is my first novel, and I naively thought making up a story from scratch might involve less fact-checking than when I have written nonfiction. It turns out that is not the case—especially when poison, police procedures, diplomats, and seasonal cooking are involved! I am indebted to the following people for their help, although it goes without saying that all errors remain my own: Dr. Alexandra Binnie, Dr. Elizabeth Brown, National Commissioner of the Icelandic Police Sigríður Björk Guðjónsdóttir (who did point out that of course there would be more officers on duty on Vestmannaeyjar than I have allowed the story to have), Dr. David Juurlink, and Chef Gísli Matt (from whose wonderful cookbook, *Slippurinn*, I have adapted some Skel dishes with his permission).

Thanks also to Terry Fallis, Jóhannes Jóhannesson, Tatjana Latinovic, Joanna Marcinkowska, Dr. Samir Sinha, Dr. Ildikó Somorjai, and Dr. Jeffrey Tanguay. Paul Mathew created the Flaming Viking cocktail. It's much tastier than I make it out to be in the book, especially because no poison is involved.

Numerous people read early drafts of this novel, and all provided helpful information. Thanks to Jonas Moody, Tara Flynn, Friðjón Friðjónsson, Karítas Friðjónsdóttir, Laurie Grassi (who offered vitally encouraging comments on a very early draft), Guðni Jóhannesson (my husband), Ambassador Bryony Mathew, Ambassador Jeannette Menzies, Vala Pálsdóttir, Allison Reid (my mother), Hugh Reid (my father), Iain Reid (my brother), and Yrsa Sigurðardóttir.

Running the Iceland Writers Retreat with Erica Jacobs Green for over a decade has taught me much about the craft of writing, and I'm grateful to all the faculty and participants we have welcomed over the years.

As usual, the team at Transatlantic Agency have been fantastic: Samantha Haywood, Eva Oakes, Laura Cameron, Evan Brown, and Megan Phillip. I'm thrilled to be working with Blink49 Productions on the television adaption of this book.

This book has been gifted with some wonderful editors who were very generous helping me navigate authoring my first mystery. At Sourcebooks in the U.S., that's Anna Michels. At Sphere (Little, Brown) in the UK, that's Rosanna Forte. And at Simon & Schuster Canada, it's Nita Pronovost and then Adrienne Kerr. After all the writing is done, of course, it went to copyediting, marketing, and sales, and I'd like to thank Liz Kelsch, Mandy Chahal, and Emily Engwall in the U.S.; Stephanie Melrose, Lucie Sharpe, and Sophie Ellis in the UK; and Rita Silva and Cali Platek in Canada.

My family were very tolerant of regular ~~gripes~~ updates about the book-writing process, and I am grateful for their encouragement and patience: Guðni, Duncan, Donnie, Sæþór, and Edda. I am also indebted to my family and my friends in Iceland and my extended family back in Canada, who raised me in a world of storytelling.

To diplomats and their families: Thank you for your efforts and for your dedication to improving relations between nations. I wrote this book partially because I admire the work that you do, often in challenging circumstances and with little wider recognition or understanding of its significance and long-term influence on the course of world history. Any errors in the day-to-day activities and roles of diplomats are my own, and I thank many of you experts for suspending your disbelief in service of the story, for example, the unlikely scenario of the refugee subplot. (Another detail for sticklers: Canada's real embassy in Iceland is so small it doesn't have a deputy ambassador or someone serving at that level. In fact, Canada has very few embassies with a position of deputy ambassador. In most countries where Canada has a mission, this role is titled political counselor.) And to those who are sometimes referred to inelegantly as *trailing spouses*: I see and value your vital contributions.

Lastly, to the people of Vestmannaeyjar, one of my favorite spots in Iceland. Thank you for the hospitality you have shown me over the years. I hope my love for your community comes through on the pages of this book. *Takk fyrir mig.*

READING GROUP GUIDE

1. Would you like to live on a small island? What are the advantages/disadvantages of living in a more isolated place?

2. Graeme cheated on Jane in the past, which she has trouble forgiving him for. What would you do if your partner did this to you? Would you be able to forgive them eventually, or would there be no repairing that trust?

3. Kristján is convinced that his husband was murdered, but no one believes him. What might you do in a situation where you believe something to be true but no one will listen to you? How would you go about convincing others?

4. Graeme speaks to Kavita in a manner she finds demeaning, though he might not see it as such. Do you think Graeme's behavior toward Kavita is acceptable behavior between colleagues? Are there things you do that might unintentionally irritate those around you?

5. Why is it difficult for a small community to part with the major company in their area, no matter how corrupt that company might be? How much power does that major company have over the people, and is that right?

6. Jane and Ben, though friends, argue and say hurtful things to each other in a moment of anger. How difficult is it to reconcile after such an argument? Have you ever said something you didn't mean when you were angry?

7. It is revealed that Ben hadn't actually written the novels published under his name and was instead stealing them from his relative. What do you make of his actions? If he had not stolen the manuscripts, would they ever have been published?

8. How do you think Jane's character changed over the course of the novel?

9. Did you figure out who the murderer was before the reveal?

10. What are your thoughts about the job of diplomats? Did the actions and personalities of the diplomats in this book align with your previous thoughts, or are your impressions different after reading?

11. Did you know about the Westman Islands before reading?

Would you be interested in visiting the Islands or mainland Iceland?

12. Do you present yourself differently in different situations, such as when you're working versus when you're at home? Do you feel like you keep parts of your personality (or other secrets) hidden from the people you meet on a general basis? How much of other people do we really know, even of our loved ones?

13. What are the assumptions we make about people based on their roles in life, whether that be wife, diplomat, or chef? Why do you think we hold these assumptions, and is it right to have them?

A CONVERSATION
WITH THE AUTHOR

What was the inspiration for this book?

I love the mystery genre and wanted to write a novel that was a classic Christie-style mystery but set in Iceland, my adopted homeland. I also have a great admiration for diplomats and the often underappreciated work they do and of which I have developed a greater understanding after serving as First Lady of Iceland. I wanted to reveal a glimpse into this world as well.

What kind of research went into creating the story?

More than I had expected! I have written a nonfiction book before and thought that would involve more research than fiction, but I was wrong! I needed to learn about poisons—for example, whether cyanide would be effective so rapidly despite being stored for so long or how Ari could be killed without arousing too much suspicion by characters other than his husband. I also wanted to incorporate the history of Vestmannaeyjar into the story. Finally, I spoke with diplomats about some of the challenges they face. The subplot about refugees working in Iceland on their way to Canada is completely made up and unlikely to happen in real life (even practically speaking, it would run through Canada's Ministry of Immigration and not Global Affairs), but I liked the idealism of it and hope the reader is willing to go along for that ride.

What was your favorite scene to write?

I wrote and rewrote the "Flaming Viking" scene where Kavita dies many times. It is seen from two different points of view, and there is a lot of choreography surrounding the preparation of the cocktail. One of my favorite moments around that was an evening where some friends and I gathered to sample various Flaming Viking cocktails—a friend prepared some real cocktails that used Icelandic ingredients and could be set on fire, and I got to choose which one would fit best in the book. Naturally, I chose the strongest tasting one!

The Westman Islands seem like a fascinating place! Can you tell us more about their history and how they fit into Icelandic culture?

There are a lot of places I love in Iceland, and Vestmannaeyjar is one of them. They have a long history, which I refer to in the book. One of the most recent notable moments was the volcanic eruption of 1973, which happened with no notice. That surprise is no longer a danger given technological advances in geological studies. But beyond that history, there is also plenty to do for the visitor. The wonderful swimming pool gets a mention in this story, but the islands are also great for taking boat trips, ATV trips on the volcano, or puffin watching. You can even visit a special beluga whale sanctuary.

Which authors have inspired you most in your fiction writing?

I grew up reading Agatha Christie from a young age, so she is most definitely an inspiration, although I would never claim to be as talented as she is! But there are so many excellent mystery writers publishing now; recently, I have enjoyed books by Louise Penny, Clare Mackintosh, Anthony Horowitz, Elizabeth George—but if you asked me in a month, I might give you different answers! Of course, we have a strong tradition of this genre in Iceland too. I dare not mention specific names because we all know each other, but I highly recommend you read some mysteries that have been translated from Icelandic.

What do you want readers to take away from your book?

I hope readers have enjoyed getting to know these characters, because Jane, Graeme, police officer Jónas, and maybe others will be returning in book two! From this story, I hope that readers get to know a part of the world that perhaps they were not familiar with before and also that they consider thinking about the work that public servants undertake and the sacrifices they and their families make in service to increased international cooperation.

ABOUT THE AUTHOR

© Saga Sig

Eliza Reid is a bestselling writer, public speaker, gender equality advocate, and cofounder of the acclaimed Iceland Writers Retreat. She was born and raised in Canada but has lived in Iceland for more than twenty years. Her first book, *Secrets of the Sprakkar: Iceland's Extraordinary Women and How They Are Changing the World*, was an instant bestseller in Canada and Iceland, a *New York Times Book Review* Editors' Pick, and translated into numerous languages. *Death on the Island* is the first of a series and has been optioned for television. From 2016 to 2024, Eliza served in the unofficial role of First Lady while her husband was president of Iceland, an adventure that greatly informed the writing of this book. A memoir of her time in the position is set for publication in 2026.

Eliza lives in the outskirts of Reykjavík with her husband and four children. This is her first novel.